The Spinner's Tale

Omar Shahid Hamid has served with the Karachi Police for twelve years. During his service, he was actively targeted by various terrorist groups and organizations. He was wounded in the line of duty and his office was bombed by the Taliban in 2010.

He has a Masters in Criminal Justice Policy from London School of Economics and a Masters in Law from University College London.

His first novel, *The Prisoner*, was critically acclaimed and longlisted for the DSC Prize for South Asian Literature 2015. *The Spinner's Tale* is his second novel.

Also by Omar Shahid Hamid

The Prisoner

The Spinner's Tale

Omar Shahid Hamid

PAN

First published in the Indian subcontinent 2015 by Pan
an imprint of Pan Macmillan India,
a division of Macmillan Publishers India Private Limited
Pan Macmillan India, 707, Kailash Building
26, K.G. Marg, New Delhi-110001
www.panmacmillan.co.in

Pan Macmillan, 20 New Wharf Road, London N1 9RR
Basingstoke and Oxford
Associated companies throughout the world
www.panmacmillan.com

ISBN 978-93-82616-44-3
Copyright © Omar Shahid Hamid 2015

This is a work of fiction. All characters, locations and events are fictitious.
Any resemblance to actual events or locales or persons, living or dead,
is entirely coincidental.

Typeset by Eleven Arts
Printed and bound in India by
Shree Maitrey Printech Pvt. Ltd., Noida

For the women in my life,
My mother, who gave me the courage to do
everything I have done,
And my wife, who has been my rock.
And to my friend Aslam, whose loss I feel every day.

Prologue

The Animal
Husbandry School

one

The Present: 21 April 2011

The desert can be a scary place at night. Darkness descends very quickly upon the barren landscape. The night brings with it a bone-tingling chill. But it is the silence that is most unnerving. The slightest noise is amplified tenfold as it echoes across the vast empty spaces. The wailing of a lonely jackal sounds menacing. The sparse vegetation casts sinister shadows and the whistling wind tosses up dancing balls of dust that look ethereal in the moonlight. In a place like this, the mind starts playing tricks on the senses. Every shape, sound and shadow brings with it an associated sense of dread.

This was especially true of the small group of policemen who huddled together over a campfire in this particularly desolate corner of the Nara Desert. Their little camp was set in the middle of two single storey buildings in the middle of nowhere. The closest signs of civilization were across the Indian border, two kilometres away. The buildings themselves were dilapidated, with doors, windows and all other fixtures having long since been removed. Only one room, in the larger of the two buildings, had a shiny new set of iron bars in the window. The road that led up to the encampment was little better than a dirt track. At the entrance of the compound was an old board, hanging from its hinges now, that proclaimed this place to be the Forestry Department's School of Animal Husbandry.

The sun had only set an hour ago, but already the desert was enveloped in darkness. The sole light came from the fire around which the men sat. It was the month of Ramadan, the month of fasting, and the policemen had had to content themselves with breaking their day long fast with some stale naan bread and soggy pakoras. But they were fortified by strong tea, brewed in a steel kettle over the open flame of the campfire. It was the first time in the day they had really taken stock of their surroundings. The morning had been spent in ceaseless activity, setting up the place and in resisting the pangs of hunger that the first week of Ramadan inevitably brought.

One of the men, the tallest of the lot, a constable called Peeral, noisily slurped his tea from the cracked china cup. 'This is not a good place to be in. I have heard stories about this place … it's haunted.'

The others hushed up, looking around nervously for any sign of the supernatural. The sudden sound of creaking metal startled all of them, making two of the men spill their tea. The stoutest of the lot, a rotund man by the name of Juman, was the only one who hadn't moved at the sound. He laughed. 'You bloody idiots. It's only the back door of the pickup. You know it always creaks, we've been meaning to get it repaired for some time. All of you know this, yet you let this village simpleton scare you. Tell me something, which chutiya ghost is going to haunt an animal husbandry school?'

The others laughed uneasily. Peeral frowned. 'It's wrong to abuse them. We don't want any passing spirits to take offence.'

'Listen Peeral, the only spirit passing this place would be the ghost of a horny buffalo who died while mounting a cow. Any self-respecting ghost wouldn't be caught dead here.'

The mood lightened after Juman's comment and the laughter was much more relaxed. Only Peeral remained doubtful.

'Okay, Juman, granted it's an animal husbandry school. But that doesn't mean there were never any people here. What if one of the researchers had died here and his spirit is still wandering about?'

'And how, pray tell, would the researcher have died? Was he struck by lightning while he was masturbating a buffalo? Yes, I'm sure you're right, there's a spirit walking around here right now with buffalo sperm on its hands.'

The men chuckled again and another of them spoke up. 'It's not the dead that I'm worried about, it's the living. Arre baba, do you even know what we're doing here? Who are we supposed to be guarding?'

'A living ghost.' Juman took a sip from his tea, allowing his words to sink in.

'Who is it?'

'Do you know Sheikh Uzair?'

'Yes, he's the one who tried to kill the President. Twice. Oh my God, is it him? He's coming here?'

'Didn't he also murder that gori journalist a couple of years ago? The one who was pregnant? But I heard he had been killed in the Sher Masjid siege?'

'Yes, the very same fellow. He didn't die, he was arrested. But after Sher Masjid, his group is the biggest jihadi group in the country now. You see their recruiting centres everywhere. Last month, they even came to my village and recruited two or three of the local boys. But this Sheikh was in Hyderabad jail. Why are they bringing him here to Nara?'

Juman relit a half-smoked beedi. The raw, unprocessed tobacco was strong, and he could feel it enter his bloodstream, jolting him out of his post-fast lethargy. 'I heard something went wrong at the jail in Hyderabad. That's why they had to move him.'

'But why are they moving him here? This is not a jail. This place is just a little shithole in the middle of nowhere. And why us? We aren't some elite anti-terrorist squad. We're just a bunch of village cops. Now his jihadi friends will come after us. I knew I shouldn't have come back on duty today. Another absence and I would have been sitting comfortably in my own home.' Peeral's whining became more and more animated.

'That's probably why they moved him here. *Because* it's such a shithole. And that's also why we're guarding him. What connection can he have to a bunch of country bumpkin cops like us? At least that's what ASP sahib's Reader explained to me.'

'Where is ASP sahib anyway? I haven't seen him since iftar. He broke his fast with a couple of dates and took a swig of water, and then he disappeared.'

'You know how he is. He has to check everything five hundred times. He probably went to check the barbed wire fence again.'

'But why did they have to pick us, yaar? ASP sahib always gets us stuck in the worst possible assignments.'

'Shut up and stop whining, Peeral. You think ASP sahib had any say in this? If it involves Sheikh Uzair, the instructions must have come from the very top. Arre baba, he's one of the most wanted men in the world. I have heard the Americans are offering a bounty for him, but the government wants to put him on trial. Apparently, they consider him second or third in importance after Osama.'

'How much do you think the Americans will pay?'

'Enough for you to buy a plot of land and as many cows as you like in your village.'

From where he stood, just outside the encampment, ASP Omar Abassi could clearly see the men laughing at Juman's light-hearted remark. He put his hands on the new coil of barbed wire, checking its sturdiness and the sharpness of its edges. He had decided to inspect the perimeter of the camp again after the fast, even though he had done it twice already in the day. But Omar Abassi had been known in the Academy for his conscientiousness. Well, some termed it being conscientious. Others, who were less kind, called it anal retentiveness.

Unfortunately, there had always been plenty of those in his life. Omar Abassi had never been good at making friends. He had never had any time for camaraderie, always maintaining a laser-like focus on the work in front of him. The son of a humble village schoolmaster, he had been a scholarship boy all his life, attending some of the country's most prestigious institutions, but always remaining an outsider. His classmates, all scions of rich and powerful families, had nothing but contempt for him. They may have shared a bench with him in school, but for them he would always be the village schoolmaster's son which, in the rather rigid class structure of rural Sindh, was no better than being a peasant. His father had nursed dreams of him becoming a doctor, but the scholarships finally ran out in his second year of medical school. Abassi was left with the choice of slinking back to a life of mediocrity in Larkana, the provincial town where his father lived, or trying to pry open the one door that was left for him: taking a long shot at passing the civil service exams that would enable him to break out of his circumstances. He took the long shot and succeeded, getting a commission in the police.

But the social awkwardness that had plagued him throughout his academic years reared its head again at the police academy. His colleagues may not all have been the heirs to landed aristocracy, but they were all his social betters, and never missed an opportunity to remind him that he was an unsophisticated provincial oaf, who didn't even know which fork was to be used at dinner. As if an intimate knowledge of cutlery was all that was needed to become a good police officer. He didn't help matters with his aloof manner, never seeing the lighter side of things and never participating in any of their banter. And so, while they advanced their careers by endlessly networking with politicians and senior officers, he kept his focus on becoming the best trainee in the batch, never late for parade, excelling academically, always ensuring that his uniform was immaculate. He never figured out that getting the trophy from the chief guest on graduation day didn't necessarily mean he would get the best posting. All his colleagues managed comfortable postings in the big cities, thanks to the connections they had nurtured while he had been bent over his books. When Abassi's turn came, there was no place left to go but the wilderness.

And Nara really was the wilderness. They said that a directly appointed ASP had never been posted here before Omar arrived. Most self-respecting ranker officers avoided the place like the plague. In fact, the post had lain vacant for a couple of years, before Omar was granted the final indignity of drawing the worst subdivision in the country. He also drew the worst boss. His district SP was the archetypal caricature policeman come to life. He was short, squat, corpulent, and didn't have an honest bone in his body. His uniform was always sloppy, his belly protruded over his service belt like an overhanging cliff, and he took genuine pride in the fact that he had never let go of a single opportunity to make a dishonest rupee in his entire career. He believed that the police force of the district existed to aid him in his personal enrichment. Unfortunately, having an idealistic young ASP under his wing was an encumbrance, one that he soon got rid of by restricting Abassi to this little patch of desert.

Stuck in this predicament, Omar responded in the only way he knew. He worked conscientiously and diligently at every measly task that his overbearing boss assigned to him. He kept working, as if it were the most important thing in the world. He tried to bring a semblance of professionalism even to this place, where he had been dumped and forgotten. It was the only thing that had kept him sane these past fourteen months.

That had all suddenly changed two days ago. He had been sitting in the shack that passed for his office, performing all sorts of calisthenics to ensure that the sweat that dripped from every pore of his body in the 110 degree heat did not smudge the paper on which he was so painstakingly writing another of the reports that he knew would get filed in some drawer by his boss without ever being read. His two assistants were bent over an ancient air conditioner, trying to coax it to life. But the machine only made things worse, spewing out hot air that made the room feel like a boiler. The office's solitary phone started ringing suddenly, which was an event in itself, since the only person who called was Omar's boss, and he too had stopped bothering altogether about three months ago.

But it wasn't his boss. Instead, it was a man from the Interior Ministry. When the voice on the line told him about the nature of his assignment, Omar, at first, thought it was an elaborate practical joke that some of his course mates were playing on him just to rub salt in his wounds. He hung up and thought nothing of it, until his boss showed up an hour later, ashen-faced, holding a written confirmation of the orders. He stayed only long enough to hand Omar the orders, and to inform him that he was proceeding on a month's medical leave and that Omar would now be in charge of the entire district in his absence and would thus have sole responsibility for the assigned task. When Omar asked for further instructions, his boss replied that he could utilize whatever resources there were in the district as he thought best, just as long as Omar promised never to contact him on any account. Having absolved himself of any responsibility for the affair, the SP then proceeded to zoom off in his shiny red jeep.

The orders from the ministry weren't very illuminating either. They simply stated that he was to take over the Forestry Department's School of Animal Husbandry, which was the largest and most isolated facility in the area, and to secure it immediately, so that Ahmed Uzair Sufi could be detained there for an unspecified period of time.

Sheikh Ahmed Uzair Sufi. The orders contained no further information on him, but of course, like every other person in the country who owned a television set, Omar knew who Sheikh Uzair was. Who could forget the horrific images of the Sheikh beheading the female journalist? TV networks had replayed the video clip that his group had posted on the internet again and again for months afterward, paying no heed to the propriety of the images. Omar closed his eyes and played the scene from memory. The woman, a foreigner, so obviously pregnant that her swollen belly was visible even from under the filthy shawl that she had been wrapped in, terrified, sweating, clutching a newspaper that showed the date, pleading with her eyes, unsure till the very last moment whether she would be allowed to go free or not. He stood behind her, his tall frame filling the picture on the television, wearing an elegant maroon turban, his dark, piercing eyes staring straight at the camera, besotted with an Olympian calm as he waited for his accomplice to finish reciting the list of their grievances against the State. While the speaker raised his tone to an ever passionate crescendo as he exhorted true believers to join the Jihad against the Crusaders, the Sheikh raised his blade high above the woman's head, and as soon as the recital ended, he brought it down onto her neck in one smooth motion, severing the head cleanly from the body. Even his preaching colleague seemed to stumble from his text as the blood splattered onto his pristine white shalwar kameez, and perhaps the enormity of what they had done sunk in. But the Sheikh was unwavering, unblinking, the only visible emotion was in his eyes, those smouldering black eyes that burned with a fire that surely must have been forged in the depths of hell.

Omar remembered another TV image of the Sheikh, from the day he had been arrested. The police had captured him after launching the largest manhunt in the country's history that culminated in a siege of a madrasa complex in Karachi. When his accomplices had been dragged out of the building by the police, their clothes were ripped to shreds, their faces and hair covered in dirt and dried blood, and the pungent odour of tear gas, all rotten onions and sharp ammonia, hung heavily over them. They all looked like a thoroughly pathetic and defeated bunch of individuals. Only *he* remained defiant. He had emerged from the building with his head held high, staring directly at the dozens of TV cameras that he knew would be there. He did it deliberately, so that they could capture the ferocity etched on his face, and those black eyes burning without a hint of remorse. At the time, watching on TV from the comfort of the police academy, Omar had wondered what it must have taken to have so much hate in those eyes.

Despite the paucity of official information and the magnitude of the task, Omar had stuck to it in his usual dogged manner. He had worked day and night the past two days, marshalling all the resources at his disposal, and attempting to transform the dilapidated group of sheds into something resembling a maximum security prison. Looking down on it now, he could breathe a small sigh of self-satisfaction. A double-barbed wire fence had been laid around the entire compound. Searchlights taken from police pickups had been hastily put up on the roofs of the sheds. Omar had even persuaded the electric company to reopen the electricity connection to the school that had long lain dormant. It hadn't been easy. Initially, the chief engineer at the company had been unwilling to even speak to Omar. But a quick visit to his house in the middle of the night by the local police station in charge had brought a radical change in his demeanour. Overnight, lines had been laid and connections reset. The lights weren't working yet, but the engineer had promised to have them up and running by the following day. Omar was confident that it was a promise that would be fulfilled. Workers had come in and given one of the sheds a quick makeover, installing iron bars on the windows and repairing any wear and tear on the structure. Omar had deployed police checkpoints in a 1 km radius around the school.

He paced by the barbed wire, trying to read the file in his hand by the distant glow of the encampment fire. To fill the gaps in the official information flow about Sheikh Uzair or the reason for his presence here, Omar had attempted to compile a dossier, asking a friend in Hyderabad to print out whatever was available on the Sheikh on the internet. Wikipedia had a particularly detailed entry on him. Omar was surprised to learn that the Sheikh had attended one of the best schools in the country. Referred simply as 'The School', as if that were sufficient for anyone to recognize it, it was called 'the Eton of the East'. Omar knew from personal experience how difficult it was to get admission there. A cousin of his had just spent most of the past year jumping through all sorts of hoops to get his son enrolled, and had still failed. It was not just a question of money, which his banker cousin had plenty of, but more about the fact that The School was indeed a meritocratic establishment who looked for 'the right sort'. It was unfathomable how Sheikh Uzair could ever have been considered 'the right sort'.

The Wikipedia entry contained a couple of pictures, one that was his trademark picture from the day of his arrest and another that was apparently from his schooldays. The school picture showed a youth, dressed in the school uniform of white shirt, grey trousers, and a striped blue and red tie. He had the slightly bored expression of a teenager trying to act cool in front of the camera. He was a lean, athletic-looking boy, tanned like only a sportsman can be, and in a further affectation of coolness, his school tie was loosened and drooping close to his belt. Only the dark eyes gave him away as being the younger version of the man who had walked out of the devastated madrasa. There was another boy in the picture, with his arm draped around the Sheikh, wearing cricket whites. The boy was around the same height, but with a much darker complexion than the Sheikh. He too seemed to be affecting a cool image, but a lot less self-consciously than Sheikh Uzair. He wore wraparound shades that covered half his face, had his collar turned up, and with the red patch on his slacks that indicated where he had been polishing the cricket ball, he looked like a professional fast bowler who had just completed his spell.

Had it not been for the boy's piercing eyes, Omar would have assumed that someone had made an incorrect entry on the page. The rest of the entry dealt with the Sheikh's known career, how he had been trained in Afghanistan, gained notoriety in Kashmir by kidnapping western tourists, and, of course, his infamous cases, the murder of the journalist and the attacks on the President. Omar just could not reconcile the first paragraph of the entry with everything else. How could this boy in the picture, wearing the uniform of the most prestigious and anglicized educational institution in the country, who looked as if his only concern was to look cool in front of girls and play cricket, have become the bearded, turbaned decapitator of a pregnant woman?

There was no information about the reason for his shift from Hyderabad. Although Sheikh Uzair had been arrested in Karachi, he was considered such a high profile prisoner that the authorities had decided that he would simply act as a magnet for his fanatical followers if he were to be incarcerated in the metropolis. There had been some talk in the intelligence community that his followers were preparing to launch a wave of suicide attacks to force the government to release him. That was the reason why he had been incarcerated in Hyderabad in the first place. Tucked away in a little corner, away from the media spotlight that he craved so much, everyone hoped that he would soon become a forgotten man. Obviously, that hadn't happened, thought Omar, otherwise there would have been no need to push him out into an even smaller and far more desolate place than Hyderabad.

Presently, a stream of flashing lights became visible in the distance. A convoy of police pickups and jeeps were driving at breakneck speed towards them. As the vehicles came closer, the wailing of their sirens became louder. Omar started walking toward the front gate of the compound and reached just as the motorcade entered the gate, sending a cloud of dust in his direction, coating his uniform with a layer of dirt. For a man who took pride in the fact that his uniform was normally as fresh and neat at eight at night as it would be at eight in the morning, this was a considerable irritation. His mood only grew worse when he saw the motorcade up close. Apart from the official licence plates on the vehicles, there was nothing to identify the men who got off as police officers. None of the men wore uniforms, choosing instead to dress in a variety of costumes, some wearing combat fatigues, some in shalwar kameez, and some in T-shirts and jeans. But all of them were armed to the teeth, carrying an assortment of weapons, including AK-47s, MP-5s, Glock pistols and even a couple of sniper rifles.

This motley crew took position around the central vehicle in the motorcade, an Armoured Personnel Carrier with just the narrowest of slits for windows. As the men prepared themselves, Omar was even more shocked to find that none of them paid any attention to him. None of the men had bothered to even acknowledge his presence, much less salute him. Omar was about to walk up to them and demand to see their supervisory officer, when someone tapped him on the shoulder. He whirled around, infuriated by the impudence, and came face-to-face with a rotund, jovial looking man in a safari suit. Instead of being cowed by Omar's fierce expression, the man grinned even wider as he made an attempt at a greeting that was somewhere between a salute and a casual wave.

'ASP Omar Abassi?' The fat man spoke the words with such mirth, that one would have thought he was relating an exceptionally funny joke.

'Who the hell are you?' The words tumbled out of Omar's mouth, his exasperation at the level of impertinence dumbfounding him.

'Oh, so sorry. Inspector Shahab. CID. Quite an impressive job you've done with this place in such a short time, ASP Abassi.

I used to have a cousin who worked here once upon a time. I came to see him here once. Place used to be a complete dump. There was a hole in the wall that the buffaloes used to just walk through. My stupid cousin was always chasing them around in the desert. But you've really improved it. Yes, most definitely.'

'The hole has been covered up. What does all this have to do with me?'

'What? Oh nothing really. Sorry, I always ramble on.' Inspector Shahab gave another approving gaze and took a leisurely stroll round the compound as if it were the most natural thing to do. It was a good five minutes before he finally noticed the apoplectic look on Omar's face and smiled sheepishly.

'Oh, so sorry ASP sahib. I got distracted out here by the open air. I don't get out of the city much, you know. One should enjoy such opportunities when they present themselves. But you must be waiting to receive your guest.' Shahab took another look at the compound. 'Uh, you have, I am sure, prepared a room or some sort of cell for him, right?'

'Yes, of course I have. Some of us take our responsibilities very seriously, Inspector.'

'Oh, of course, of course. A thousand apologies.' He signalled to the men who were surrounding the Armoured Personnel Carrier, and they turned to open the back door of the APC. A uniformed officer emerged from within, holding a chain linked to his belt. At the other end of the chain was a man, wearing an ancient pair of shackles.

At first, Omar didn't recognize the manacled figure that emerged from the APC. The Sheikh Uzair on television had seemed taller. This figure appeared bent over. He wore a simple prayer cap on his head, and the black, bushy beard had been reduced to a neatly trimmed two weeks' growth. He still looked young, not older than mid-thirties, Omar guessed. His eyes were shielded behind a pair of spectacles that gave him a sort of middle-class respectability. He was dressed in a plain white shalwar kurta and wore a pair of plastic blue flip flops on his feet. As he slowly raised his gaze from the ground, he seemed to lock onto the young, uniformed ASP. Omar noticed that the Sheikh ignored the rest of his surroundings, but kept staring straight at him with a kind of quizzical expression on his face.

'Uh, yes ASP sahib, just a couple more things before we hand the prisoner over to you. If you would come this way, please.' Shahab had noticed the interest that the Sheikh seemed to have taken in Omar, so he walked a little distance from the rest of the assembly, and lowered his otherwise jocular tone. 'I don't know quite how much our superiors have told you about this affair, but I would guess that they would have pretty much kept you in the dark about things.'

'Well, they haven't told me anything. I don't even know why he's being brought here, or what I'm supposed to do with him.'

'Ah yes, well that's typical of them, isn't it? The first part's the easy one. You obviously know who he is. After his arrest, he was shifted to the maximum security Hyderabad Jail, because it was thought that his presence in the jail in Karachi would attract too many of the crazies who worship him. In any case, there are a lot of these jihadi sorts in Karachi, so he would have plenty of the wrong sort for company. Hyderabad was supposed to be out of the way, isolated, a place where we could dump him and forget about it. Unfortunately, it didn't work out that way. You see the Sheikh is a particularly charming fellow. He started preaching to his guards about how meaningless the comforts of this world were, and that their true calling was to work for God. He brainwashed them completely in a matter of weeks. It started with them growing their beards. Then, they began shunning western dress, refusing to wear even their uniforms to work. The jail superintendent didn't make the connection, thinking that maybe they were just peculiar, so he allowed them to wear their ankle high shalwars. But that wasn't all the Sheikh was making them do. He was passing messages to his comrades on the outside, using the stupid guards as couriers. We found out purely by chance, when we happened to arrest one of his followers and found a message in his possession. They had been making plans to blow the jail up and help the Sheikh escape. The plan had been in quite an advanced stage. That's when the alarm bells started going off and the government decided to shift him to the most isolated location they could think of.'

'Who the hell would have thought of this godforsaken place?'

'Ah, well, for that, I confess my guilt. You see, that's where my cousin comes in. I remembered this place from when he used to work here, and I suggested it to the higher ups, because I couldn't think of a more ideal place for the Sheikh.'

'You said the second part of my question was harder. Why?'

'Well, in a way. I guess it's not difficult to figure out what to do with him. Basically, do whatever you feel is appropriate under the circumstances. Had this place still been functioning as an animal husbandry school, you could have put him to work inseminating the cows, I suppose.' Shahab guffawed at his own joke. 'No, the difficult bit is *how* you go about handling him. You see, after the episode in Hyderabad, we've figured out that the Sheikh can be extremely persuasive. So we don't want him becoming too chatty with anybody. The prison guards weren't some green youths on their first job. They were men with fifteen or twenty years' experience, and they had been used to guarding high profile, dangerous prisoners. But he flipped them as if they were children. So, now we don't want him talking to anybody. You have to ensure that.'

'How the hell am I supposed to do that? Whoever came up with such a stupid plan?'

Shahab smiled for a moment at Omar's outburst, nodding thoughtfully in the manner of a parent trying to explain something to an errant child. 'ASP sahib, I'm sorry. I think perhaps I haven't been able to convey to you the seriousness of this situation. We recovered large quantities of C4 explosive, sewn into a jacket, from one of the prison guards we arrested. The Sheikh had convinced the man to become a suicide bomber and blow up the prison. The man was willing to take his own life, as well as the lives of dozens of his own colleagues whom he had known for years, just to get the Sheikh out of prison. Another of the guards had prepared lists of his co-workers' families, along with their addresses, to pass on to the Sheikh's followers so that they could take them hostage. Can you imagine the level of diabolical genius required to convince men to do things like that? So please, please, take what I am saying to you very seriously. On no account are you to allow any kind of fraternization between him and your subordinates. It helps that, out here, most of the guards probably only understand Sindhi, which he can't speak. But nevertheless, you have to ensure this. And you yourself are also not to communicate with him either, except when you want to command him to do something. I know him, and I saw the way he was trying to size you up right now. He will try to charm you, try to be friendly, but you are not to respond. Just keep in mind that whatever he says or does, his only interest is to try and get out. This man has no value for human life. Now, if you could just point my men in the direction of his cell, we'll escort him there and leave you to it.'

The story had made an impact on Omar. He would have been loath to show his reaction in front of Shahab, but the change in his attitude was evident. So far, Omar had been happy to carry out his task without question because after having been ignored for so long, he had been thrilled to have finally gotten an important assignment. Of course, he hadn't been naïve enough not to understand that such an assignment would obviously have an element of risk. After all, that was exactly why his boss had disappeared and left him in charge. But this was the first time someone had actually spelt out the dangers in such an explicit manner. He offered no more rebukes to Shahab, but turned and silently led the group towards the old shed that had been prepared for the Sheikh.

Sheikh Uzair had observed the exchange between Shahab and Omar in a kind of disinterested manner, preferring to take in his new surroundings. As Shahab's men started marching him towards his cell, a few metres from the shed door, he hesitated and cleared his throat.

'Assalam Alaikum, brother.'

Involuntarily, Omar froze. He glanced sideways at Shahab, who had turned his head and was glaring at the Sheikh. He signalled to his men to prod the Sheikh to move. The Sheikh himself had a disarming smile, as if he were oblivious to the mischief he was causing.

'Forgive my impudence, brother, for speaking in English, but I noticed from your shoulder decorations that you are an ASP. I figured you must know English. I haven't spoken it in such a long time, that I could not resist it. I was wondering if you would know the result of the Pakistan India cricket match.'

Shahab grunted his disapproval. 'Keep walking. No one speaks English over here.' He uttered the words in Urdu. One of his men prodded the Sheikh a little harder to push him along.

The smell hit them with the force of a physical object. The old shed was pitch dark, and so Omar had to feel his way forward, until Constable Peeral came up behind him with a flashlight. The cell, such as it was, was essentially the corner stable of the shed, just wide enough for a four legged animal to stand in. It had been secured and reinforced on all four sides, and new iron grilles had been placed on the one window which was the sole source of light in the room. A narrow cot with a single sheet had been placed in the cell, making it even harder for more than one man to manoeuvre inside it. Omar's efforts over the past two days had gone into making the building as secure as possible. In the process, he had overlooked the cleanliness of the place. Now, as he stood in the dark shed, the stench of buffalo urine almost overpowering, the floor beneath his boots a wet and slimy mixture of excrement, hay and God knew what else, he regretted having done that. For all the work he had put in over the past two days, this place wasn't fit for human habitation. Even for a monster like Sheikh Ahmed Uzair Sufi. Omar stole a glance at the Sheikh, in his pristine white shalwar kameez, a slight discoloration on his forehead, the mark of those who prayed five times a day. Whatever sort of monster he was, there was no denying that he was a religious man. Omar felt guilty as he pictured the Sheikh bowing his forehead on the filthy floor.

'It's not, uh, as clean as it should be, but uh, we have secured it properly. I was told that was the priority. I'll, uh, get someone to clean it up in the morning.'

'Oh that's fine, ASP sahib. This cell will do very nicely. I'm sure it'll be fine for Sheikh sahib.'

Shahab seemed almost pleased with the filthy condition of the cell. The Sheikh himself had not said anything. He continued to take in everything in the room, staring at the floor, then at the small window by the ceiling. His eyes lingered on the plastic bucket that had been placed in one corner of the room.

'Would it be possible to get some clean water in that bucket? I would need it to perform my wudu.'

Peeral, who seemed as embarrassed at the condition of the shed as his boss, picked up the bucket immediately, muttering under his breath in his half Sindhi half Urdu that clean water for wudu – ablution before prayers – was a man's right after all.

Shahab nodded one final time, and his men took the shackles off the Sheikh. The party withdrew from the cell as the Sheikh settled himself down on the edge of the cot. Peeral secured the door with a giant iron padlock, and after taking one last look through the slit in the door, Shahab, satisfied with the day's work, walked out into the cool desert air.

'Ah, that's most refreshing. Thank you, ASP sahib, for your cooperation. Good luck with him. You'll need it. If you need any kind of help, or advice in how to manage him, here's my card. Don't hesitate to call, and please drop by my office next time you're in Karachi.'

'Wait a minute. Karachi? But didn't you bring him from Hyderabad?'

'Oh yes. He was in Hyderabad. But when this mess happened in the jail there, the powers that be thought it best to call me from Karachi to escort him to his next destination. You see, I was the officer who arrested him, so I have the most background on him. Well, we must get a move on now. I'd promised my cousin a chicken karhai dinner if I ever came to this place again, and I guess he's won that bet. Did I tell you he used to work here? Oh, but of course, I did. Sorry, I have a habit of rambling on, as you may have noticed.'

'How long am I supposed to keep him here?'

'Oh, you mean they haven't even told you that? God, they really have thrown you into the deep end, haven't they? I don't know anything about how long he'll be here, as our job was to merely transport him from one location to another. But I reckon it won't be too long. They also realize that this is not a permanent arrangement. I would estimate, maybe, three to four weeks. Oh, by the way, one more thing. I almost forgot.' He fished around in his breast pocket and took out a torn envelope. 'He was trying to pass this to one of my men, as we were bringing him here. It's in English, so none of my men could understand it, and as for me, well, all of my English is written by my munshi. Since you're in charge of him, you get to keep this as well.'

'What is it? And what do I do with it?'

'It's a letter of some sort. You can read it if you like. You're the English expert. I'm sure you'll figure out the right thing to do. Doesn't matter to me, it's all up to you. Good day, ASP sahib.'

Shahab's men were already in their vehicles revving their engines by the time he trundled into his jeep. The motorcade did a quick about-turn and sped off, leaving Omar to stare at the envelope in his hand. The paper felt like a burning brick. He could not believe Shahab's casual attitude, in not having even tried to read or understand the letter on his way here. How could such an important piece of evidence be neglected like this? At the same time, he was strangely drawn to the letter, wondering what sort of secret instructions a terrorist mastermind would have jotted down. The lives of hundreds of people could depend on what was written on those pieces of paper. For, possibly, the first time in his career, Omar felt what it was like to be at the centre of events, privy to the inside track. It was a feeling he enjoyed.

But his curiosity and excitement soon gave way to dread. He cursed Shahab loudly, because he finally understood exactly why the Inspector hadn't bothered to read the letter. Knowledge was a weapon, but it was a double-edged sword. It was convenient for Shahab to hand the letter over to him, because with it, he had transferred the responsibility of dealing with the letter as well. What if, as Omar suspected, the letter really was a set of instructions to conduct a mass genocide? What should Omar do with it? There was no one here to help him. This was exactly why his SP had disappeared. In his elation at finally having something to do, Omar hadn't even bothered to find out who he should contact in case of an eventuality like this. If a hundred people were killed in a bomb blast tomorrow and it transpired that the plan had originated from the Sheikh, Omar's SP would say that he had left him in charge. Shahab would dutifully reply that the letter had been duly handed over to the young ASP. It was very important that he do exactly the right thing with this letter. One misstep and Omar Abassi's dreams and aspirations of a lifetime would shatter.

He suddenly found himself standing in the middle of the compound, paralyzed with fear. He forced himself to snap out of it and took a look around the compound. He would get himself out of this by doing the thing he did best, methodically preparing for any situation. He shoved the letter into his pocket and threw himself into giving instructions and checking every last detail of the security of the compound. Doing this reassured him. It was familiar. Whatever poison pill the letter contained would have to wait until he was ready to deal with it.

The men had by now supped and prayed and the night shift was preparing to stand on duty. Omar had made a special four-man detail who would supervise the prisoner, and this detail included both Peeral and Juman. He briefed them, in Sindhi, about the strict rules regarding communications with the prisoner.

'But sir,' asked a particularly perplexed Peeral, 'what if he communicates with us?'

'I made it clear to you that you are not to respond to him at all. Is that understood?'

Juman and Peeral exchanged a look, which made it obvious that, in fact, the matter was not at all clear to them. Juman then spoke up after some hesitation.

'But sir, how do we ask him if he wants to eat? It is Ramadan, and we don't know if those escort fellows fed him while they were driving him down. I'm sure he must be fasting, and if he hasn't eaten and we don't feed him, then the sin will be registered in our account. But if we ask him about it, then we violate your orders, which as you know, are sacrosanct for us.'

Omar shook his head in frustration. 'Just prepare a plate of food and put it in the cell. If he wants to eat, he will. Got it?'

The men dispersed, apparently satisfied with ASP sahib's eminently logical answer. Omar took one last stroll around the camp, and then turned towards the tent his staff had set up for him in a corner of the compound. The tent was lit by a kerosene lamp and had a simple cot bed on one side. The lamp was set on a small portable table, on which his orderly had left a plate of cold dal and a roti. Omar realized that he hadn't eaten anything except a date at iftar, so he took off his belt, sat on the bed and started dipping pieces of the roti into the dal. He suddenly felt light-headed as the entire day's fatigue swept over him. His eyelids were heavy with drowsiness. Omar was thankful for the thermos of tea that his orderly had left along with the food. He poured himself a cup and patted his pocket again to see if the letter was still there. It was. How stupid. Where else would it have gone, he thought to himself as he sipped the hot tea. Finally, after another couple of minutes' procrastination, he knew he could not put it off any longer.

The envelope had been torn open. It had no other writing on it, except a PO box number of a remote town near the Kashmir border. The letter itself had been written on two pieces of old newspaper. Omar had to stare at the paper for several seconds before he could decipher the English words, written by a pen that had probably been running out of ink at the time, against the background of Urdu newsprint. At first, the words didn't seem to make any sense to him. In truth, being stuck out here had rusted his comprehension skills. It wasn't like there was regular English correspondence out here. Therefore, it took him a couple of moments to understand the flow of the words. But then he started to read.

two

13 April 2011
Hyderabad Jail

Dear Eddy,

I know you are angry with me. To be sure, our last correspondence didn't end well. It's my fault and subsequently, I tried to write to you to apologize, but it was on the day that I was arrested, so my letter would never have gotten to you.

I can't sleep these days. I think of her often. No, not Sana. The other one, the journalist. I see her in my mind's eye, so cocky and confident the first time I spoke to her. You could tell she was sharp from the moment she walked into my tanzeem's office. She had gotten the address from some second-rate fixer, who had assured her he could secure her an interview with a 'Jihadi sort'. Total scam. You remember, in those days western reporters had descended into the country like a swarm of locusts. Everyone wanted to be on the 'frontline' of the War on Terror, whatever that meant. Local fixers were having a field day, making their local mosque imams out to be jihadi commanders, and charging the stupid goras 1000 dollars a day for the privilege of interviewing them.

But she wasn't stupid. She had done her homework on me before she came by the office. She argued forcefully with my people, who were trying to brush her off, trying to convince them to let her interview me, unaware that I was in the next room all the time, staring at her through a partition, planning her death. I think I took the decision to kill her in that moment itself. Sitting there in the outer office, drinking that horrible tea and trying to look demure in a shalwar kameez, but unable to hide her obviously pregnant state. It was just too good an opportunity to let slip.

I can't stop thinking about her. It is a boiling April day in Hyderabad, but I cannot stop shivering. Is this guilt? After all I've done? A bit late now, don't you think? Or is it fear? Perhaps that is why I am writing to you now. When the shadow of one's own mortality falls upon you, you turn to what was most familiar in your life.

I confess, the authorities have found out about some of my extracurricular activities here. Let's just say, they haven't taken kindly to their families being threatened. I don't know why people take these sort of things so personally. But as a result, I have heard they are going to shift me from here, but not to another jail. That is the worrying part. Jails have rules, manuals that the jailers have to follow. My hosts grow tired of my little games. I fear they may have decided upon a more permanent solution for me.

I don't think I am scared of dying. After all, a man like me who has cheated death so many times has no excuse to fear it. It's dying alone that frightens me. I have spent years building walls around myself, so many walls that even I do not know how to get past all of them. I made strangers of my family. I wonder if anyone will truly mourn my passing. I mean I know, my father will observe my funeral rights, the family will observe the obligatory three days of mourning. Deghs will be cooked and distributed among the poor. Relatives will come to condole and eat. And my followers will pray for my soul, call me a martyr and plaster posters of me all over the city. If they feel really enthusiastic, they might even burn a few buses.

But I wonder if anyone will really miss me. Posters get torn or are covered with newer ones. Relatives decamp to the next occasion, happy or sad. And I think, deep down, my father will be glad to be rid of me. My wife might also breathe a sigh of relief, and perhaps look forward to marrying a more reliable, more caring man the second time round. As for my son, I am just a photograph on the wall for him. He is young. He will forget. After all, how many people still remember the journalist, so many years after her death?

I know you will remember me. Just as I will always remember you. You and I have travelled very different paths since our last day in school, all those many years ago, but the bond between us has never been broken. We both kept our word, to never lose touch, no matter where we were. In truth, the nature of our friendship changed, inevitably, as the distance between us and the worlds we inhabited increased with each passing season. We became less companions and confidants, and more like silent spectators in each other's lives, always watching, learning, but never participating.

4 November 1987. The day I first met you. Pakistan vs. Australia. World Cup semi-final. I remember it as if it had happened last week. The schoolyard was virtually empty because most kids were staying home to see the match. Nobody wanted to miss it, everyone was caught up in the moment. The first World Cup to be held in the subcontinent, and Pakistan the favourite to win. Playing a semi-final, and that too, in Lahore. What else could one ask for? Do you remember, there was a group of about sixty students who actually travelled to Lahore for the match? Of course, they were all placed on detention by the Principal the next day after they had been prominently seen cheering on television.

You and I were part of the handful of unfortunates who were still in school that morning, because our parents did not believe that an international cricket match, no matter how important, was a good enough reason to miss school. My parents believed truancy was the first step on the road to hell. Having subsequently become something of an expert on the subject of hell, I can now safely discredit their theory. But at the time, my humble suggestion had been greeted with the back of my father's hand.

If I close my eyes tight, I can still hear snippets of the commentary wafting through the schoolyard. Munir Hussain in Urdu, and Ifti Ahmed and Chishty Mujahid in English. I was desperate to find out where the sound was coming from, and then I found you, sitting under the boxing ring, your transistor held close to your ear. When I asked you the score, you offered it to me, saying, 'Here, you can have a listen.' And so we sat together, long after the break bell rang, bunking class, hiding in nooks and crannies around the school to avoid detection from the prefects, imagining every ball bowled and every shot played in our minds. When the home time bell rang, we both rushed to the gate, eager to run home so that we could catch the Pakistan side batting on TV. It was only then that I first bothered to ask your name.

But that wasn't the day we became friends. No, that happened the next day. In the aftermath of Pakistan's defeat, the entire country was in depression after having their dreams shattered by eleven Australians, and no one wanted to hear about cricket. They were fickle, following the fortunes of a nation, and not the game. I was a purist, and I did not think that there was another like me until I saw you again the next day, sitting under the boxing ring and listening with the same intensity as India's spinners tried to squeeze out the English batsmen in the other semi-final. And when you explained to me in the greatest detail the variations that Maninder Singh was bowling in his left arm spin, I knew then that we were going to be friends for a very long time.

The fact that we both loved spin bowling really cemented our friendship. At a time when every sane twelve-year-old dreamt of becoming a fast bowler like the great Imran Khan, we took the opposite path. The spinner's art is the hardest in cricket. It requires patience, perseverance and a maturity beyond your years. It needs for you to have an inordinate amount of imagination, especially when you have to bowl on a concrete school pitch for years. I have always marvelled how you had those qualities even back then. Wheeling away with your leg spinners, never flustered when you got hit for a four or six. Why you chose this difficult path, I will never know. But I'll let you in on a secret. I took up spin bowling because I thought it would help me to get into the team. I was always a decent bat, and then I discovered that the average batsman found my loopy left arm spin difficult to hit. Things just worked out for me after that. But I was a utilitarian, you were the original romantic.

I miss school. What a privileged life we led! If only I could return to a world where my only concern was how to get through my O levels. Becoming friends with you changed my life. Before you, everything about The School intimidated me. I hadn't been there as long as you had, and I didn't come from the same background as most of the others. I wasn't even used to constantly speaking in English, like everyone else did. But you made me feel so comfortable, that I forgot my own inhibitions. I remember the first time you made me speak to Sana. I had admired her from afar for some time before I finally spilled my guts to you, thinking you would be my one confidant. I could have killed you when you dragged me in front of her then and there, and said in that confident, somewhat pompous voice of yours, 'Hi Sana, have you met my friend Ahmed Uzair Sufi? We call him Ausi for short.' I don't know how you made up that nickname on the spot, but I know that it made me feel cool. My world changed when Sana turned around, and in her typical aloof, sultry voice, she said, 'Hi Ausi. What a cool name!' Never again would I answer to Ahmed in school from now. I was Ausi. How could I not be? Sana had said so.

Thanks to you, the three of us became inseparable. But you never embarrassed me in front of her. You didn't tell her that I liked her, like so many of our other friends would have done. I now sit back and laugh at my own foolish insistence that she never find out about my feelings. I was so scared of being cast out of her court, of her no longer confiding her secrets and insecurities, and not giving me the exalted, but ultimately worthless position of being her 'best friend'. That was an exile that I could not have borne.

I pass my days in prison reliving our memories. I replay every match we played for the school team, ball by ball, in my head. I remember each detail of those days, what Sana wore, how her hair used to look untied, and her bright orange scrunchy on her wrist. I see each of Sana's boyfriends getting dumped by her. I see their teenage heartbreak and how she turns to us and gives her justifications for dumping each one of them. I see your eyes roll upwards when I try and console her and tell her that, of course, it wasn't her fault, and that they don't deserve her. I see all of this in my mind's eye, and it's the only thing that ever brings a smile to my face.

Do you remember the first letter you wrote to me from college? We had promised each other we would write when you left for the US, but then I didn't hear from you for two months, and I was bitter that you had forgotten me so quickly. The letter was an effort on your part to reassure me about our friendship, but I think it was an act of catharsis too. You were in a new world and you needed an old friend. I remember reading that letter and thinking that you must have been the loneliest man on the planet. That is how I feel today. I need a friend and I wish you were here.

Your friend always,
Ausi.

three

The Present: 22 April 2011

Omar awoke after a restless night. He had read and re-read the letter several times, obsessing over it until sehri – the obligatory meal before the fast – came as a welcome distraction. He forced himself to sleep for a couple of hours after the morning prayer. He had wracked his brain all night, but he was unsure of what to do. His head could not get around the letter. The only explanation for it was that it was some kind of code, a way of relaying instructions to the Sheikh's followers.

He got out of bed just as the cool of the morning was receding and the desert sun was making its presence felt. He splashed some water on his face and instinctively called out to his orderly for tea, before remembering that the fast had begun. Omar could feel the craving for caffeine and the incessant pounding in his head. It was always like this during Ramadan. He had decided long ago that God must have derived some perverse pleasure from watching humans muddle about like a bunch of zombies while fasting.

As he stepped out of his tent to take stock of the situation, he found that things were actually going well. His men had not slept after the morning prayer, preferring to do all their duties in the morning coolness, so that they could sleep in the long afternoon, when their hunger increased as the breaking of the fast drew nearer. The guard shift had changed, and the compound had been cleaned up some more. Peeral and Juman had even managed to make the Sheikh's cell bearable. It was brighter, the floor was visibly cleaner and a portion of the door had been cut out to create an opening through which the Sheikh could receive his meals without actually having to communicate with anyone. Peeral and Juman had come up with the idea of the cut-out on their own, as they explained to him, grinning widely. However, nothing could be done about the lingering smell of buffalo piss.

The electrification of the compound also continued apace. His office staff, glowing in the reflected glory of his temporary elevation as the head of the district police, had wasted no time in throwing his weight around to ensure that all the things he had asked for were duly completed. And just to think, that barely three days ago, he had been the ASP that time forgot. In a strange way, he had the Sheikh to thank for the improvement in his status.

The thought of the Sheikh brought him back to the letter. What should he do with it? The logical course was to inform his superiors. In this case, with his SP having run away, that meant communicating with the Deputy Inspector General in Sukkur. That was an option that did not particularly enthuse Omar. The DIG was known to be a notoriously difficult boss. He was honest, but his honesty made him cranky. In all the time that Omar had spent here, the DIG had never bothered to enquire after him, had never bothered to make him more comfortable, despite the fact that he was aware that the young ASP had been stuck with a notoriously corrupt SP. If Omar called him up now, the old man would probably find some reason to berate him. The DIG was a real stickler for doing things by the book. He worshipped the 1934 Police Rules, believing that, like all holy books, the answers to all of life's problems lay within those pages. If Omar went to him before having questioned the prisoner first, he was likely to get an earful. The DIG was unlikely to accept the argument that Shahab had told him not to talk to the Sheikh. No, as Omar thought more about it, it was better to take a chance on communicating with the Sheikh and asking him about the letter first.

Peeral dutifully reported that the Sheikh had been cooperative when the cell had been cleaned in the morning. He had not tried to talk to either Peeral or Juman, but instead, once they had finished, he had simply thanked them very humbly for having made it possible for him to pray in the cell. Or at least, that's what they thought he must have said, as their comprehension of Urdu was very rudimentary. That didn't sound too bad. The only question was where to interrogate him. The cell would have been the obvious choice, but it wasn't big enough to hold two people, and besides, Omar wasn't sure he could stand the smell. But the rest of the shed was more spacious, and better lit as well. In one corner of it stood an old battered desk and a couple of broken chairs, and it was here that Omar sat down, instructing Peeral and Juman to bring the Sheikh. As a security precaution, one of the two sentries were to stay in the room with Omar.

As the Sheikh came out from his cell into the outer shed, Omar was astonished to find that the prisoner seemed sprightlier than his captor. The Sheikh's face seemed to have been freshly scrubbed and the layer of dirt and dust that had covered him the previous evening was gone. Despite the shackles on his feet and the effect of the miserable little cell, the Sheikh carried himself with a certain dignity. Omar looked at his face, still handsome, though prematurely aged and hardened by life. The Sheikh sat down on the broken chair that Omar offered to him, and bowed his head in acknowledgement.

'Assalam Alaikum.'

'I, uh, called you here because I have some questions that need to be answered, and the easiest way to solve this would be for you to cooperate with me.'

'Assalam Alaikum.'

'What?'

'It is customary, when two Muslims meet each other, irrespective of their relationship towards each other, that they greet each other with Allah's blessings. Only then can they move towards any other business. The proper response, as you know, should be "Walaikum Assalam".'

'Walaikum Assalam.' Omar was flustered by the Sheikh's patronizing tone. He also noticed that the Sheikh had addressed him in English, despite his having spoken in Urdu.

'Now, ASP sahib, tell me what it is that I can help you with.'

Omar could see the ease with which the Sheikh had taken control of the conversation and he realized that he had to alter this very quickly otherwise any attempt at getting any meaningful information from the prisoner would be useless.

'Now look, Sheikh Uzair, or whatever your name is, you had better behave here. This is not the jail, where you could dupe a bunch of simple-minded wardens to do your bidding! What we do with you ultimately, will rest on how you behave over here and how much you cooperate with us. The *gornmint* is considering a number of options for you, and not all of them are particularly nice as far as you are concerned. Therefore, I suggest you mend your *ettitude*.'

Omar was nervous about his spoken English. It was not as polished as the Sheikh's. He had a typically Sindhi pronunciation of certain words like 'government' and 'attitude', and this gave away his rural origins. In all of his years as a student, he had always been far more confident of writing, rather than speaking English. He knew that this fact would be plain for someone like the Sheikh, whose pronunciation was so effortless. For some strange reason, this was a source of irritation for Omar, as if his lack of proper grammar skills somehow gave the Sheikh an edge over him.

The Sheikh smiled at Omar and paused, as if sizing him up. Then suddenly, he changed his tone and became far more submissive. 'I apologize, ASP sahib, if I have given you offence. I did not mean to. I acknowledge your power over me and am ready to cooperate with you in any way possible.'

Omar took the letter out of his pocket. 'Did you write this letter?'

Sheikh Ahmed peered at the letter through his spectacles. 'Can I see it?' He took the letter in his hand and pored over it with the curiosity of a scientist who has discovered a new element. He finally nodded. 'Yes, I wrote this.'

'You admit this?'

'Yes, of course. Why wouldn't I?'

'This letter seems to me to be in code through which you are trying to communicate with someone. What are you trying to convey through this letter?'

'My emotions. If you have read the letter, I would have thought that was pretty clear to everybody.'

'That is what you say. But the letter has a hidden meaning as well, which you are even now trying to conceal. Who is this Edhi, or Eddy? Is he one of your followers or is he a facilitator? Has he provided any financial or material support to jihadi causes?'

'Eddy? He's just my friend. He's not a follower of mine,

and, as far as I know, I would be extremely surprised if he had ever financed a jihadi cause. Although, you can never tell with people these days.'

'These references to countries: India, Pakistan, Australia, England. Are these targets? Have you selected targets for bombing in these countries?'

'ASP sahib, with all due respect, I think you're really taking this letter in the wrong spirit. I can assure you, it has no references to any target in any country…'

'Shut up! Do you think I'm stupid?' Omar realized the minute the words were out of his mouth that he was letting the Sheikh get to him, and so he held back a further outburst and took a moment to calm himself. 'I am afraid, Sheikh Ahmed Uzair, that your responses to my questions are not helping your case. I will ask you one final question. You mention Sana in the letter. Now I know that Osama bin Laden's mother was born in Yemen and San'aa is the capital of Yemen. Isn't that true?'

'ASP sahib, I haven't the faintest idea where Osama bin Laden's mother was born.'

The Sheikh's last answer was met with a stony silence from Omar, who pursed his lips and stared at him for a long instant and then walked out of the shed. The interrogation was over. It was frustrating because, for all his anger at the Sheikh, the truth was that he himself didn't know if the letter was a code, or just some random jottings. He had never worked on a terrorism case and he didn't have any background information on the Sheikh other than what he knew from the media. He had only known about bin Laden's mother because he had read it in a book. There was no way to sift out the truth of the letter. What was worse, from a personal point of view, was that he had been exposed as a typical unprofessional, small town police officer.

Sheikh Ahmed would be laughing now that he had seen the competence level of his captors. Omar cursed himself for having gone in to meet the Sheikh so unprepared. Still, what was done was done. Now he would have to figure out some other way to decipher the letter.

Going Out into
the World

four

The city always intimidated him. Every time he rode down the Super Highway into Karachi, past the new vegetable market, past the settlements of illegal squatters, perched at the edge of the city that seemed to grow larger every time, swallowing up every tract of available land. The city spread like a cancer, random and menacing. Omar would always shudder with awe because Karachi confounded him. This untamed metropolis, with its hustle and bustle, teeming with millions of strangers, all of them living their lives in a fast-paced frenzy, oblivious, for the most part, to their fellow citizens.

It wasn't like Omar hadn't spent time in the city. His more affluent cousins, all bankers or accountants, lived here. He had moved in with them for several months when he was preparing for his civil service exams. The casual callousness of the city never failed to shock him. He would read the newspaper every day, and every day the paper would be filled with horror stories; of people getting killed in the streets; policemen getting shot by gangsters; women mugged at gunpoint inside their homes. Riots were a daily occurrence and, as his cousins joked, you hadn't had the authentic Karachi experience if your car hadn't been snatched at gunpoint. For a boy from the village, where the smallest event, whether it was a lost buffalo or a bereavement, impacted the entire community, the big city's attitude of shrugging, getting up and dusting off everything was unfathomable.

But there was also another, deeply personal reason why Omar disliked Karachi. This was where he had fallen in love for the first time. It had happened unexpectedly, one of the few unplanned events in his otherwise meticulously planned existence. He had joined a study group of other prospective civil service exam takers, but none of the other participants could match his level of preparation. They came from comfortable family backgrounds, and their drive to excel in the examinations could not match his. Inevitably, he became the mentor in the group, tutoring the others even as he fine-tuned his own preparations. She had joined the group very late, when the exams were just a month away. Her name was Aroosha, and from the minute he laid eyes on her, Omar had been infatuated. She had walked into the library, dressed in six inch heels, a smartly cut shalwar kameez and a large Gucci handbag on her shoulders. Her lipstick was bright red and her long, dark waist-length hair blow-dried straight. Omar had never seen anyone like her.

He had never expected her to speak to him but, having sat at the edge of the table and observed the group for five minutes, she had figured out that he was the only one who could help her. So she had got up from her seat and approached him, and spoken to him in that friendly, yet vulnerable, whiny way that some women have when they want men to do something for them. She had pleaded for his help and sworn that if he didn't help her, she was bound to fail the exams. To this day, he couldn't remember what she had wanted help in, whether it was some basic principle of Forestry, or the clauses of the Congress of Vienna, but the instant she had opened her mouth, Omar Abassi had fallen for her hard.

The next six weeks had been a dream for him. The two of them spent hours together in the library every day, bent over some textbook or the other. Afterward, she would go with him to one of the food stalls near the library to grab a bite to eat. They began to share jokes and all the other small intimacies that develop between two people who spend so much time together. It was the first time that Omar Abassi learned to laugh at himself. Once the exams started, they would meet outside the exam centre at seven each morning, and he would quiz her on all her notes, reassuring her in a gentle tone that she had covered everything. They would wish each other luck and enter the classroom, and while he sat through all his papers, Omar would find his mind wandering towards her, thinking about how she was faring. He couldn't wait for each paper to finish, so he could rush out and be reunited with her. They would sit in a nearby park, or go to a restaurant, and she would nervously replay her entire paper for him, asking him after every question if he thought she had done okay. It never struck him that she never ventured into the details of his papers, but he didn't care. All he cared about was being able to soothe her anxieties. Besides, all the members of the study group had long ago reached the conclusion that his position in these exams was guaranteed.

By the date of the last paper, Omar was in a state of bliss. He was confident that he had managed to do very well in the exams, well enough to merit selection in one of the top services. And at the same time, he was convinced that he had found the woman of his dreams. More importantly, he was convinced that she was as besotted with him as he was with her. He had already mapped out his future strategy. They would wait till the exam result was published before he formally sent a proposal to her family. After all, the chances of their refusing a successful civil service candidate were bound to be negligible. And though it would be a bit taxing on them to be together while he was at the Academy, he wasn't willing to wait till the end of his training to get married. So that was that. Of course, it never entered his mind that she would have a slightly different take on their relationship. Two days after the exams, when the old study group had organized a celebratory get together at a coffee shop close to their library, he asked her to come earlier than the others because he felt it was time to speak the unspoken. He had never expressed his feelings to a girl before, but he was so sure about her that this was hardly going to be the same as walking up to a stranger and telling her you liked her. And so her reply came to him like a cold, hard slap in the face. She confessed that she had never felt about him in *that* way. To her, he was just an extremely helpful friend. Besides, it was incredibly presumptuous of him, a *village* boy, to consider himself equal to her in matrimonial terms. She was a city girl, from a prosperous family. Her high heels and handbags cost more than he would expect to make in a month. How had he imagined to keep her in the style that she was accustomed to?

Omar had never bothered to consider any of these things. He had been so enchanted by the allure of her company that he had never asked about her background. And since he had never really had the time for girls in college or medical school, this was his first experience of his own social limitations. But what hurt more than any of this was the realization that she had used him to get through her exams. He had been nothing more than a study aid for her. And it was this realization that made him feel, more than he had ever before, like a small town village boy. He was reminded of this every time he came to

Karachi. Reminded of her, and how inadequate she had made him feel. How inadequate this city made him feel.

But, this time, the circumstances of his visit to the city were a little different. A week had passed since Sheikh Uzair's arrival. Omar had dealt with the immediate dilemma of the contraband letter by typing up a comprehensive report on the matter and forwarding it, post-haste, to his DIG. That way, even if something happened, at least no one could say that the appropriate letter had not been initiated. He knew he was playing a game of bureaucratic Cover-Your-Ass, but there was little else he could do at the moment. He was completely tied up in ensuring foolproof security for the Sheikh. Plus, his boss's continuing absence meant that Omar had to increasingly tend to the more mundane problems of the district. Nonetheless, he had managed to establish a first rate facility at the Animal Husbandry School. The Sheikh was being monitored round the clock by a handpicked team of his men. Peeral and Juman were in charge of feeding him and taking him out for his daily half-hour exercise. Even the smell of buffalo urine had almost dissipated from the cell. Omar had been extremely careful in ensuring that all the men on the Sheikh's detail spoke nothing but Sindhi. Shahab's warning had stuck in his mind and he didn't want to take any chances of his men fraternizing with the Sheikh.

By the time the DIG's summons arrived at the camp the previous morning, Omar had started to feel pretty self-satisfied with his efforts. In fact, he had almost forgotten about his report on the letter, and so the message from the DIG, ordering him to come to Sukkur to discuss his report, took him by surprise. He had hurriedly dressed in his best uniform which, he was alarmed to find, was now several shades lighter than its original colour and had developed tears where his nameplate was pinned on. Trying as best as he could to ignore these wardrobe malfunctions, he had read and reread the letter, trying to decipher anything new that he could tell his boss. After all, the DIG was a stickler for detail and Omar didn't want him to glean something from the letter that he himself had been unable to do so. That would be terribly embarrassing and what's more, the DIG would never let him forget it.

Sukkur was several hours' drive from the Animal Husbandry School and Omar arrived at the colonial building that housed the DIG's office well in time for his meeting. Expecting to be made to wait, he was again surprised when the orderly ushered him into the DIG's presence immediately. The office, in contrast to its grand exterior, was a mess inside. Files were stacked against the walls and on all the chairs. Only one chair, directly opposite to that of the occupant of the office, lay vacant.

It took an eternity for the DIG to acknowledge his presence. He was a wiry-looking man, with a slightly receding hairline, which he had compensated for by letting his silver hair grow long over his collar. The pair of half-moon bifocals that were perched on the bridge of his nose gave him the look of a stern school headmaster. The DIG was also a short man, and Omar had to crane his neck to see his forehead behind two high mounds of papers that rose from the desk like twin towers.

The DIG was referred to as the 'Englishman' by his subordinates, for his formal and brusque manner, and for his habit of diving straight to the heart of the matter. Today, he did not disappoint.

'What are your apprehensions regarding the prisoner Sheikh Uzair, and the contents of the letter that was found on his person?'

The speed of the delivery and the clipped English that it was delivered in made Omar hesitate, for just half a second, in which time the DIG fired another fusillade.

'What do you think is the nature of the threat? Is it a jail break, a terrorist attack or a kidnap attempt?'

'Sir, I…'

'Because if it is a jail break, then I would suggest you re-evaluate your own contingency plans. His security and safekeeping are exclusively your sphere of responsibility. You must ensure that there are no loopholes in your security measures. Are there any?'

'Yes sir … I mean no, sir. I know his security is my responsibility, sir, and rest assured that I have taken painstaking measures to ensure that the location is escape proof. Tripling of the guard, double barriers of barbed wire in a 1 km radius of the compound…'

'Good. Well then, I don't see a problem. If it is a terrorist plot, is it going to be executed in the Sukkur region, or elsewhere? And if it is a kidnap attempt, will he abduct a local, or go for a foreigner again?'

'No sir, I mean I don't know, sir. That's the problem, sir. I don't know what to make of the letter. I have never worked a jihadi case before. I don't know their codes nor do I understand their way of thinking. I just felt that, well, since the letter was handed to me, it was my duty to report it to someone who might be able to decipher it.'

For the first time in the exchange, the DIG peered up at him from his papers and looked at him in the manner of a botanist examining some rare new breed of plant. 'So there is no imminent threat, then?'

'I don't know, sir.'

Abruptly, the headmasterly scowl reappeared. 'I have referred the matter to the head of CID in Karachi. They will investigate it further. I have also reviewed your reports on the security of this Animal Husbandry School. Your efforts appear to be satisfactory.'

'Sir, with due respect, it was the CID staff who discovered the letter on him, but they didn't pursue the matter. I don't think they will undertake a serious investigation of the matter.'

'They are the experts on him. What alternative do you propose? Certainly none of my other officers can investigate the matter. I don't see what else can be done. Do you wish to pursue it yourself?'

'Well, er ... sir, maybe I can make some inquiries with the CID inspector, Shahab I think his name was ... If my SP would allow me to leave the district for a day or so, then I could...'

'Very well, if you want to pursue it. But let me remind you that the custody of the prisoner is still your primary responsibility and should anything happen to him while you are out conducting your investigation, I will not absolve you or exempt you from any future inquiry. You may go.' The DIG then returned to his paperwork as if he had never stopped.

Stunned, and not sure whether he should have felt elated or disturbed, Omar saluted and turned on his heels. His hand was on the door knob when the DIG called out to him again.

'Oh and there is no need for you to ask your SP. He didn't wish to deal with this Sheikh Uzair matter so he had himself transferred to another district. Under the circumstances, it will be foolish to send a new officer to your district. Therefore, I have appointed you the district SP. Make sure nothing goes wrong.'

When he came down the stairs, he found his former boss's shiny red jeep waiting for him in the driveway. He was a little nervous, and tempted to go back to the Animal Husbandry School to conduct yet another check on his arrangements. After all, the DIG had made it perfectly clear that it would be his head on the block if any negligence occurred. But then, for once in his life, Omar Abassi decided to do the spontaneous thing. He sat in the passenger seat of the jeep, and asked the driver to rev the engine and drive full speed to Karachi.

As the traffic of the Super Highway gave way to the urban sprawl, Omar couldn't help but reflect on his return to the city. Back then, after the Aroosha incident, he had run out of town with his tail between his legs, like the impoverished student he had been. He returned today, like a conqueror, replete with bodyguards and an escort, the unquestioned master of his little corner of the earth. So what if that corner was the godforsaken Nara Desert! A district SP was a district SP, after all. It was this last thought that brought a smile to Omar's face.

It was almost evening, close to iftar, the breaking of the fast, by the time they got close to their destination. It took a while for his driver to navigate his way to the CID office, which was located in the congested city centre. The problem of locating the office was exacerbated by the fact that when Omar's driver asked for directions to the CID headquarters, no one had the faintest clue what he was talking about. They went through about seven or eight pedestrians before one finally had a faint glimmer of recognition.

The CID building, or Bhoot Bangla as it was commonly called, was a dilapidated colonial-era structure, surrounded by tall glass and concrete monstrosities that Karachi's builders were so fond of calling 'Plazas', and which had been liberally peppered all over the city over the past thirty years like smallpox scars on a handsome face.

The place seemed to be falling apart. The building had an imposing slanting roof, covered with ancient terracotta tiles. Parts of the roof had fallen in, creating such large holes that whole flocks of pigeons had taken to nesting among the exposed rafters. There was no sign to indicate that this was the CID headquarters, nor did there appear to be any human habitation in the compound, until suddenly a man appeared from the shadows and raised the barrier at the gate to allow their convoy to enter. Curiously, the sentry didn't bother to check their identity, and before Omar's driver could ask him where to go, he wordlessly pointed to a parking spot that was, as the painted sign on the tarred road read, for visitors only.

Again without asking any questions, the same sentry pointed Omar toward a decrepit wooden staircase that creaked loudly as he began to ascend it. At the top of the stairs, waiting to receive him, was Inspector Shahab, wearing his trademark safari suit and wide grin.

'ASP sahib, what a pleasure to see you again! Welcome to CID. Have you broken your fast? I'm sure you haven't. Not to worry. One of the advantages of having our office in the heart of the city is that we have access to some excellent dining establishments. What would you like to eat? Actually, I might as well get a little bit of everything and you can pick and choose as you like.'

All of a sudden, as Shahab was delivering his staccato monologue without any break, the haunted house seemed to come to life. More men appeared out of nowhere. One of them took Omar's beret and stick, while another shoved a glass of cold water into his hand. Shahab himself led Omar by the arm into a little office to the side of the staircase. In sharp contrast to the exterior of the building, the office was modern. A powerful air conditioner had made the small room uncomfortably cold. Shiny tiles covered the old floor and walls. The room had a small desk and a very large, decadent office chair, one that seemed well equipped to accommodate the girth of a man like Shahab. Behind the desk and chair, a video console with six screens had been set up. Four of the screens showed closed circuit images of the main gate and the area surrounding the compound, while the remaining two screens were focused on the lockup cells.

Omar had barely sat down when an orderly swept into the room, having brought food with impossible swiftness. His arms balanced several dishes that gave off the most enticing aromas. Shahab moved with a balletic deftness that belied his size, managing, in the same motion, to guide Omar to a seat, removing the papers from his desk and popping a chicken drumstick into his mouth. He seated himself on the big chair, and dealt with the various dishes placed in front of him like a maestro playing a concerto. He piled the food onto a plate with an artist's touch, a mound of rice here, a sprinkling of dal there, a dollop of chicken curry on top, and he shoved the plate into Omar's hands.

Omar had a dozen questions, but in truth he was starving and the sight of such rich delicacies proved too much for his natural reserve. He dug into his plate, but hesitated after four or five mouthfuls, suddenly remembering that he had not come here alone.

'My men...'

Shahab raised his hand like a traffic warden and motioned to one of the video screens, where Omar could see that his escort and drivers were digging into a huge bowl of biryani.

'How did you know I was coming?'

'I didn't.'

'What? Then how did you arrange all of this?'

Shahab grinned that big Cheshire cat grin of his and wiped a bit of chicken gravy from his cheek. 'Don't distress yourself, ASP sahib. I had told you to look me up next time you were in Karachi. Besides, we saw your motorcade on our cameras, and I spotted the Khairpur number plates. We quite like having visitors at CID. Unfortunately, we don't get many. Well, not voluntary ones at any rate.'

His whole frame shook as he giggled, overly pleased with his little joke. Omar for the life of him couldn't figure out how or why anyone would regard Shahab as a competent officer. But he restrained himself. In their previous meeting, he had gotten off on the wrong foot and now he needed this man, whatever his personal impressions may have been.

'Well, now that I have taken care of my duties as a host, ASP sahib, please tell me, how may I help you? I hope our friend isn't troubling you too much? He hasn't tried to escape, has he?'

'No. No, he's fine. Well actually, he's quite a difficult problem. Not physically, but professionally. I … well, I don't know quite how to say this, Mr Shahab, but … well, I haven't worked on such cases before. You know, jihadis, high profile criminals … So I don't quite know what to make of him, or how to judge whether what he says is true or not.'

'That's an easy one, ASP sahib. Don't believe anything that he says. I was on his trail for a very long time, and the one thing that I learned about him is that I don't think he has ever been truthful with anyone in his entire life. I told you this when I visited you. He will try to seduce you like a woman. Don't make the mistake of falling for it.'

'But that's just my point. I don't know anything about him. No background, except for what little I read in the newspapers. So I don't know what to make of any of it. Like the letter you handed to me before you left. I don't know whether it's a code of some sort, or just gibberish written by a man who has been locked up for a while. You know him, you know how he thinks. You said it yourself right now. You were on his trail for a very long time. Please help me to understand him. If he is to remain in my custody for god knows how long, I must be able to decipher him.'

Shahab smiled benevolently. 'Shall we have some green tea? It will help to digest that meal.' He pressed a buzzer on his desk and an orderly appeared, tray in hand, with two steaming cups of green tea. 'My staff is very good. They anticipate my wishes before I need to verbalize them. It comes from having been with me for so many years, I suppose,' he said by way of explanation.

He squeezed a thin lemon slice into the porcelain cup, and stirred it slowly. 'I sympathize with you, ASP sahib. You have been lumped with a very precarious problem indeed. And I am sure, knowing our wonderful department, that everyone else must have washed their hands off you. I heard that your SP got the Chief Minister to transfer him to another, more lucrative district. He was always a politically shrewd man. I did my Sub Inspector's promotion course with him. I knew then that he was going to go places. And then there is your DIG. Don't expect anything from that bastard, unless something goes wrong. Then he will be the one standing right next to you, fashioning the noose around your neck. Anything goes wrong and it's your fault, as I'm sure they would have made it abundantly clear to you. It is very unfair. You're a young officer and cannot be expected to manage this on your own. In truth, I now feel partially responsible. I was the one who suggested the Animal Husbandry School, though I had no idea that you were posted there. I don't think there's ever been an ASP posted there. Somebody upstairs clearly doesn't like you. But I just suggested the place because everyone wanted to dump the Sheikh somewhere where he could be forgotten, and, well, I'm sure you can testify to the fact that if there's one place you can be well and truly forgotten, it's the Nara desert in Khairpur.'

Omar shrugged his shoulders with an air of resignation. Professional pride was one thing, but Shahab had summed up his situation perfectly. There was no point denying any of it.

'Can you help me?'

'I will certainly try. Though you may find the extent of my knowledge about him to be quite limited, ultimately. Yes, you are right, I was on his trail for years, and I do know him, in the way that a hunter knows his quarry, but to say I know how he thinks … well I don't think there's anyone alive who knows how he thinks. I have been doing this job for a long time, ASP sahib. I came into service as an Assistant Sub Inspector in 1981, and I have seen all sorts of things in my career, but I can tell you without exaggeration that I have never come across a man like the Sheikh. But I am getting ahead of myself. Let me begin at the beginning, as they say.'

Shahab leaned back in his massive chair and placed both his hands on his paunch with an air of self-contentedness.

'CID was formed shortly before 9/11. You see, at the time, there had been a spate of sectarian murders. Sunnis killing Shi'as, Shi'as killing Sunnis. No one in the police had any real experience of this sort of thing. So they decided to set up a new unit that would specialize in these cases. I volunteered because I figured it would be an easy job, no having to come to a police station on time, no uniform, good money. How was I to know that 9/11 would happen a month later and the sky would fall on our heads?

'We were so naïve, I swear, in the beginning when an informer used to come and tell us that the SSP had killed someone, we thought he was talking about the Senior Superintendent of Police, rather than the Sipah Sahaba Pakistan.

'And then the woman got kidnapped. Rachel Boyd, award winning BBC journalist.' He opened a drawer in his side table and took out an old, laminated press pass. Under the grime, was a picture of a pretty Caucasian woman, who looked to be in her mid-thirties, in a typical passport-photo pose.

'She had joined the flock of western journalists who came here after 9/11, looking for a new story, a new angle on what was going on. Nothing exceptional about her, nothing exceptional at all, except her ambition. She was the only one, out of 450 international journalists who entered Pakistan, who was seven months pregnant when she got here. Apparently her doctors in the UK had advised her not to travel in such a state, but she said she couldn't sit by and watch the biggest news event of the century unfold from home. Afterwards, we questioned the immigration officer who allowed her into the country. He said that she was so obviously pregnant, he had stopped her at the airport counter. But she became indignant and told him that he should be ashamed of himself for making fun of a fat woman. Can you imagine? Such confidence. The entire immigration staff was so embarrassed, they carried her bags all the way to the taxi.'

Shahab chuckled, and took another sip of his green tea.

'You sound as if you met her.'

'No, unfortunately not. But,' as he spoke, Shahab took out a thick folder that had been lying under the press pass, 'I spent so long trying to find her, I learned up everything there was to learn about her. She became like a member of my family.'

He leafed through the folder, taking a pair of spectacles from his breast pocket as he did so.

'She was here a week, didn't stay at the bigger hotels, the Sheraton or the Marriott, because, as she told her producer, that's where the media pack all were and she wanted to get away and find the real stories in this country. She opted for the Embassy Inn, on Shahrah Faisal, a hotel with a slightly dubious reputation for providing guests with prostitutes, but still, a nice clean place.

She tried to contact various individuals in the jihadi underworld, sometimes using fixers, sometimes just calling them up directly.

'Somewhere along the line, she got in touch with Sheikh Uzair. He hid his true identity from her, and introduced himself as a marginal figure in jihadi circles, but one with excellent contacts. He threw her some bait and she took it. He set up a one-on-one meeting with her, on the pretext that he would take her to meet some Al-Qaeda type, and she was never seen alive after that.'

'Did he always intend to kill her? What was his motive?'

'That was the thing that we never understood. He had no apparent motive. At the time, although he was a major jihadi figure, he hadn't gotten involved in any of the fighting against the Americans in Afghanistan. There was a story, though he never confirmed it when we finally arrested him, that shortly after Ms Boyd's kidnapping, he had been picked up by one of the intelligence agencies. They slapped him around and asked him some general questions, but never bothered to question him about the Englishwoman. They never imagined that he would be involved in any way. So, after keeping him for a day or so, they let him go. And all this time he had the girl, but never told them a thing! Can you imagine?

'Anyway, after he had kept her for a month or so, without any prior indication, no ransom demand, no list of political demands about colleagues he wanted us to set free or anything like that, he just decided to kill her. He made a production of it, filming the whole thing, as you must have seen. All the other jihadi groups condemned his action. They felt it was against their code to kill a pregnant woman. They all felt he had crossed a line. But then, that was Sheikh Uzair. Always willing to take the one extra step that no one else was willing to take.'

'What happened after that? How did you catch him?'

'Oh, his trail went cold after the murder. We spent a month looking for her before he released the video, and then almost another month looking for a body to confirm that the video hadn't been some kind of sick hoax. Ultimately we found her, on a small farmhouse on the outskirts of the city. Or what was left of her, after the dogs had gotten to her. God, the smell was awful inside that farmhouse. Just thinking about it makes me gag.'

Shahab covered his mouth with his fat hand, just to emphasize the point. 'Anyway, we picked up a couple of the small fry, the fellows who had guarded the farmhouse, but who had no idea of the overall plan. We couldn't get near the Sheikh though. He had vanished like a ghost.'

'Where did he go after that?'

'I found nothing on him. Every source, every informer of mine, I cracked down on all of them. Even the guards we arrested didn't know his real name. For all I knew, the fellow in the video, who cut the girl's throat, could have been a paid actor. The only evidence I had of his existence was a couple of recorded messages on the hotel phone. You see, ASP sahib, the Sheikh has a very peculiar way of speaking English. He is well spoken, for one. His diction, his grammar, is perfect. Not like the way we speak, always mixing Urdu words with English ones. Of course, I do not consider myself a great linguist, I am not a PSP officer like yourself sir, and I am sure your English is far better than mine, but I would wager that even you could not hold a candle to the Sheikh. You see, we speak it like a second language, or in your case, even a third language. We still think in Urdu, or Sindhi. He thinks in English, so he speaks it like a native. You know, of course, that he went to The School?'

'I think there was some mention of it in the internet entries that I read about him. But I assumed that was just a myth. After all, the people who go to The School are from the elite class. They go abroad to study and end up as doctors, lawyers, big shot corporate types. How would someone like him have even gotten into a place like that?'

'Oh no, it's absolutely true. I checked the school records myself. He was there, but I doubt if anyone even remembers him at school. I got the impression that he must have been a non-entity of sorts. Anyway, as I was saying, a year passed after the Boyd murder and all I had was this voice recording. Then, the twin attacks on the President happened in Islamabad. Massive operations, superbly planned, and almost achieved the objective too, if it hadn't been for a donkey cart driver who lost control of his donkey and came in the way of the vehicle that was supposed to ram the President's motorcade at the last minute.

'Well, the army fellows went ballistic after that. They were desperate to trace out the case. They scanned all the mobile phones in the area at the time of the incident to pick up any clue. Like looking for a needle in a haystack. But lo and behold, I found the needle. There was a call, almost at the exact time of the attack, and a man spoke in English, cursing when the attack failed. The voice was the same as the one on my recordings from the hotel. So now we knew he was behind the attack on the President. But we still had no trace of him. The entire army, all the intelligence agencies and the CIDs of four provinces were on his trail, and we couldn't find a thing.'

'How did you catch him then?'

Omar could see that Shahab was obviously getting into his storytelling. His voice intonations went up and down with the dramatic highs and lows of his narrative, and his hands moved about like the conductor of an orchestra, dictating the rhythm of his music.

'Ah, now that is another interesting tale in itself. Months went by. Then a year. And then another year. The sense of urgency wore off. The army and the intelligence agencies went back to their work, and we went back to ours. Then one day, out of the blue, I heard him again. We had been monitoring the comings and goings of some jihadis in a nondescript madrasa complex in Korangi, here in Karachi. We had the phones of the madrasa tapped, and we would go through the recordings every day. Very tedious task, as there were hundreds of calls daily and most of them were nonsense stuff, students calling for fast food deliveries, or the occasional local Romeo chatting with his Juliet for an hour or two. One day, I was listening to the recordings, and I heard a short call, made by someone speaking in English. It was him! I recognized the voice and the way he spoke. He was living in the madrasa. Of course, I compared it to the earlier recordings, and the intelligence boys ran their computer generated voice analysis tests, but I didn't need to see the results of the tests to know it was him.

'I didn't know if we would ever get such a good chance again. I wanted to raid the madrasa. But that presented problems. It was a huge complex, and it would have to be a massive operation. Even then, there was the chance that he might slip away. Funnily enough, we never expected them to resist the way they did. Eighteen hours, the firing lasted. We fired so many tear gas shells into that godforsaken building that the entire neighbourhood stank for a week afterwards. But his men had a fanaticism I had never seen before. They were so desperate to protect him that when our assault team entered the building, they started throwing pots and pans at our men because they had run out of bullets. Can you imagine?

'And then, once we had them all, they wouldn't reveal which one was him. He had totally changed his appearance since the

Rachel Boyd episode. I was the one who finally found him. I'm not good with faces but I always remember eyes, and his eyes set him apart from all the others. They smouldered as if a volcano sat beneath them.

'When we brought him here, still he didn't say a word. He wouldn't even give us his name. We strung him up for two days, before he uttered anything. And the curious thing was, he wasn't trying to save himself. When he spoke, he didn't deny anything. In fact, he proudly admitted to the killing of Rachel Boyd and the attacks on the President.'

'But if he was going to admit everything anyway, why did he hold out for so long?'

'I asked him that, after he started talking. And do you know what his answer was, ASP sahib? He said he didn't want to make it easy for us. The whole thing was a game for him.'

Shahab laughed and slapped his knee, as if he had been reminded of a particularly mischievous favourite nephew. 'I have a theory about him. I don't believe he does whatever he does for religion. I mean, that's what he tells his followers, and the other jihadis. But he's not like them. They have either been misled, or they have their own twisted version of what is right and wrong. They are willing to give up their lives, but he isn't. He plays with the lives of others. He's a survivor. Life is like a chess board to him. But he is the only one who sees the whole board, who understands perfectly why he does something and what the result will be. And he does what he does because he enjoys it.'

Shahab had leaned towards Omar while saying the last sentence, as if letting him in on a big secret. Now he nodded sagely, looking at Omar, trying to assess if his message had gotten through.

Omar was quiet for a minute. He absent-mindedly sipped the now cold green tea.

'Shahab sahib, were there ever any other letters? From him, I mean. Did you ever find any kind of correspondence on him when you arrested him?'

A look of surprise crossed Shahab's face. He had not expected this question. He picked up his spectacles and placed them on the rim of his nose, while he picked up the thick file once again. 'Letters? What a curious thing to ask. I don't think so ... hang on, why yes! It says here that a letter in a sealed envelope was found on his person when he was arrested from the madrasa. Hmm, the letter should be in this file ... ah, there you go!'

Shahab pulled out a grime-encrusted brown envelope from the back of the file. Omar's heart jumped as he felt the rough texture of the paper. He had asked the question as a long shot, not really expecting that there would be a letter. Yet here it was, written on a few scraps of yellowing notepaper. It was in English, and had a heading that said simply, 'Final Letter'. It was addressed to the same person, Eddy, as the earlier letter. Omar's eyes widened further as he quickly glanced through it. He had the urge to run away and read the letter in private, like some lovesick school girl. He felt it somehow inappropriate to read it in front of Shahab, as if the Sheikh had meant to share this correspondence with him, and no one else.

'That's full marks to you, ASP sahib. I don't know how I forgot this little detail. The note here is written by one of my subordinates. The envelope had a mailing address on it, of the post office in the town of Fatehpur, district Kotli, in Azad Kashmir. The note says that we had the address checked, but it was a drop box at the local post office. Local authorities said it hadn't been used in ages. We never pursued it further. But at that time, we were so swamped with work, and he was singing like a canary anyway. He was a huge catch, we all got promoted, I got a medal and the reward money, so unfortunately some of the details got overlooked. I must never have gotten around to asking him about the letter. Well, now you can ask him about it.'

'Do you think I should go and ask him?'

'Oh certainly, ASP sahib. Look, you had an instinct about something and you followed it up. And you seem to be on to something here. Undoubtedly. Question him about the letters. But be very careful of one thing. He will try to charm you, try to speak in English, talk about cricket and all that sort of nonsense. But he's only doing it to gauge your weaknesses. He wants to know what makes you tick so that he can use it against you when the time comes. Always be on your guard. And above all, never forget that he is a very dangerous man.'

Omar felt the envelope between his thumb and forefinger, and nodded wordlessly. He had made his decision. He would find out the truth behind Sheikh Ahmed Uzair Sufi. Come what may.

five

23 October 1994
Haileybury College, Ridgefield
New Hampshire

Dear Ausi,

How are you man? It's been two months since I got here, and I haven't heard a peep from you. What the hell, bro? Whatever happened to your promise of keeping in touch? I'm the one who's gone to a new place, I'm the one whose life is changing. The least you can do is take five minutes out of your 'oh-so-busy' schedule to drop me a line. You obviously haven't forgotten how to write, because I spoke to Sana in Boston yesterday and she was raving about the letter you wrote her. That's convenient. I was the one who drove you to Boat Basin every time you wanted to cry over her, yet she's the one who gets the correspondence. Yeah, fuck you too, pal.

Look, I'm sorry for that. I wanted to start this letter in a very different vein, but my emotions got the better of me. I just miss you, man. Sana told me what you wrote and I guess deep down I feel a bit guilty. I know you feel like we've all moved on to a new life and you're still stuck in dirty, violent, screwed up old Karachi through no fault of your own. I realize that it should have been me who made the first move to reach out to you, but you know I'm really bad with these sort of things. Sana has always been much better at stuff like this, remembering people's birthdays, sending them thank you notes and what not. I remember you used to flip every time you got one of her cute little scented slips. Hell, I always made fun of her for being such a sop. But I guess that's why you responded to her, because she made the effort to write to you first. Maybe I should have done that too.

I wish I could tell you that I hadn't written because I was just so involved in my new life here. I actually first thought of writing to you about a month after I arrived. I wanted to tell you about how engaged I was in every aspect of campus life; the frat parties, the chicks, sports, booze. But I would have been lying to you if I had done that. It's actually been really hard for me to adjust over here. There isn't any one thing in particular that's got me down, not the college itself, not my studies, not my friends, being so far from home, but a combination of all of these things. Most of all though, it's just me.

Let me start by telling you about this place. Haileybury College is in a dead end town in the middle of nowhere. I cannot believe that I was dumb enough to actually choose to come here. You know better than anyone how I did my college selections. I just looked at the places which had the best female-male ratio. By my calculations, it was either here or Miami State. And since my Dad wasn't going to pay for a Bachelors in Beach Volleyball, it was here. I wish I'd actually bothered to look at the prospectus. It would have at least told me how far from civilization I would be. Three hours' drive from Boston, and another four from New York in the opposite direction. If you don't have a car here, you're dead, and my father says he won't buy me one till the end of my sophomore year. Sana's lucky, she may be homesick, but at least she's sitting in Boston, studying English Literature, the great dream of her life. I haven't even figured out what I want to do. Studying here is so tough, man! Back home, I always had you to cheat from. I attended a class here the other day, and the professor had expected us to read 300 pages in a week! And everyone else had actually done it! I felt even dumber when I left the class and stopped to have a drink from the water fountain. And man, I am only admitting this to you because you're my best friend, but I actually stood there for about ten minutes trying to get the fountain to work. I didn't know how to operate it. I'd never used one before. Everyone there was giving me these looks like I was either some spoilt rich kid or a mental retard. Finally, this one nice Chinese girl, obviously assuming I was in the latter category, showed me how to do it.

You know, Ausi, back in Karachi I never really thought of myself as privileged. We were all, you know, regular guys. With my grades, I was never going to get a scholarship like Sana or you. It was just always assumed that my father would send me abroad to study, like he did with my older brother. He's always said that he wanted us to get some international exposure before we joined the family business. Over here, I see all of these kids working their asses off and I feel guilty because I think they all look at me and see a guy who's only here because his Dad could afford it. I know, I sound like some poor little rich boy, but believe me, it is not a very comfortable feeling to have all the time. You must have guessed that all of this isn't exactly conducive to making friends. I've always been a sportsman, Aus, used to being in a team environment all the time, used to being the centre of attention. We were the kings of our closed little world in school. Here, no one gives a shit if I was the most popular guy in school, or if I went out with Saira Khakwani, the hottest girl in school, or whether I picked up four wicket hauls in our last three matches. I don't think anyone over here has even heard of cricket.

I came here with a lot of attitude, Aus, thinking that college would just be an X-rated continuation of school. It isn't like that. You know, before we all left, the guys used to talk about how we were going to walk out of immigration at JFK and there'd be nice American girls just lining up to have sex with us. College isn't like that at all, bro, and anyone who tells you different is lying. It's really hard to make friends over here. The thing is, all the friends I have, I've known since like kindergarten or something. You're probably my newest friend and I've known you ten years. I don't think I know how to make friends. I have never felt so lonely in my life.

Man, I miss home so much. I miss everything. Some days, I wake up in the morning and think of all the stuff we did last summer. I relive every single moment and I feel like crying. The thing I miss the most is the team, Aus. Wow, what a season we had! It's like a fairy tale when I think about it now. How we ended up winning the Willis Cup I will never understand. We were like Imran's cornered tigers in 1992, coming back from the dead. You and me bowling in tandem, like Tauseef and Iqbal Qasim at Bangalore '87, Ram and Val at the Oval 1950, Laker and Lock in '56. And Eddy and Ausi at the KGA in '94. Spin twins forever.

But it's not just the cricket I miss. It's all the little things. Sending Ram Lal to get us halwa puri through the back gate early in the morning, and then convincing Sana to bunk whatever class she was sitting in. She was constantly complaining about how we were making her education suffer, but she was a sucker for a greasy puri! And then our late night drives to Boat Basin, the only place in the world perhaps where you can get a fresh sizzling kebab roll at four in the morning. And yes, while a lot of the time was taken up in your hopeless pining for Sana, we also had some great non-pathetic conversations there.

Speaking of which, I was surprised how you left things with Sana, dude. I know that you are the world's biggest chicken when it comes to all things Sana, but I really expected you to ask her to go with you to the Victory Ball. I think she would have liked to go with you too, because I know that she didn't want to go with her ex. She only did it 'cuz she didn't have a better option. There was no point in you giving her attitude for having done that. You should have stepped up and just told her how you felt. What's the worst that would have happened? I mean school was over anyway. And where the hell did you dig up that strange Polish exchange student as your date? Seriously, Ausi, only you can come up with crazy shit like that.

Anyway, shortly after we came to the States, Sana told me she was going to write to you. She wasn't happy about how you'd left things with her, and I'm pretty sure she suspected your feelings for her. She's not stupid, you know. She did get into Tufts after all. So when I spoke to her last week, she said she had written you a letter and asked you point blank whether you had ignored her because you had feelings for her. And what reply did you give?? I can't believe you lied to her. You told her that you had had a crush on her briefly, but that you got over it a long time ago! And that you considered her one of your two best friends in the world and you had only been upset because you thought she was going to get hurt if she got back together with the evil ex!! I had to sit there and act like I was some kind of moron and nod while she gushed over what an honest and forthright guy you were. Jeez man, the things I do for our friendship. If you had been here right now, I would have forcibly driven you to Boston and held a gun to your head till you confessed the truth to Sana.

You know, the one thing Sana and I both wish for above anything else is for you to have been here. Oh man, the world would have been a different place. I'm really sorry about what happened Ausi. I know it was hell for you to know that you had gotten the scholarship to McGill, but could not go just because your Dad refused to pay your airfare. Look, I realize that your Dad was in the Postal Department and that you were on a scholarship even in school, but dude, in this case, it wouldn't have cost him anything. Couldn't he have just borrowed the money for the ticket? You really deserved it, Ausi. I also know how you've always been very proud when it came to money matters but I wish you'd just approached me once. I would've gotten my Dad to put up the ticket money. We could have considered it a loan between us. I thought about just getting you the ticket because I know how anal you are about asking. I even discussed it with Sana, but we both decided that you would never have accepted it and gotten pissed off with us in the process. Still, maybe you can defer the admission till next year. When I get back in December, we can think about ways to raise the money. I can correspond with the university on your behalf. They've got this new thing here, called the Internet, which has made it easier to communicate through the computer. You don't have to send stuff in the mail anymore. I haven't used it yet but I'm sure it will be a lot easier to talk to the admissions guys at McGill.

Let's talk about something a little less heavy. I started writing this letter because I thought it would cheer me up. Instead, I feel more depressed now than when I began. What's happening in cricket? I am absolutely starved for information. I got my Mom to mail me some sports pages from home. I cannot believe I missed this amazing test match in Karachi against Australia! One of the best test matches ever played, happens in my home town, two months after I leave for college! Inzamam and little Mushy hung on to win us the match! Unbelievable! I didn't think much of making Salim Malik captain, but he certainly has produced results. But this Shane Warne is really talented. I mean it's easy to pick up wickets in England, because they don't know how to play spin to save their lives, but I had thought that Warne was overrated and would have problems against subcontinental teams. It's pretty impressive that he still managed to pick up nine wickets in the match. You lucky devil, I bet you went to the National Stadium to see every day of the match, while I'm stuck here in freezing New Hampshire, in the middle of my semester.

Sorry bro. I just realized I was being a little insensitive. There's my poor little rich boy routine again. Man, I'm beginning to get why these kids don't like me here. I wouldn't like me if I were one of them. Gotta go now. Still have to read 150 pages of some crap for class tomorrow. I just wanted you to know that I miss you Aus, and I can never turn my back on our friendship. Can't wait to hang with you in December.

Take care,
Eddy

six

Dear Eddy,

I'm sorry I missed your visit in December. My mother told me that you swung by our house. I'm very impressed that you found the new place. Lalookhet is such a maze, it took me about a month before I could stop asking people for directions to my own house. I don't imagine anyone from school has ever come to this side of town. I don't blame them. Why would they, it's such a dump. Yeah, we had to move pretty suddenly because some politically connected colleague of my father's had the Jamshed Road house allotted to himself. My father tried to challenge the decision, but they sent a police mobile over and we were told to clear out in a week or else we'd be thrown out on the street. This place was the best we could afford at such short notice. That's why you didn't get any response on my old phone number. We applied for a new phone line about four months ago, but you know how it is. The lineman wants some 'kharcha pani' to expedite the process and my Dad isn't willing to cough up. Still, I must say, full credit to your keen detective skills in tracing me down.

The good thing was that they did forward our mail and I got your letter. Thanks yaar, what you wrote meant a lot to me. Thanks for the offer to talk to McGill, and by the way, yes, we provincials do know what the Internet is. The thing is, my Dad wanted me to try for medical college and after you guys left I gave the test and got through. I wasn't that keen on it, but my parents are totally hooked on the idea of me becoming a doctor. So I guess that's what I'm doing for the rest of my life, whether I like it or not.

Things have really changed in my life since you guys left. You have a very rosy picture of home when you think about it sitting so far away. Things aren't so pleasant here, my friend. Especially when we step out of the cocooned environment we were in when we were in school. I got the shock of my life the first week I went to medical college. You know, I had always considered myself a pretty level headed guy because of my family background, not like some of our other friends who never ventured beyond their palatial houses in Defence or Clifton. Of course, I don't count you among that lot, even though your palace is the biggest one in Clifton. But you've always been pretty chilled out in that sense. When I got to college though, I was a complete misfit. Everyone started out by calling me a 'burger'. By the way, to explain for your benefit, Mr Haileybury College, a burger is someone who is totally out of touch with the local scene, a 'wannabe gora', you know, someone who is so westernized that they only eat burgers, as compared to salan roti. Basically, everyone in school would be a burger and if you ever came by here, they would call you a 'Mr-Burger-with-Cheese'.

No one wanted to really talk to me in the beginning because they automatically assumed that since I was from The School, I must be a typical arrogant snob. My second week here, I went for cricket team trials. They didn't even want to give me a chance to bat. This one guy there asked me where I had gone to school, and when I told him, he said, 'What the hell would you know about cricket?' Apparently, our successes in the Willis Cup don't count for much here. I must admit though, that the boys there were seriously talented. They had all played at least club cricket and some had even played a few first class matches. But my ego was damaged, so I argued with them that the least they could do was give me a chance. So they did. And Eddy, I had never been so pumped up ever. I smacked everything out of the nets. I even got a couple of wickets with my spin. Overall, I thought I had put in a pretty impressive performance, but the next day, when the team selection sheet went up, my name wasn't on it. When I went to ask the coach why I hadn't been selected, he admitted that I had played well, but he was never going to select me because I had no sifarish. Every slot in the team was doled out on a quota basis. There are ethnic quotas, there are quotas for the various political student organisations, and quotas for the boys who have some powerful patron among the faculty or in the government. I didn't fit into any of these slots. In school, I had been one of the best players on the team and here, I didn't even merit a place as an extra.

I have learnt that the smallest action here has overtones. In one of my first days, I made the mistake of talking to one of the female students. I was just asking if she needed any help with her work, like I would have asked Sana or Saira or any of the girls in school. When I came out of class, this fellow with a beard came up to me and asked why I had spoken to the girl. I told him it was none of his business. All of a sudden I was surrounded by a bunch of goons who started grabbing me by my collar. The bearded fellow slapped me in front of everyone in the yard. There were teachers there, faculty members, other students, but no one came to help me. They would have beaten me senseless. I had to beg them to forgive me and I had to promise that I would never speak to another girl on campus.

It was so humiliating, I couldn't bear to go back to college for a couple of days afterward. And when I finally did go back, I found I couldn't look a girl straight in the eye. I would just go to college, attend classes and then head straight home without talking to anyone. It made me furious that these bloody mullahs had made me fear doing something that I used to find to be the most natural thing in the world. But no matter how angry I got, I couldn't get over my fear. I started to despise myself for becoming like them. I mean what was the big deal in talking to a girl!

I turned to writing poetry. You remember I used to dabble in it in school, more because someone had to participate in the Urdu debates, and all you English-medium types used to think it was beneath you to speak Urdu, let alone recite poetry in it. But now I started composing my own shairs. A few weeks after the incident with the girl, there was a mushaira at college. I was so sick of hiding that I decided to enter it to recite a few couplets. Maybe it was the fact that I hadn't spoken to anyone in a couple of weeks or that my emotions were close to boiling over, but when I got up on the stage, I recited my couplets with such passion that I surprised even myself. The next day this guy called Sohail, who I knew was with the student wing of one of the political parties, came up and congratulated me.

'You have a real passion within you,' he said. 'And you speak so well, you can spellbind an audience.' I thought he was pulling my leg, but he assured me he wasn't. 'My friend, there were people in the crowd yesterday who had tears in their eyes when you finished. We could use people like you in our Party. Why didn't you say you were one of us, when the Beards picked on you? We would have backed you up.'

'What do you mean by "one of us"?'

'You know, a mo ... uh, from Lalookhet.'

'Why should it make a difference?'

'Arre bhai, it does. You don't understand this yet because you come from a privileged background. If we don't stick together, the other groups will pick us off one by one. The only strength is in unity.'

He invited me to come and hang with his Party boys. They were all nice guys, all from lower middle class backgrounds like myself, and it was only when I started talking to them that I realized what a struggle life really was for ordinary people in this city. These were all bright boys, Eddy, not miscreants of any sort. They weren't even interested in politics before they joined the Party. But every day, they suffered harassment just because of who they were. If you would just hear their stories, Eddy, it would really open your eyes to what goes on in this city. Getting pulled over by some bloody tullah for random checking, just because you're wearing jeans and a kurta. Can you imagine that? Or being forced to call your girlfriend your sister just because some damn 'fundo' student who has never had the guts to speak to a girl in his life, doesn't approve of your relationship? Missing out on a job placement because of where your parents came from? It all sounded crazy to me. I finally understood what they meant when they said I came from a privileged background. My father may not have had money, but due to the opportunities he provided, he kept us all sheltered from these sort of problems. For the first time that day, I stopped resenting him for having forced me to join medical school.

So I started hanging out with them, helping them out on their errands for the Party. I didn't tell my parents, because they would totally freak out at my joining a political party. But I wanted to do it because it made me feel good. All of a sudden, my status in college changed. I wasn't a pariah anymore. Instead I was someone who had the backing of the largest political organization in the city. The teachers started paying attention to me. I actually found that I had regained the confidence to talk to girls again. I admit though, the first time round, Sohail came with me, and we stood in the middle of the college yard and he deliberately made me speak to the same girl that I had spoken to the day I was manhandled. The Beards kept staring at us from a distance but they didn't dare touch us.

After that, I was sold. I started spending more and more time involved in Party affairs. I quickly became one of the top organizers in college and was acknowledged as being Sohail's right-hand man. He introduced me to some of the Party's ex-ministers and central committee members. They had all heard of the work I was doing and they all praised me. From them, I heard stories about how the police bastards picked up innocent boys, took them to the police station, and tortured them into confessing all sorts of 'acts of terrorism'. When the police have made enough false cases on a party worker, they pick him up and kill him in a 'police encounter'. It sounded all too fantastic, until one day Sohail came to the dorm room we use as a Party office and said he had to leave town for a bit because he was on a police hit list. There were five of us there, so we decided it might be fun to travel to the north of the country together. That was around the same time you came looking for me. We spent about two weeks out of town, until things had cooled down a bit. Normally, the college would have us all thrown out on account of such lengthy absences, but all the professors knew we were with the Party, so they would automatically mark us as present. You've got to admit, it's a pretty good system, eh?

So, as you may have gathered, there's quite a lot going on in my life at the moment, none of which I had imagined would happen when we left school. As for what you said about Sana, look, I just feel that nothing would have been gained if I had admitted my feelings to her. Even if she turned around and said she reciprocated my feelings, what would happen? She and I are a million miles apart, living in two completely different realities. We could never be together. Besides, from her letter, I got the distinct impression that there was a gora in one of her classes who she liked. That's Sana. I don't fit in to that picture, so I would just like to cherish the memories of the great friendship that we shared. Please do me a big favour and just leave things as they are, Eddy. And you need to cheer up, my Punjabi friend. Things will get better for you as time passes. You couldn't be in a worse predicament than I was, and look what happened to me. Good luck in your semester, and I'm looking forward to hanging with you in the summer.

Regards,
Ausi

seven

The Present: 4 May 2011

It was morning by the time Omar returned to the Animal Husbandry School. He had driven through the night to get back from Karachi, frantic that something may have gone amiss in his absence. But when he got to the district headquarters at Khairpur, still several hours from the Animal Husbandry School, he found himself exhausted by the journey. A call on the wireless confirmed that everything was all right with the prisoner. So he chose to treat himself to a night in a real bed in the district SP's bungalow. It was, after all, his official residence now and he figured that he was entitled to enjoy the perks of his office, however brief they may prove to be.

He also needed time to think about what Shahab had said. Omar was surprised at his own newfound sense of determination. Shahab's acknowledgment that he was onto something had meant a lot to him. A sense of professional pride was taking root. At first he couldn't understand it. Shahab wasn't his senior. He wasn't even a peer, just a ranker inspector. But underneath the bumbling exterior, Omar had spotted the truth about the CID man. That he was a cop's cop. It couldn't have been easy, hunting the Sheikh for so many years, but Shahab had done it, and in the end, he had got his man. And by doing so, Shahab had won not only medals and promotions, but the respect of the entire department. That's why they had called him from Karachi to Hyderabad to deal with the Sheikh. Because he was the only one who could.

That was what Omar secretly hankered for. Recognition. If he could solve the riddle of Sheikh Uzair, then all the previous slights would be forgotten. His humble background wouldn't matter anymore. After all, they didn't look at Shahab's background when they asked him to investigate the attack on the President. His old course mates from the academy wouldn't be able to snicker at him anymore, because no matter how many postings you could wrangle by marrying the daughter of a senior officer or a politician, none of that held a candle to bagging Sheikh Uzair, or re-bagging him in this case. A hundred rejections from a hundred Arooshas wouldn't matter anymore. The Sheikh would be Omar Abassi's silver bullet, his way out of the morass of his life. If he could just manage to figure out these letters, he could transfer out to CID, become one of the elite jihadi hunters, like Shahab. He would get a medal, a Sitara-e-something or the other, and every time he made a bust, it would make the headlines on Geo News. Wouldn't that be something?

It wasn't going to be easy. It wasn't as if the Sheikh would just sit there and spill his guts out. Omar was still working on a strategy as he drove into the Animal Husbandry School the next morning. In his absence, his staff, now reinforced by members of the district SP's office, had established a fully functioning bureaucracy in this desolate outpost. There was now a proper encampment where formerly his tent had stood alone and the clacking of a portable typewriter could be heard along with the sounds of the almost continuous construction that was going on at the school. One of his subordinates had even thought to bring out the SP House cook, who informed Omar that he was preparing egg fried rice and chicken manchurian for iftari. It was a long way from the soggy pakoras of a few days back.

Omar walked toward the cell, where the ever-reliable Juman was on duty. He enquired about the prisoner, and was informed that everything was in order. Peeral and Juman had progressively improved the condition of the cell. There was plenty of clean hay on the floor, giving the cell a more cheerful look, and a makeshift desk and plastic chair had been placed as well. Omar sat down and had Juman bring the Sheikh out. This time, he was careful not to make the same amateur mistakes he had made in his first interview.

'Assalam alaikum, Sheikh Ahmed Uzair Sufi.'

'Walaikum salaam, ASP sahib. And how are you, this morning? I hadn't heard from you in a while, and so I started to worry, but then I heard the good news. I believe congratulations are in order.'

'Huh? What do you mean?'

'I overheard some camp gossip that you have been promoted and made the district SP.'

'You can understand Sindhi?'

'Not really. A few words that I picked up here and there. But I understood enough from the repeated references to your name and the words 'district SP' to make out what had happened.'

'Well, uh, thank you. Yes, I was away sorting out some things. I hope I didn't disturb you, but I wanted to have a chat with you. We might have gotten off on the wrong foot and I wanted to make amends for that. Maybe there is something that I can do for you to make you a little more comfortable, and maybe there are some things you might be able to help me with.'

'Tut tut, ASP sahib. Sorry, SP sahib. Just our second meeting and you want to pump me for information. I think somebody's ambition is getting ahead of them. You need to learn to be a bit more subtle than that. *'Maybe I can make you more comfortable and maybe you can help me?'* The Sheikh mimicked Omar's squeaky voice. 'You wouldn't need to ask me anything if you picked up some pointers from Shahab. Those CID wallahs can make a man admit to anything they want. You spend four days with them and you'll admit you crashed one of those planes into the World Trade Centre.'

Omar could feel the anger rising within him, but he bit his lip to suppress it. 'Is that what they did with you? Did they beat a false confession out of you?'

The Sheikh smiled mischievously. 'Oh no. I'm the exception to the rule. I actually did everything they said I did.'

'I am sorry Sheikh sahib. I am new at this. I am not an expert, like Shahab. I am from a small town and one of the first virtues we learned was to be straightforward. But I am afraid that virtue is useless in this job. Perhaps that's why I am stuck here in the middle of nowhere. I have never handled as big a case as yours, so I was just curious. I will not bother you again, but I will assign someone from my staff to look after your requirements.'

Omar got up to leave, but just as he did so, Sheikh Uzair held out his hand in a conciliatory gesture.

'SP sahib, please sit. I apologize for my bluntness. I seem to have forgotten my manners during my years in captivity. I enjoy talking to you, because I can at least practice my English. I haven't had the chance to speak it in years. Please stay, I would like to talk to you.'

Omar sat back down. His gambit had been a long shot, but it seemed to have worked. 'I know you are very interested in cricket. The other day you had asked about the result of the India

Pakistan semi-final, but Shahab stopped me from answering. However, I see no harm in the question. I think Shahab gets carried away with his rules, sometimes. Unfortunately, Pakistan lost the match. I'm not much of a cricket fan, but I understand that they got themselves in a very good position by bowling India out cheaply, but then the batting collapsed.'

There was a look of genuine pain in the Sheikh's eyes. 'Saaley Indians, they always manage to beat us in the World Cup. But you say Pakistan bowled well, do you know who took the wickets?'

'Uh, I think the spin bowlers shared them. There was Afridi, the captain, and one or two others. I am sorry I don't know the names, but I don't really follow cricket.'

The Sheikh smiled. 'I'm glad the spinners did well. I always said that it was a good idea to make Afridi captain. He's a naturally aggressive fellow, and he has the instincts of a spin bowler. Perfect combination. You're looking at me as if I'm speaking Greek, SP sahib. You should follow cricket. It's one of the things that defines us as Pakistanis. It gives us a sense of self-belief as a nation and brings us together. We have a unique cricket culture and others envy us for the way we play. You learn that when you go abroad. I remember when I was in prison in India, our team would beat their team almost every single match and every time it happened, the guards would go crazy. They would be infuriated by their team's inability to win, and they would take it out on us, as if beating us would make up for their team's loss. I didn't care. I would smile during the beatings. Our victories proved that our resolve, our faith, was stronger than theirs. But alas, we seem to have lost our way in recent years. That's why they keep beating us in the world cup matches.' The Sheikh sighed regretfully.

'I never thought about it that way. Did you ever play? Cricket, I mean.'

'Back in school. But I'm sure you already knew that.'

Omar ignored the comment. 'Is it true that you went to The School? I mean it seems very...'

'Unlikely? Yes, if you look at me in my present state, it does sound very unlikely. But I assure you I did. But you have my letter to verify my claim.'

'Ah yes, of course. Your letters. I actually found another one of your letters, lying with Shahab. I believe they found it on your person when you were arrested.'

For the first time, Omar saw a flicker of interest in the Sheikh's eyes.

'Uh, I have it with me, were you trying to post it when you were arrested? It's addressed to the same person as in your other letter, the one I questioned you about earlier. Eddy, isn't it? He is a friend of yours, yes?'

'Yes SP sahib, he is.'

'But I take it, he's not one of your, uh, colleagues. I mean he isn't a jihadi...'

'No SP sahib, as I told you at our last meeting, I don't believe he is. He is a friend of mine from The School.'

'Oh. I am surprised that you are still in touch with anyone from The School.'

'Yes, Eddy is the only one.'

'He must be a very close friend. If you were thinking about him when you were arrested, and again, now when you were being moved here, he must be very special to you.'

'Don't worry, SP sahib, its nothing sordid. Eddy has been my friend since school, my oldest friend, and now, perhaps my only friend. He is my last link to my old life. I fear that if I lose him, I will lose a part of myself.'

'You have sacrificed a lot for the path you chose. Don't you regret that?'

'SP sahib, I spent a year and a half being tortured in an Indian jail, and then I got out and slaughtered a pregnant woman in front of a camera, like you would a goat on Bakra Eid. Do I strike you as the kind of man who suffers from any regrets?'

'Why didn't you mention Eddy when you were arrested? There is no mention of him in your interrogation report.'

'I was never asked. Besides, he had nothing to do with my current activities.'

'But if he wasn't involved in your jihadi activities, why did you lie to Shahab's men about him?'

'I never lied about Eddy.'

'Yes you did, Sheikh sahib, but they never caught your lie. When you were arrested, they found a letter on your possession, a letter addressed to Eddy. But the postal address on the envelope was a PO box in a small town in Kashmir. Shahab sent a team to Kashmir, but they found nothing, just as you knew they wouldn't. Because you and I both know, Sheikh sahib, that Eddy was never in Kashmir. Eddy is in Karachi. During the siege of the madrasa, you knew you were going to be captured. You even say it in your letter. So you scrawled the wrong address on the envelope, to throw Shahab's men off the scent. You are a very intelligent man, Sheikh sahib. I suspect that even if they had bothered to actually read the letter and questioned you about it, you would have sent them off on some other diversion. Now please tell me where I can find Eddy.'

There was a twinkle in Sheikh Uzair's eyes as he laughed out loud. 'But I am evidently not intelligent enough to have fooled you with the same trick. I admit to what you say, but Eddy has nothing to do with my world. What would you do with Eddy?'

'Call it my intellectual curiosity. All right, tell me this. Where are the other letters? My understanding from reading your "final" letter is that there were others. I'm sure you kept them safe. Where are they? Surely, if they have nothing to do with your criminal activities, then there is no harm in letting me have a look at them.'

The Sheikh did not reply immediately, pondering Omar's words. His eyes glazed over, as if looking at the distant past. 'Very well, SP sahib. I have a proposition for you. You and I will play a little game. I won't tell you where Eddy is because I don't know myself, but I will tell you how to locate him. But you will have to come back here and tell me what you found. And when you come back, you will bring my letters with you and hand them over to me. Because, as you correctly assumed, they are very dear to me. This deal is non-negotiable. Either you accept my terms, or I don't cooperate. Of course, you could always try and beat it out of me, but others before you have tried that, with limited success at best.'

'Is everything a game for you?'

'The simple answer to that question is yes. Come on, SP sahib. I am giving you the chance to become a hero. Take my offer.'

'Why would you willingly give me any useful information that might incriminate you?'

'Maybe I want to get caught. Or maybe it's nothing. You'll only know if you play along with me.'

At that point Omar wished he could have walked away from that miserable shed, from this strangely compelling man. But the Sheikh had read him well. He bowed to the inevitable, sighed and nodded his assent.

'Very well, I will play your game. But I warn you, don't try and make a fool of me by sending me on some fool's errand.'

'I would never make a fool of you. I respect you. I respect the fact that you had the courage to accept my offer. Not many would. Whatever you find will be genuine, and if your aim is to try and understand me better, I can assure you that it will help you in your purpose, even though the final result may surprise you.'

'All right. Now what?'

'The answers are in the letters. You have two of them. Over the years, I have tried to save as many of them as possible, though even I have not been able to retain all of them. But they should lead you to Eddy. You have a keen mind. You will be able to deduce it.

'And you were right. They were never in Kashmir. A few years ago, when I started moving around almost constantly to evade capture, I collected all the letters I could, and placed them in a safety deposit box in a bank in Karachi. The United Bank branch on Sunset Boulevard. The box is registered under the name Adnan Shah. The number of the deposit box is 77824. You will find the letters there. I swear on my honour.'

Wordlessly, Omar got up and walked out. His legs trembled with excitement, yet, somehow, he managed to get to his tent without stumbling. He almost had a sip of water before remembering that it was Ramadan and he was fasting. He started laughing at his own giddy enthusiasm. He was sure the Sheikh wasn't lying. The real key to finding Eddy would be to interpret the letters correctly.

eight

January 1996
Kashmir and Karachi

The wind feels icy on his face as it blows through the open window of the bus. The passengers shiver but do not complain. The fresh cold air acts as a shot of oxygen, keeping the driver alert. A journey from Kotli to Rawalpindi that usually takes three hours has stretched to ten because of landslides on the mountain roads. Ausi doesn't mind though. He sits by the open window, loving the smell of pine and walnut, and the sight of the coniferous trees winding around the road as it follows the path of the Neelum river. He tries to commit these images to memory, taking a mental photograph of Kashmir, a place he has come to love.

As the bus draws closer to Rawalpindi and the Punjab border, his heart grows heavier as he notes each passing town. Even their names sound romantic to him. Gulpur, city of roses; Sehr Mandi, the market of dawns. Six months ago, when he got here, Ausi could not have imagined that he would grow so attached to this place. When he arrived at the Muzaffarabad bus depot, he was the stereotypical city boy, cranky at not receiving his daily dose of carbon dioxide poisoning. He didn't think much of either the place or the provincials who had come to pick him up. They were his mother's family, whom she hadn't really kept in regular touch with since she married and moved to Karachi with his father. But true to their rustic generosity, they had welcomed him with open arms in his time of need. They hadn't asked him why he had run away from the big city, or what he was doing here. They just took him into their family as if his mother had never left. When he had been there a few weeks, he had asked one of his mother's cousins why they had never asked him any questions. The cousin had responded by simply saying that when they saw him at the bus depot, there was such a look of despair in his eyes that they all figured that he needed love and not questions. Besides, his mother was still their sister, even if she had moved away twenty-five years ago. They figured that he would tell them whatever they needed to know in his own good time.

Kashmir proved to be a revelation for him. It was a beautiful land, with forests and mountains and streams, truly a vision of heaven on earth. The Indian side was supposed to be even more spectacular, a fact that was particularly grating for his mother's village, situated as it was so close to the Line of Control. Many of them were refugees from villages just across the border, who could still see their homesteads across the rolls of concertina wire and rows of fortified bunkers. These were people who, without any formal education, had become experts in international law by dint of their personal geography. In six months of sipping endless cups of Kashmiri chai with them, Ausi learned more about 'the Kashmir Problem' than he ever would have had he followed every debate on the issue at the UN in the past fifty years.

He thinks back on that now. All those years in school, observing Kashmir Day on February 5th, or watching PTV, the state channel, drone on about humans rights abuses in Kashmir, he had never bothered to pay attention. All of that was just something that was always going on in the background, something to sit through while waiting for the late night highlights from Pakistan's latest overseas tour. But for the people here, it is a daily reality. He remembers Kashmir Day last year, when a handful of Kashmiri students had come to see him and Sohail, to ask for help in organizing a 'dhamakedar' protest, since Sohail and he were the experts in that sort of thing.

Sohail. It always comes back to him. Ausi closes his eyes, trying to hold back the tears, but it's too late. Sohail's memory has triggered them. Sohail, the man who became more of a brother to him than his own brothers. His inseparable companion in Med school. Sohail, always smiling, always quick with a joke, or a friendly putdown. Except when he lay in the mortuary, his body filled with bullets. Remembering is painful beyond belief, but now that it has come up, he relives everything.

It is May, and he has virtually stopped living at home, having told his parents that it is more convenient to study in the dorm. They are impressed with his new-found dedication to the medical profession. In reality, he crashes in one of the Party's hostels and helps Sohail and the others with their political activities long into the night. Sohail has one weakness. He spends the entire day either on campus or at the Party headquarters, but every evening, at dinner time, he goes home to eat with his mother, who has lived alone since his father's death years ago. Ausi teases him mercilessly about this, calling him a mama's boy.

One night, Sohail is late in returning from his mother's house. It is worrisome for Ausi and the others, because they know that Sohail is wanted by the police in several cases, and the danger of him being arrested is an ever present one. But standard procedure in such a case is to usually get word back to the Party's central headquarters, so that they can mobilize their political resources. This isn't too difficult, since someone would always have seen the police arrest Party activists, whether it was relatives or colleagues, or even passers-by, and they would get word to the Party. But here, several hours pass and there is no word on Sohail. Finally, around four in the morning, there is a call to the dorm room from Party Headquarters. There is a rumour that there has been a police encounter near where Sohail lives. Since Ausi is the only member of the campus unit without a criminal record, he is sent to the police station to make inquiries.

At the police station, he is told to go to the mortuary at Jinnah Hospital. At the mention of the mortuary, it begins to dawn on Ausi for the first time that something serious may have happened to Sohail. Up till this point, he has been in a state of denial. By the time he gets to the mortuary, his hands shake uncontrollably. The only people there at that time of night are the medico-legal officer, finishing up a post mortem examination, and a police sub-inspector from the station. Before Ausi even has the chance to open his mouth, the sub-inspector asks him if he is here for the body of Sohail Commando. His heart sinks but he still isn't sure if it is his friend they are talking about. The sub-inspector grabs him roughly and drags him into the mortuary and forces him to look at the dissected body that the medico-legal officer has been examining. 'Is this him?' The sub-inspector is shouting in Ausi's ear, but his voice seems to be coming from a thousand miles away. On that cold metal table, his face half blown away, his hair hanging awkwardly on top of his exposed cranium, it is undeniably Sohail. Ausi sees an ant crawl over his flesh and deposit itself in what is left of his jaw.

In a trance, Ausi slowly nods his head in response to the sub-inspector's repeated query about the identity of the body.

The policeman yelps triumphantly and races out of the room, while the medico-legal officer hands him some forms to sign. Ausi signs them wordlessly, unable to take his gaze off Sohail's corpse.

There is shouting outside the room. He hears someone say, 'We got him, we got him, the reward money is ours!' and as he turns, he is confronted with a more senior police officer.

'What is your name?' This officer has a smarter uniform than the sub-inspector, and Ausi notices that his polished brown boots shine like mirrors.

'Ahmed Sufi.'

'What relation are you to Sohail Commando?'

'I don't know any Sohail Commando, I just know my friend, Sohail, who's lying in there.'

There is a commotion behind the officer. Someone says, 'Get him, he's also with the party, we'll bag another one.' The next thing he knows, he is grabbed by several pairs of hands and dumped into a police pickup. So many months later, on the bus to Pindi, the subsequent events still remain a blur to Ausi. He remembers shouting at the policemen, begging them to let him inform Sohail's mother. He has a vague recollection of being tossed into a police station lock up with a couple of spaced out heroin addicts. But his own state of shock is so intense, that he seems to be the one on drugs. The cops decide to let him cool off before they start working him over in earnest. His good fortune is that someone at the hospital informs the Party and they inform his parents. Ausi sees his father enter the station with the dawn. To this day, he doesn't know what his father says to the police officers, whether he pleads with them on the basis of being a fellow government servant, or whether he pays the shiny booted officer the first bribe that he has ever given in his life. Whatever it is, they let Ausi go home.

His homecoming is straight out of a bad Bollywood movie. A lot of histrionic crying and shouting from his mother, and his father slapping him and saying he has ground the family's izzat into dust. Both alternately beg and threaten to get him to break off all ties with the Party. Ausi hears all of this without offering a defence because his mind is numb with grief. As soon as his father's tirade ends, he rushes to Sohail's house. The neighbours inform him that Sohail's mother has suffered a stroke on hearing the news of her son's death. The only one left in the house is his little sister. After his father's death, Sohail's mother had made ends meet by slaving over an ancient sewing machine, stitching clothes for rich housewives. The irony that she may well have stitched clothes for the mothers of many of his old schoolmates never leaves him. But no one knows who will pay her hospital bills now. A delegation from Party headquarters arrives while he is there. They declare Sohail a martyr of the Party and pledge to keep his family like their own. But at the end of the speech, they leave Sohail's sister with five thousand rupees for his coffin.

Five thousand rupees. Even now, on the cold bus, Ausi thinks about the money. The exact price for martyrdom. In retrospect, he should have realized at that moment that all political parties are the same, that they use workers for their own ends and then discard them. That the Party would use him, as they had Sohail. But he was blind to everything except the need to make someone pay for Sohail's death. He wanted to set the world on fire, and the Party egged him on, right or wrong.

It starts with Ausi wanting to shut down the college for a week, as a mark of respect for Sohail. When he takes his proposal to the principal, he looks at Ausi like the lunatic he has become. So he does the only logical thing and holds a gun to the principal's head until he agrees to his demands. For the first time in his life, he experiences true power, when a man his father's age, a respected man, a professor of medicine, sinks to his knees and blubbers in front of him like a baby.

Ausi and his fellow Party activists take over the college, beating up lecturers, setting fire to tables and chairs, and forcing students out of their classes to attend compulsory 'memorial services' for Sohail. The Party, of course, does nothing to stop them, in fact encouraging them to more radical action. After a couple of days, the government decides it has had enough, and sends the police in. They come with a vengeance, with tear gas and lathis, breaking heads and arresting whoever comes within their grasp. Somehow, Ausi manages to evade capture and reaches Party Headquarters. But now he is a wanted man, and suddenly, the Party wants nothing more to do with him. One of the Party's MPs, the same one who had earlier egged him on, now berates him for having been disrespectful to his teachers.

He does not know what to do. If he goes home, it is more likely that his father will personally hand him over to the police. He calls his mother, who tells him to go to her people in Kashmir, and sends his brother to deliver a train ticket and some expenses. As he waits, Arshad, one of his fellow Party activists from the college, shows up. He too has evaded capture, and has also managed to salvage the collection box which they had set up in the college yard to elicit donations for Sohail's family. The donations have been generous, not least because those who elicited them came with guns in their hands. Arshad tells Ausi the amount is close to two hundred thousand rupees, but with the police now cracking down on all Party offices and Party workers, it is impossible for them to get the money to Sohail's mother.

Arshad too, is in much the same position as Ausi. Unable to go home, and with an equally precarious financial position. They sit there wordlessly, sipping a couple of bottles of cold Pepsi that Arshad has bought with the last pennies in his pocket, staring at the collection box. Two hundred thousand rupees solves a lot of problems but they are wracked with guilt. How can they take money meant for Sohail's family? Finally, after several minutes of agonizing, and the staff at Party headquarters urging them to leave as the police are on the way, Arshad overturns the box on the floor. He divides the pile of money into two roughly equal halves and shoves a handful of notes towards Ausi, while stuffing his own pockets with his other hand. 'Let's just consider it a loan from Sohail.'

The money, however tainted, frees him and allows him to come to Kashmir and press the reset button on his life. And now, as he exchanges an uncomfortable seat on the bus for an even more uncomfortable seat in a third class rail compartment, he feels a sense of dread. And as the cold air of Kashmir turns into the warmth of the Punjab plains and then the sub-tropical heat of Karachi, the dread only seems to grow. He does not want to go back and he has deliberately delayed his return till now, to avoid getting sucked into the vortex of party politics during elections. He feels strange as he gets off at City Station, returning to the city of his birth, but also to a city that holds a lot of bad memories for him. A few days after his return, he pays a visit to Party headquarters. He is, after all, still a registered activist, and besides, Party headquarters is now a different place, bathed in the glow of electoral success and the promise of favour and patronage. He runs into Arshad, and the two embrace like survivors of a war. Arshad is dressed in designer clothes, having apparently done well for himself working as a bank robber in Lahore.

And as they sit there at Party headquarters, enjoying the previously unimaginable luxury of a ten-rupee fruit chaat, Arshad takes out a thick wad of bank notes from his breast pocket.

'Remember our loan? I saved this from my bank jobs, so we could return the money to Sohail's family.'

'Were you really a bank robber?'

'Of course. What other job can a medical college dropout with a talent for guns aspire to? I hung out with a gang of rich kids who wanted to get their kicks, but didn't really care about the money. I knew how to plan things so I became their leader. Anyway, when I came back, I didn't know if you would be here and I was planning to go to Sohail's house on my own, but then I heard some things about his sister, and I didn't have the heart to go myself. Here, you take it and deliver it.'

'What do you mean? What did you hear about his sister?'

Arshad hesitates before speaking. 'The first day I got back, I was chatting with a couple of the old boys. One of them was from Sohail's old neighbourhood. He said that a few days after Sohail's soyam, one of the Party's central committee members had come by the house. Sohail's mother was still in hospital, and only his sixteen-year-old sister Kiran was at home, struggling to learn the sewing machine so that she could cover her mother's hospital expenses. The committee member was very understanding. He put his hand on her head, and told her she didn't need to worry about anything. All her needs would be looked after. And then he slipped it down to her breast. Nobody knows what she said or did, but since then the committee member pays frequent visits to their house, at all hours of the night and day. And all of a sudden, all of their outstanding bills have disappeared.'

'I don't believe you.'

'I didn't believe it either. I didn't want to believe it. But it's true. I don't want to confront the truth so I can't muster the courage to go to Sohail's house. That's why I want you to deliver the money. It's your burden now.'

The next day, Ausi goes to Sohail's house to see for himself what has happened with Sohail's sister. He remembers her vaguely, as a shy girl in pigtails, whom Sohail would occasionally bring to the dorms. But the moment he reaches Sohail's house, Ausi knows instinctively that all the rumours must be true. Gone is the shy pigtailed girl and in her place stands a woman, her hair cut stylishly, wearing lipstick, eyeliner, nail polish, and the whole nine yards. She wears a designer shalwar kameez that shows off her hour glass figure, and she holds a cigarette in the fingers of one hand. Ausi remembers that Sohail's mother had been such a strict woman that Sohail would leave his packet of cigarettes in the dorm, for fear that his mother might stumble upon them at home. It is inconceivable that the vision in front of him can be Sohail's sister.

She recognizes Ausi and hugs him, another unnatural reaction for Sohail's family. 'Ahmed bhai, it's so good to see you. Just give me one minute while I send Amma off with the driver for her physiotherapy session.'

His bewilderment is obvious from his face, for she immediately points to the Suzuki Alto with government number plates parked outside the house, with a liveried driver standing next to it. 'Oh, Wasim has arranged a regular slot for her with the head of Jinnah Hospital's physiotherapy department. The car is also thanks to him, otherwise it would be so difficult to take Amma to the hospital. He's become a minister now, you see, so it's from his ministerial pool.'

As Ausi steps inside the house, he can see that Sohail's simplicity has been swapped for the latest television, gaudy sofas and fridge-freezers with the plastic still on them, all the trappings of new wealth. 'How come Wasim bhai is being so helpful?'

'This is what the Party does for the families of all its workers.'

'You and I both know that's not true. The only thing the Party was willing to give was five thousand rupees for Sohail's funeral. Don't tarnish your brother's name by acting like this.' Ausi feels the anger welling up inside him.

'How dare you, you bhenchod! How dare you accuse me of tarnishing my brother's name! My brother isn't here anymore, and like you said, the only thing the Party was willing to give was five thousand fucking rupees for his coffin. So somebody had to do something. Wasim gave me an offer and I took it. If you want me to be direct about it, I will. Yes, I fuck him. I fuck him and he gives us things. I fuck him and as a result for the first time in my life, I am not wearing second-hand clothes. My mother gets quality medical care because the doctor knows that Wasim is his Minister. Sohail can't help us because he died trying to uphold some stupid ideal of the Party that never existed in the first place. They fucked Sohail for years, but he never got any benefit out of it for himself. The only difference between me and him is that I know how to get something back for myself after being fucked. I got an opportunity to improve my life and I'm going to take it. My advice to you is to do the same.'

He has no idea how to respond. He has never heard a woman swear like this before. He deposits the envelope of money on the table and mumbles something about a donation. As he gets up to leave, she throws the envelope back at him. 'Here, take this with you, I don't need your measly contribution. Wasim can give me double that amount just for sucking his cock.'

Ausi is shaken by his encounter with Sohail's sister. He does not want to associate with a Party that makes whores of its martyr's sisters. And he really needs to get out of this city that he is learning to hate. He volunteers for the graveyard shift at Party headquarters, so as to avoid meeting anybody. One night,

Arshad tells him about a scheme the Party is running for some of its loyal workers. Those who are considered to have suffered at the hands of the police during the Operation are helped to settle in England. It isn't easy to get on the list, and Ausi can hardly qualify as one of the most persecuted workers of the Party, but he has one advantage. The wad of Sohail's money that remains untouched, in his pocket.

He knows this is his only chance to escape from his present misery. Thus, the right palms are greased and within weeks, he receives a letter confirming that his visa has been approved. Overnight, he finds that a new world has opened to him. He suddenly has prospects in life, a fact that is even acknowledged by his father, who has refused to speak to him since his return from Kashmir. Although he still refuses to speak to him, Ausi's mother prevails upon him to somehow put up the money for a one-way air ticket to London.

As the date of his departure comes closer, his excitement grows. He finds himself writing to Eddy, reconnecting with the world of school that he has moved so far away from. He has never travelled abroad before, but he feels he already knows London, from the stories Sana and Eddy used to tell him during their summer vacations. Edgeware road. Leicester square. Madam Tussauds. Women dancing naked in a magical place called Soho. Even Pakistan's defeat at the hands of India in the World Cup quarter-final cannot dampen his spirits. He wants, more than anything, to see Eddy and Sana again. Even though it has been less than two years since they finished school, it feels as if an eternity has passed. And so, as he finally sits down in his seat on the plane and watches with fascination the airhostess going through the safety instructions, he cannot deny that despite his guilt, Sohail's two hundred thousand rupees have been the best investment of his life.

nine

'I love you.'

   'I want to marry you.'

   'Will you marry me?'

Eddy Shah looks at his own reflection in the mirror and cannot help but giggle. He looks idiotic, saying these lines out loud to himself in the freezing marble bathroom but it's the only location that affords him privacy. He has woken up especially early, to ensure that he doesn't wake Nicole and ruin the surprise. After all, he doesn't want her to catch on that he's going to ask her to spend the rest of her life with him.

He stares at the piece of paper that he has been holding in his hand. It's the long overdue letter that he has been trying to write to Ausi for the best part of a year. Things have been so crazy, that he hasn't even gotten round to telling his best friend about the girl who has changed his life.

Nicole. The only word he has been able to pen down on the piece of paper. Eddy grins wryly and reflects that really, he owes everything to Ashish Patel. If it hadn't been for that 200 pound

Gujarati gorilla giving him a black eye, he would never have met Nicole.

It is fall, six months and eleven days ago. The miserable time that Eddy endured as a freshman has carried over into his sophomore year. He still hasn't made any new friends, and his hopes of reconnecting with his old friends over summer vacations are dashed by the fact that Sana stays in Boston for summer school and Ausi has disappeared into the Kashmiri mountains.

He has even contemplated moving back to Karachi. Sana tells him to hang in there and stick it out, but Sana is just a voice on the phone, sitting 200 miles away. The only relief that he gets from loneliness is the pickup tape-ball cricket games that he has started to play on campus with a couple of other Pakistanis and a bunch of Indians. But he knows that the onset of winter will bring an end to this small mercy.

That Sunday, the 14th of October, is a brilliant day though. Crisp, but not cold, and sunny. The cricket session is so keenly contested that the flood lights have come on over the tennis court, which serves as their makeshift pitch, by the time Eddy bowls the last over. Despite the informal nature of these matches, a degree of competitiveness is impossible to prevent, especially when all the Indians are on one side and all the Pakistanis on the other. Eddy has never minded that though. It makes it all the more fun to rub the opposition's faces in it. He is by far the most talented player on either side, managing to extract sharp turn from the electric tape wrapped tennis ball. With the Indians needing 12 to win off his last over, Eddy concedes no more than 4 and takes a wicket. The only people who seem unpleased by the result are a bunch of loud American-born desis, who have been sitting in the bleachers all afternoon, steadily getting more and more drunk.

Seeing their friends sink to an ignominious defeat, they start baiting Eddy. And that's where Ashish Patel steps into his life. He calls him a cheating Pakistani, and asks him if he is for sale, like the Pakistan cricket team. The obvious reference to the recent match-fixing scandal the team has been implicated in incenses Eddy, who rushes into the stands and responds with his fists. Unfortunately, Ashish Patel's fists are a little bigger.

He is lucky that someone calls the campus cops, and Ashish and his buddies decide to curtail their efforts to remodel his face. No one wants a hassle with the cops, and so Eddy too struggles to his feet and makes a run for it. Having left his cherished cricket kit behind and been abandoned by his companions, his misery knows no end. He staggers into the campus cafeteria, looking for ice to numb the pain in his face. And that's when he sees her. She is in line waiting to get a burger and, observing his swollen eye and cut lip, she comes up to him and asks if he is okay. No one has spoken to him in such a caring and concerned manner since his arrival at Haileybury. It takes all of his strength to not start bawling like a baby. He tells her that he is and explains that the fight was about cricket. She has no clue what he's talking about, so over the next couple of hours, using the salt and pepper shakers as props, he explains to her the laws of cricket.

The even more amazing thing is that she actually enjoys his lecture, giggling as he explains some of the more eccentric names of fielding positions: Silly Point, Fine Leg and Extra Cover. Eddy doesn't think he has seen a more beautiful girl on campus. And it's so easy to talk to her. The conversation moves seamlessly from cricket to their experiences at Haileybury and their families. Nicole's family is originally from Eastern Europe. Her grandfather arrived in New York on a boat as a penniless immigrant and now her father is a God on Wall Street. Welcome to America!

They finally decide to call it a night when the cafeteria staff throw them out. They have been talking for hours and Eddy knows that he has to see this girl again, otherwise he will regret it for the rest of his life. With great trepidation, he asks her out to dinner the following night, and to his immense relief, she says yes. It is his first date in almost two years, a tremendous fall for somebody who was known as the King of Cool in Karachi. But there is no artfulness, no act that he puts on with her. What is there between them is an obvious mutual attraction. After dinner that night, he walks her back to her dorm and kisses her chastely at the door. She takes his hand and invites him up to her room. The rest is history.

Eddy looks out of the bathroom window at the rolling upstate New York countryside and has to pinch himself to believe that he is actually here. This is Nicole's father, Jim's estate in the Catskills. It's a mansion set at the edge of a lake and it's got everything: indoor and outdoor pools, jacuzzis, stables, a games room. It's the perfect place to get away from the stresses of being a Wall Street 'master of the universe', as Nicole's father is. It complements perfectly the penthouse on the Upper East Side and the beach house in the Bahamas. Eddy has always considered himself to be from a wealthy family. They own a factory, have a huge house in Clifton, and are able to go on a couple of foreign holidays a year. But until now, Eddy has never understood what it is to truly enjoy money. In a typically desi fashion, his parents keep competing with their social peers in little things. Who buys how many tables at the Layton Rehmatullah Ball, whether you upgrade from a Honda Accord to a Mercedes saloon that year, or whether you get an appointment from one of Karachi's top designers in time to order a jora for the shaadi season in December.

To Eddy, all of this now sounds distinctly middle class. His parents wouldn't know what to do with more money if they had it. No, having money is about being liquid. It's about changing your mindset. It's about being able to get on to a jet and fly to Switzerland just to ski on a whim. It's about blowing 20,000 dollars in a club in one night, just because you can. Like Jim's friends do. That's what Eddy wants.

Up till now, he had presumed that he would return to Pakistan after graduation to join the family business, just like his brothers did before him. For them, college had been a four year break before the drab reality of working in the motorcycle spare parts trade really sank in. As a result, they concentrated on partying and enjoying themselves, and never even contemplated the possibility of doing something else. But that's no longer the life Eddy wants. He has seen his father, wasting his life, dealing with petty problems. Fighting with his brothers and cousins over pieces of the family business. Shitting a brick every time one of his shipments gets delayed due to some silly labour dispute or a shutdown in the city. Besides, with two of his brothers already there, Eddy has to ask himself just how many executive directors can one spare parts factory have?

But hopefully, if all goes as planned this weekend, he won't have to worry about that life anymore. This weekend will be Act One. The proposal. Once Nicole completes the formality of saying yes, they can think about setting a date. He would prefer a long engagement period, a couple of years, to give them time to wrap up college and for him to establish himself in the finance world. Her family certainly isn't a problem. They have accepted him into their lives from the first day, despite the fact that he had thought they might have an issue with their daughter dating a Paki boy. Nicole's father has been extremely helpful acting as a kind of mentor, and with the help of his contacts, Eddy figures it should be a cinch to get a job on Wall Street. This weekend has further opened his eyes to the extent of Jim's influence and how big shots are lining up to do him a favour. Eddy finds it hilarious that he has been mixing martinis and playing water polo with corporate CFOs and law firm partners who his professors would give an arm and a leg just to be in the same room with.

Of course, not everybody is happy with his plans. His mother does not approve of him dating Nicole, leave alone wanting to marry her. Nor is she thrilled by his plans to stay on in America after graduation. His weekly phone calls home become progressively more histrionic, until two months ago, when he finally exploded. He hasn't called home since.

Sana is another critic. She has been dismissive of his feelings for Nicole from the beginning. The first time he told her about Nicole, about a week after they had started going out, she coolly told him that he was suffering from Alabaster Skin Complex, a disease peculiar to desi boys, who get whipped by the first white pussy they see. He finds her insufferable, in her new pseudo-intellectual avatar, as if Jean Paul Sartre had crawled out of her ass. Eddy also detects a hint of sour grapes. His relationship has flourished at a time when Sana's have not, and naturally, since he began seeing Nicole, he has paid less attention to her. Their friendship has suffered, but it's only to be expected.

His increasing apathy about home further estranges her. She jumps on him when he tells her he doesn't care anymore about what goes on back home. This country is beyond saving in his opinion and he doesn't understand why he should be singled out for wanting to turn his back on the whole damn thing. But she has a new group of Fresh-Off-the-Boat, 'politically aware' desi friends, who think they will bring revolutionary change to the country by digging up articles about the government's corruption on the internet and handing out copies of these to all the other desi losers on campus. In a fit of pique, he sends Sana a copy of Ausi's last letter, just to punch a hole in her rose-tinted vision of home. In his anger, he even tells her about Ausi's feelings for her, as evidence that she has such a blinkered outlook that she couldn't even figure out how her best friend felt about her. He knows Ausi wouldn't approve, but someone has to give Sana a reality check. And it works. It shuts her right up.

The truth is that the extreme contrast between his past and what he hopes is his future, makes him uncomfortable. On the one hand is depressing news from Karachi, of growing violence, a Kalashnikov culture, rampant corruption. And on the other side is Nicole and her preppy friends, all Choate and Exeter and summers in the Hamptons, all looking as if they just stepped out of a J Crew catalogue, living a life of privilege, parties and endless opportunity. He wants so desperately to belong to this new world. And so he has decided to jettison the vestiges of his old life. He lies about his origins, telling people he is Turkish, rather than Pakistani. He goes to any length to stay away from desis, even missing the World Cup quarter-final between India and Pakistan. It is an unthinkable act for him, all the more so because it is India and Pakistan at Bangalore, but he does it, because he knows the only people watching in the common room will be South Asians. When his new friends ask him about the match, he is dismissive, saying how he much rather prefers basketball and questioning how cricket can have a 'world cup' when only nine countries play the game? And as he says the words, he feels pangs of guilt, as if he has cheated on his first love.

Cricket makes him think about Ausi once again. He can just imagine the tirade of Urdu curses that Ausi would have unleashed on him had he heard about his betrayal of the great game. But he just thanks God that Ausi has finally managed to find a way out. He is the only one from home who Eddy wants to meet. Perhaps, if his Wall Street internship gets delayed in the summer, he might try and fly to London to see him. Perhaps.

ten

Summer 1996
Whitechapel, London

Dear Eddy,

Since you haven't bothered to reply to my last six letters, I will begin by recapping all the abuse I gave you in the previous six: *Saley, bhenchod, dullay, kutay, kaminey, gaandu!*

Where do you want me to start? At the fact that it is so blatantly obvious to everyone except you that you are totally pussy-whipped by this gori? Or that you spend five minutes with a couple of hot shot bankers and you think you are now moving in their world? That everyone else from your past is now somehow beneath you? Including your mother and your family? I called your mother in Karachi last week, and she told me you hadn't spoken to her in five months. She is worried sick about you. What the fuck is wrong with you?

And don't even get me started on your blasphemies on cricket. 'Just a game desis play?' You think basketball is a global game? How is it a world championship if one team is from Chicago and the other is from New York? Please!

Back in school, you used to be the most self-confident person I knew. You never doubted yourself, even for an instant. I really admired that about you. I remember, of all the girls you went out with, you never pandered to any of them. You were the trailblazer, the one whom all the rest of us followed. What happened to that Eddy? You're trying so hard to fit in, you're so desperate for this thing with Nicole to work out, that you see her world and you're convinced that this is what you want in life. I mean, okay, I'm not discounting the fact that you may be in love with her, but you can't throw out every aspect of your old life just because it doesn't fit with your new one.

Look, I understand that you have been getting this shit from everyone. I spoke to Sana a couple of weeks ago. She was angry with you too, but she was also really worried. She thinks that Nicole may not feel the same way about you as you do about her. She told me that she had tried to explain to you that you were moving too fast, and a girl like Nicole wasn't likely to be ready to settle down before even finishing college. Look, I haven't met her, so I don't know how she feels about you. Maybe you're right and Sana's wrong. But it wouldn't hurt to give it some time. Step back for a minute to gain some perspective.

Anyway, I don't want to go on nagging you for the rest of this letter, so I'll stop here. Except to say one more thing; call your mother. You know, we never realize how much our mothers do for us, until it's too late. That's always the case. Trust me, I know because I spent all those months away from my mother in Kashmir. And now that she's not well, I'm here in London. Every day, I wish I could go back, just to be with her, to sit at her bedside and take care of her, because I know my Dad is hardly an emotive kind of person. But I can't. I'm here on asylum, and if I went back, they would reject my papers. I don't know how my Mom feels after her treatments, I don't know whether she has her medicines or not, and every day I wish that I had spent more time with her. So take it from someone who's suffering, buddy, call your Mom and talk to her.

Okay, enough depressing talk. I have so much to tell you! So, as you know, I have now been here for about seven months. I landed here without really knowing anyone. I initially stayed with a relative of my Mom's (yeah, they're the useful ones. My Dad's family doesn't seem to live anywhere further than Liaqatabad), who had moved here from Kashmir in the '60s. But they were the sort who came to London but never became a part of London. My Mom's uncle was very religious, he insisted on waking me up at four in the morning for prayers every day. On the drive home from Heathrow, he informed me, with great pride, that in thirty-five years of living here, he had never allowed his kids to eat at McDonalds, because it wasn't halal. Can you believe that? My heart sank. I had been looking forward to eating my first Big Mac, since Sana and you always used to tell me about going to McDonalds in London on your vacations. And now this guy tells me that he would be damned if anyone living under his roof had any of that Kafir food. I felt really bad for his kids. They just didn't know how to fit in with their surroundings. Can you imagine that someone like me, who had never travelled abroad before in my life, still had a better cultural understanding of the west, just from having read magazines and watched TV, than these kids who were born here! All of them had this perpetually morose expression, as if they had never had any fun in their lives.

I knew that if I wanted to avoid getting hopelessly depressed, I had to get out of this house. But I also didn't really want to get involved in the Party setup over here. After all, that was the very thing I was running away from. So I met up with a group of guys who had also come here on the Party's channel but were no longer very active at headquarters. They were also trying to avoid Party activities as I was, and they offered me a job and a place to live. They have a flatshare, by which I mean that there are six of us in a two bedroom, one bath flat in Whitechapel, just off the Commercial Road. The guys all work in a Perfect Fried Chicken in Leicester Square. The place is open till 3 am to cater to the post-clubbing crowd, so there is always a need for an extra guy. The owner is hardly ever here, but he is a real slave driver, and so all of us usually work long hours for shitty money. Food is free, but it's gotten to the point where I live, breathe and sleep fried chicken. No matter how many times I bathe, or how much cologne I put on, I can never get the smell of the fryer off me.

Still, I can't complain. It has been a real treat, exploring London. It has to be one of the greatest cities in the world, so diverse, so accepting of anyone who comes from any corner of the globe. And these guys are really cool. I've really grown quite close to them, since we all have so much in common, what with all of us being cricket mad Karachi boys. One of the guys, Salim, is a real fixer, and he set up a scam where, every Friday afternoon, on the pretext of Jumma prayers, we would sneak off from the shop, taking a half dozen boxes of chicken and chips with us. We set up a fake stall outside the Oval, sold some of the boxes, and 'donated' the rest to the stewards at the gates, so they let us in to watch Surrey's county matches. I, of course, enjoy watching any level of cricket, but Salim had a more insidious plan. We kept doing this all summer, so that, by the time the Oval test rolled around in late August, we were on such good terms with the stewards, that they let us in to watch every day of the test. All of us took three days off after Salim told the owner that the health inspector had come by and was threatening to shut down the shop for hygiene reasons, but that we were trying to 'resolve' the situation. The owner got so scared, he ran off and didn't come to check for a week afterwards.

But it was great for us, because we got to see the entire test match. By the way, if you want to get back your interest in cricket, this is the series to watch. I managed to get some video highlights of the series for you, and I'm posting it with this letter. Watch it, gandu. Don't worry, you will forget your stupid basketball. This is the essence of good cricket. England vs. Pakistan. Every match was gripping. And what amazing spin bowling. Yaar, you know these past two or three years I haven't had a chance to really sit and watch a lot of matches, but over the summer, I really observed Mushy. He has matured so much in the past couple of years. He bowled us to victory at Lords and at the Oval. Watching him live is just something else. He has so many variations, he's just too good. And it was also great to see Wasim and Waqar live. But you know me, I really only appreciate the spinners. The fact that the leggie did so well this summer made me miss you even more. Anyway, I am confident that if you take one look at this series, you will be back in the cricketing groove.

Salim and the guys keep coming up with the craziest things to do, usually totally free of cost. One day, we were all at our flat, cursing our daily diet of fried chicken and wishing for some good old-fashioned home-cooked biryani. My uncle's son Mustajab, who is becoming a proper little mullah thanks to his father, had come to see me. He's just started university, and, predictably, the first thing he did was join the Islamic society. He was handing out invites to the soc's annual dinner, where, he assured us, there would be a huge vat of biryani. The Islamic socs always hold a big dinner at the beginning of term to rope in all the 'fresh Muslims'. The poor kids are all new to college, probably missing the comforts of home, so the invitation to partake of some home-cooked desi food proves irresistible. There, the guys start working on the kids, encouraging them to come after Jumma prayers to participate in debates and other cultural activities. Next thing you know, these gullible suckers are standing on street corners, handing out pamphlets about the injustice in Palestine or advocating modesty among women. Sometimes I think that these Islamic socs get all their funding based on the amount of garbage they manage to distribute. Doesn't matter if anyone came to your event or not, or even if they read the damn pamphlet, just as long as you handed out three tonnes of paper every term.

Now, the six of us decided to take up Mustajab's offer. It's true that we were also going there just for the free food, but we were different from those green kids. We were, after all, veterans of a political party and worldly-wise to such manipulations. On the appointed day, Mustajab picked us up and took us to his university, which was in a particularly grim-looking building near the edge of East London. The function was in one of the common rooms that had been cleared of its usual debris of lager glasses and ashtrays overflowing with stale cigarettes. The six of us did stand out from the rest of the crowd of fresh faced undergraduates, but the members of the Society invited us in nonetheless, and kept adding 'Brother' as a prefix to our names when they spoke to us. It reminded me of the time you and I saw the Malcolm X movie on video, and how for a week afterward, we would address each other as Brother Eddy and Brother Ausi, because we thought it sounded cool. Coming from the Islamic Soc guys, it just sounded dorky and we were all having a smug giggle about it until it struck Salim that when we had been in the Party, we used to do the exact same thing, by calling each other 'Bhai'. That took the smirks off our faces real quick.

The function began with prayers, as it was Maghrib time, and even though I had developed an aversion to prayers after they were forced down my throat during my brief stay at Mustajab's father's house, my stomach was grumbling, and I figured, it was a worthy sacrifice of five minutes of my life so that I could get my hands on that biryani. Or so I thought. After the prayer ended, one of the 'brothers' stood up and announced that, as a special event, the Soc had invited an 'expert' on the Israeli-Palestinian problem to address the congregation. We all looked at each other, suitably impressed, assuming that we were going to be lectured by some imminent academic, but the guy who stood up couldn't have been much older than us, tried to carry off wearing a dishcloth round his neck as stylish, and was obviously having a problem growing a beard on his sensitive skin, as was evident from the red blotches under his shave.

'Brothers and sisters (there were a few of them in the room too), for decades, the Jews have enslaved the people of Palestine. They have denied the Palestinians their basic human rights and stolen their land, and the west sits quietly and allows them to do whatever they want.'

Among the numerous talents I acquired as a result of my stay in the Party (knowing how to disassemble and reassemble a pistol is another), attending so many Party meetings and jalsas had also fine-tuned my critical appreciation of public speakers. To say that this 'Palestinian expert' was unimpressive was an understatement. He was hardly the most physically imposing speaker, what with being short and having the blotchy face, and on top of that, he had a squeaky voice, as if he was going through delayed puberty. When he tried to sound like a real firebrand, as if he felt the pain of the people in Gaza, and wanted to make us experience it too, he ended up sounding like a whiny kid.

'Brothers and sisters, it is time for us to make a personal contribution to jihad. We can all fight a personal jihad and make a difference to help our fellow brothers in Palestine.'

'How can we personally partake in jihad while sitting in London, brother?' To our surprise, it was one of the 'sisters', suitably draped in a head scarf, but looking particularly militant, as if she would be quite happy to get on the next plane to Israel to help the poor Palestinians, if only it hadn't been for the Econometrics term paper that was due next week.

'That's an excellent question, sister. What we can do, is mobilize ourselves, putting pressure on the politicians and businesses here, not to do business with Israel. So, like we should stop shopping at Marks and Spencer because they are owned by the Jews.'

Now, up to this point, the six of us had been quite impressed with this strategy. We hadn't expected such logic from this fellow. But the minute he mentioned Marks and Spencer, Salim firmly shook his head and whispered loudly, 'No way am I giving up my favourite double chocolate cake, even if the Israelis take all the fucking land from the Palestinians!' I had to squeeze his hand to hush him up.

Thereupon, started a debate amongst the congregation about which other supermarkets were guilty of complicity with the Israelis. If Tesco stocked Jaffa oranges, did that condemn them to the same sanctions as Marks? We all rolled our eyes and looked longingly towards the backdoor, where we could see some stirring, presumably signifying the start of dinner preparations.

Mercifully, the 'talk' ended with the serving of the promised biryani. The six of us piled it onto our plastic plates and sat down in a corner by ourselves and started wolfing it down like we hadn't eaten in a week. We didn't even bother getting forks or spoons, preferring to use our fingers. Unfortunately, our efforts to keep to ourselves were unsuccessful. The blotchy faced Palestinian expert came and sat down with us and started asking where we were from. When we said we were Pakistani, he grew especially animated.

'Mashallah, brothers, we have great expectations from Pakistan. You know, if the Muslim Ummah could just get together and pool its resources, we could defeat the kuffars.'

'What can Pakistan do to help the Palestinian cause, brother?' I asked, somewhat puzzled.

'Oh you know, Pakistan has a great army and F-16 jets, and with the right leadership, they could lead the fight against the Israelis. We could use the modern jets against Israel.'

None of us knew quite how to answer such a stunning piece of political naivete. But the biryani was admittedly excellent, and we also had our eyes on dessert, which was a nice kheer. So instead of berating Blotchy for being the moron he was, we all looked down at our biryani and mumbled our assent. Salim tried to change the topic towards more practical solutions.

'Why don't you lobby your politicians here, like Tony Blair and the Labour Party? You have such a large Muslim population here in Britain, if you organized yourselves, you could get them to change their policies.'

'Yeah brother, but you know Blair and all these other goras are just hypocritical kuffar. You can't change anything politically. This whole British system is corrupt, but inshallah one day we will overthrow the government and bring Shariah here as well.'

Not wanting to be indicted as co-conspirators for treason against the Crown, we all increased the speed of our eating, and I tried to change the topic as quickly as I could. 'Uh, so what do you do, brother? Are you a student at the university?'

'No brother, I don't study here. I'm on the dole.'

We emptied our plates and made our getaway as quickly as possible, not even stopping for dessert. Some of these universities have some real nutters. The six of us talked about this episode for several days afterward. We just could not understand these people. Do these people think this way because they have the luxury to do so? I would have given an arm and a leg for the opportunities that some of these people have over here. People like Blotchy will never be able to do anything. How can you contemplate overthrowing a government when you can't even be bothered to get a job? Armchair revolutionaries, Sohail used to call them. There were plenty of them in medical school too, guys who would make big statements about what we should do, but when the time came to do something, they couldn't be found anywhere. Sohail had a good eye for them. 'If you don't have the courage to spill someone's blood, you cannot bring about any sort of revolution. Ideology shydeology, that's all bullshit. This is the only thing that matters.'

Anyway, moving on to less serious matters, our other major occupation, as six young, single and extremely horny guys, is girls. Specifically, how to get laid. Well, let me rephrase that. If any of us got laid, that would count as a major achievement. I mean, it would be a brave girl indeed who would get into a shitty flat with six penniless guys, in one of the seedier areas of London. So no, our major preoccupation is simpler; how to get maximum physical contact with a girl. Occasionally, we sneak into one of the clubs next to the shop an hour or so before closing time. At that time, the bouncers are also less particular, and of course, the established bribe of a box of chicken and chips works as well on them as on the stewards at the Oval. As 'players' on the clubbing circuit, I would say we are roughly divided into two categories. There are a couple of us, like Salim, who suffer from an excess of confidence, for no apparent reason. These guys will go up to a hot girl, throw her a really cheesy line, and get slapped in the face for their trouble. It never fails. Then there are those, like me, who are just too overwhelmed to go up and talk to a girl. So we usually congregate together on the dance floor, and dance with each other like a bunch of morons. We've mastered a technique where we none-too-subtly shift our positions close to a group of girls who are dancing by themselves, and then just kind of 'accidentally' bump and grind with them. We dance with our palms held face up in front of our thighs, so that when a girl is pushed towards one of us, we can feel up her butt. I know, it sounds really lame, but hey, these are desperate times my friend, and believe me, we are desperate men.

All of the others claim this technique has at one point or another, gotten them to score with a girl, although in my time here, the only one who actually brought a girl back to the flat was Salim. And well, actually, calling her a girl would be stretching it a bit. She was more of a baby whale, and so piss drunk that she kept calling him 'David' for some reason. Frankly, I couldn't have gotten it up for someone that fat and ugly, but as a smiling Salim told me the next morning, 'It's not about quality, yaar, it's about quantity.' No arguing with that logic, I suppose.

So, keeping in mind my unsuccessful clubbing record, my friends decided that on my birthday in July, it was time for me to finally break my cherry. They pooled some money together, and got me an appointment with a prostitute. You know all those calling cards that are posted in London phone booths? Well, we collect them and paste them on a wall in our flat. They're good to use for, you know, and if one of us is really randy, just for kicks we call up one of the numbers and ask the girls their rates for different services. Well, my friends got me an actual appointment, and sent me off with the money in my hand. In front of the guys, I was thrilled and very macho about the whole thing, but once I got on to the tube to reach the girl's flat in Red Lion Square, I started getting nervous. I mean, I haven't done anything with a girl. And then, for some stupid reason, I started thinking about the moral implications of what I was doing. How God would shun me, how my mother would be ashamed of me. By the time I knocked on the door of the flat, I was a mess. I was hyperventilating, soaked in sweat, and worst of all, I had no libido whatsoever. Anyway, I followed the girl (who was very nice, blond, pretty, nice tits) into the bedroom, and she took the money from me and very matter-of-factly started taking off her clothes. I just froze, until she turned to me, now completely nude, and said, 'Are you planning to shag me through your clothes, love?' It took me about thirty seconds to register what she meant, and it was only when she tugged at my belt and informed me that she didn't have all day, that I understood, and started taking my clothes off.

So by this time, things were getting a little better, confidence-wise. The sight of a naked woman is great for pushing all other thoughts to the back of your head. She started going down on me, and it was fantastic until I caught a whiff of her perfume. It was the same fruity scent that Sana used to wear. And that triggered another mental image in my retarded brain. What would Sana think if she saw me in this state, my trousers around my ankles, in a strange flat with a strange woman's mouth on my cock. And that was it. Instant deflation. After that, no matter what the blonde did, I couldn't get it back up again. After ten minutes of her increasingly futile efforts to arouse me, she gave me a weird look, and asked if I was a 'batty boy'. I assured her I wasn't, but that I just couldn't perform at that point in time. She was understanding about it, commenting while I was getting dressed that I was probably 'thinkin' about my girl'. But not understanding enough to give me a refund. I felt really guilty about the money my friends had 'invested' in me, so I begged her to give me an old pair of panties so I could at least brag to my friends, however untruthfully, that I had been with a woman. I got even stranger looks, but either she sensed that I was really pathetic, or that I was some psycho-stalker whom she wanted out of her flat as quickly as possible. Whatever it was, she went to her laundry basket and handed me a pair of moth-eaten old panties.

After that, I just couldn't get Sana out of my mind. You were right, after you spoke to her, she did get in touch with me. She sent me a letter at my uncle's address. She felt very upset that we hadn't been in touch for so long. She told me that she considered me her best friend and that she always wanted me in her life. She sent me her number and said she would be stopping in London on the way back to college in late August. I didn't know how to deal with that. A long time ago, I had tried to reconcile myself to the fact that that part of my life was over, that while I would always remain in touch with you, and occasionally even Sana, I couldn't go back to the way things were when we were in school. But no matter what I do, I have never been able to exorcise Sana from my mind.

I didn't respond to her for weeks. I really wanted to see her, believe me when I tell you Eddy, I needed to see her. I wanted to know how college had changed her. But it was just too complicated. What would I say to her, that I have been madly in love with her for six years? And how was she supposed to respond? I'm not the Ausi she knew in school. I've fallen a long way, Eddy. I'm a medical college dropout who works at a chicken and chips shop in Leicester Square. How could I ever be her equal?

Anyway, before I could come to a decision, fate intervened in the form of my mother. One fine day, I got a call on my mobile and it was Sana. She had reached London. My mother had given her my number when she had gone to visit her in Karachi. And Sana being Sana, she came straight to the point.

'I realize that you may not want to see me, but I want to see you, Ausi.'

We decided to meet at a coffee shop near my workplace. I was dying to catch a glimpse of her, Eddy. You know, it's funny, we were in school together for years, and we were so used to seeing each other on a daily basis. When all of a sudden that stops and you meet someone like that after a long time, you keep thinking that the other person must have radically changed, and you worry whether you'll even recognize them when they walk through the door. It's stupid, because after all, it's only been two years since we left school, so how much could any of us have changed, right? It's really insecurity that drives these fears. We want things to be the same way they were when we last parted. You are desperate to hold on to that particular moment in your life, as if it were a snapshot, frozen in time.

I need not have worried about not recognizing Sana. She can still hold a room, bro. When she walked in, every guy turned and stared at her. She has a real trick of doing that, because she never makes it obvious, yet no one can ignore her presence. She was as beautiful as I remembered her, even more so. She had cut her hair short. It was shoulder length rather than trailing down to her waist like it used to do in school. But it brought out the beauty of her face. And she's filled up a bit, though in a good way. She actually has breasts now. Her pink lips were still puckered, like in school, and stood out against her soft, pale skin. She was elegantly dressed in tight jeans that showed off her magnificent legs in a way that the school uniform shalwars had never been able to do, and a slightly oversized sweater that nonetheless didn't hide the curve of her bosom. Wow, when we were in school, I could never imagine a time when I would say the words Sana and bosom in the same sentence.

She walked up to me and hugged me in a way that had every male in the restaurant eyeing me jealously. I will never forget that moment for as long as I live. That's the snapshot in my life that I want to preserve and keep. We sat down, ordered some coffee, she smiled at me and looked into my eyes and asked how I was and how she had missed me so much. And then she went and broke my heart.

A

eleven

22 December 1996
Haileybury College,
New Hampshire

Ausi,

What happened man? You left me in total suspense!
What did Sana say to you to break your heart? Or
was it something you said? Did you finally admit your
feelings to her?

I cannot believe I got this letter so late. Apparently,
it's been doing the rounds of the university postal system
for a while. I had moved dorms, and even though, in
theory, I had left a forwarding address, I got this letter
only yesterday. Since then, I have been going crazy
trying to figure out what happened between you two.
If Sana hadn't already left for Christmas break, I would
have driven down to see her in Boston. I called her up in
Karachi and blasted her for not having even mentioned
this episode for three months. But all I got out of her,
after speaking for an hour and running up my credit
card bill, was that you would tell me when you thought

it appropriate. What the fuck! Why are my two best friends so exasperating?

Anyway, I have threatened to beat the truth out of her when she gets back in January. The good thing was I had a heart to heart with Sana after ages. She told me it was good to hear the old me on the phone after such a long time. I told her I had missed talking to the old her, the friend I used to have in school. In recent times, all I had got was this know-it-all, opinionated bitch who thought that her current fad was the answer to the world's problems. But we had a really good talk and cleared the air between us.

I can only speculate about what happened between you guys, but I will ask you to be a little understanding with Sana. She's had a couple of really tough years. The truth is, she and I have been drifting from each other ever since we fought over Nicole, so I never saw the warning signs and I never chose to inquire as I should have because I was angry and too caught up with Nicole.

I think that when Sana first arrived in Boston, college overwhelmed her, as it did so many of us who had to step out of our safety zones for the first time in our lives. It was the same with me, but in my case, I only wanted to make some friends and fit in. I never had any pretensions about wanting to be one of the eminent scholars of the age. Sana had come from a perfect world, where she had been a straight A student for as long as she could remember. Everybody in her life thought she was perfect. Her family encouraged her, her teachers thought she could do no wrong, and her friends were people like you and me, who were always there to reassure her all the time about what a wonderful person she was, no matter what she did. She got into the perfect college, studying what she had wanted to study all her life. And all of a sudden, everything wasn't peachy-keen anymore. Competing against people from around the world, she found she wasn't as good as she had thought she was. Added to that was the fact of being away from home, having to do everything on your own. No loving Daddy to worry about your bills, no mother who made sure your favourite food was always available, so that you could concentrate on your studies, no servants to wash your clothes and clean up your room. When she had to cope with all these things herself, coupled with the academic pressure of a sort she had never known before, her system kind of overloaded. But she was too proud to ask anyone for help, because that would have been an acknowledgment of defeat. So for two years, she just kind of floundered, sinking into academic mediocrity, coming up with new forms of denial, whether it was protesting against a 'culturally discriminatory' grading system, or claiming that college wasn't about the grades, but about the experience, or just finding alternate distractions, like her political advocacy.

I can only assume that part of your heart break must be related to what she told you about her love life these past two years. That has been as chaotic and confused as everything else. You see, even in school, Sana viewed men as accessories, something that would look good on her side. That's why she always had to go for the smartest guy, or the best sportsman, or the funniest guy, rather than the nice guy. Any other girl would have totally picked up on your feelings for her. But Sana had this weird, almost selfish focus, where she didn't see anyone beyond her immediate requirements. We all had small parts in the epic movie of her life in which she was the star. I know this makes her sound like a horrible person, which she isn't. She has always been an amazing friend to the two of us, maybe because we were the only two who transcended her fantasy and gave her the occasional reality check. Well, I did at any rate. You were just the perfect friend who always gave her his shoulder to cry on and never wanted anything in return. That's why she kept hurting you in school, because she actually believed that you never thought of her in 'that way'.

Her relationships in college followed the same theme as school. See, Sana falls in love with an idea of a man. When she first got to college, she had eyes for this very typical, preppy American guy, whom I wrote to you about once. In her mind, he was the epitome of brains and brawn. He was in her Literature course and he was on the Crew team. Can you get more clichéd than that? He was from one of those unimaginative families who put a number at the end of their names because they can't be bothered to change it. Chet the third, or fourth, I think he was. Anyway, I met him for five minutes and told her he wasn't going to stick around. She was trying to engineer the perfect romance, (the highlight of which was a couple of lousy kisses) and for all his worldliness, at the end of the day, he was a freshman walking around with a perpetual hard on. The minute he got an opportunity to get laid with some big chested blonde, he ran for it, even as Sana continued to live in her delusion that this guy was going to 'complete' her, if only she could get him to fall in love with her. I remember telling her that the only way she might have accomplished that was if she took off all her clothes the next time she saw him and allowed him to do whatever he wanted with her body. I remember my rather blunt suggestion did not go down well at the time.

Unfortunately, she did take up my advice, quite literally, in her next relationship. That was with a greasy-haired Eurotrash guy, Marco, or was it Mario? In her second semester, Sana decided that Marco/Mario was her thing, because only a European, with their rich culture and love of fine things so intertwined in their blood, could truly understand her. And this time round, she dropped her inhibitions and gave in to her sensuality. She slept with Marco/Mario and he, of course, being her 'sensuous Italian' had no qualms about being indiscreet in their lovemaking. I would get calls here in Haileybury, from people I knew on her campus, telling me stories about how the 'wild' Pakistani girl would do it anytime and anyplace that her boyfriend wanted. When I told her to cool it because she was developing what we used to call a 'reputation', she told me to fuck off because I was a hypocrite. Why was it okay for me to have sex with Nicole, but not okay for her to fuck Marco/Mario? I tried in vain to explain to her that like it or not, unfortunately, we came from a society where there were double standards for men and women, but she said it wouldn't matter because she had already met the man she wanted to spend her life with.

And then, just as quickly as Marco/Mario had appeared on the scene, he disappeared. In those days, because I had just started going out with Nicole, my check in phone calls with Sana weren't as frequent as usual. One day I called her and casually inquired about the Italian stallion and she said she was so over him because, 'Like all men, he had never managed to fully sever the umbilical cord that tied him to his mother.' When I asked exactly what that meant, she said something about Marco/Mario treating her like a domestic servant, expecting her to cook and clean for him like his mama mia! I don't know, I don't understand half the stuff Sana says.

But the worst of the lot was the Asshole Lahori guy that she started seeing at the beginning of this year. She met Asshole during her 'bringing the revolution to Pakistan' phase. He was new in college and it was his first time abroad. He was from a slightly different background from us. Now I'm not class conscious Ausi, you of all people know that, but this guy was rougher, and he had a street cunning to him that we could never possess. He'd obviously seen and done things that were fascinating to Sana. It started with them hanging out together while doing research for their little 'anti-corruption society' (she actually referred to it as a Think Tank!), but soon enough she was infatuated. I only met the guy once, very briefly, when Nicole and I had driven up to Boston for some event and I decided to meet up with Sana for a quick coffee. But I just couldn't see what she saw in him. The other two had at least had some redeeming feature. Asshole was short, not good looking at all (trust me, this isn't just my subjective opinion. Nicole saw him when she came to pick me up and said Sana and him were like Beauty and the Beast). And he had the personality of a tin pot dictator. Haughty, overbearing but not too bright, and he thought rudeness was a virtue.

When I called Sana the next day to give her my impressions of the guy, she snickered and said that's exactly what she had expected me to say. According to her, I couldn't deal with anyone who hadn't been in The School with me for at least ten years. Apparently, she liked Asshole because his 'earthiness and humility' (?!) were symbolic of 'real' people in Pakistan. The only friend of hers who would ever understand and get along with Asshole was you, just as soon as she got around to telling you, because you were 'real' like him. Anyway, this just caused me to lose my shit and I got into a shouting match with her and slammed the phone down, swearing to myself that this was the last time I was ever going to give a shit about what sort of loser Sana went out with.

This was also around the same time that the troubles began for Sana's Dad. The new government suspended him and started investigating him. There was some talk about him having granted preferential licences for the Prime Minister's sugar mills or something. It shattered Sana to discover that her Dad was one of the very same people who she and her friends had been protesting against. Her friends hadn't quite figured out that Safdar Hussain was her Dad and she was desperate for it not to become public. But Asshole knew and he deliberately, and very publicly, humiliated her by revealing her secret in an email sent out to all the members of their little club. Not only that, in the same email, the motherfucker informed her that he was dumping her because he couldn't contemplate being with a girl whose father was a corrupt bureaucrat, and moreover, the father's morality had obviously rubbed off on the daughter, who was so promiscuous that she was willing to sleep with anyone who gave her a bit of attention, including him.

I don't mean to go through the list of Sana's affairs to rub salt on your wounds, Ausi. I just want you to know, in case she hasn't told you, what she's been through and to view any hurt she may have caused you through that prism. Hell, I didn't find out about the Asshole's email until three months later! She never told me, and I was so mad at her from before that I had stopped calling her. Someone I knew at her college told me that this drama had been the talk of the desi community in Boston for weeks, and that Sana had gone underground to avoid having to meet people. By the time my friend told me, she was in Pakistan, and though I wanted to call her, I just didn't know what to say. So I wrote her a very awkward email that didn't at all convey my concern for her. I wasn't there when she needed me, and that will always be an eternal regret of mine. Your letter provided me with an opportunity to make an opening to her, and it was only now that we were able to talk about these things and I was able to tell her that I was there for her if she needed a friend. God, I wish I could have killed that Asshole, but I heard he transferred out to some other college.

The past couple of months have been a period of some soul searching for me as well. Sana was the first person I told, during our call, and you're the second to get the news that Nicole and I broke up two months ago. Rather, she dumped me. What happened, you will ask. Well, the short and painful version is that you and Sana were right. I was so crazy about her that I never really saw that she didn't have the same depth of feelings for me. I was an exotic experiment, like buying a Chihuahua instead of a Labrador, just to show your friends that you can do something, or someone, different.

I guess maybe that isn't fair. It is my own fault. I got carried away by the world she showed me, Ausi. I really believed we were in love. The problems started when we got back to college after summer break. Thanks to her father's recommendation, I got an internship at a Wall Street bank and so stayed on in New York, for three months, while Nicole went on a Mediterranean cruise. I really busted my ass those three months, enduring 16 hour work days and getting no appreciation, just humiliation, from my colleagues. As one of the guys explained to me in a relatively tender moment, 'We treat interns like shit, so that you remember, and that way, when you're working here, you can treat your interns like shit.' I don't know how that logic is supposed to teach me anything about banking, but that's the way it works over here, and this is what I wanted to do because it fit with the life I saw with Nicole.

I was so glad to get back to Haileybury when term started, and for the first month, things were great. I used whatever money I had made at work to buy an engagement ring for Nicole. I wanted things to be just right, and I planned to propose to her on my birthday in October. But she picked the same time to tell me her future plans as well. Suffice it to say, they didn't nicely dovetail with mine. Initially, she told me she wanted to break up with me because she felt I was 'suffocating' her in our relationship. Then, after a couple of rounds of my arguing increasingly desperately, she admitted that she had cheated on me with some Russian millionaire during her summer cruise. Only, she didn't really consider it cheating because she felt that she had 'outgrown' me and by that time our relationship was, in any case, a 'sham'. Now, it was better for us to end this, before it dragged on for longer and became more hurtful. Women can be really something when they rip our hearts up, can't they? They make themselves sound like surgeons, as if amputating us from their lives is somehow good for us, and to do it quickly is better before the gangrene of the relationship spreads to other limbs. The way they make it sound, you almost want to thank them for looking out for our health.

I was crushed, but my pride wouldn't allow me to show it. No girl has ever done this to me. So I walked out of Nicole's room, and out of her life. I moved out of the dorm and stopped talking to all of our common friends. The break up made me re-evaluate what I had been doing for the past year and a half. I'd drifted from my family and my old friends, and I had no clue what I was doing academically. I was taking all these courses that I thought would help me in this fantasy life I was creating. Can you believe, I took a course in Art Appreciation last year, just because I felt that I needed to know what to say when Nicole and I went to her friends' art exhibitions! I hated every minute of my internship, but I stuck with it regardless. And now, in one stroke, that world was over for me. So I started doing the only thing that made sense to me. I drank heavily.

It's taken me a month to get all of this out of my system. It would probably have gone faster had I contacted my friends and family, but somewhere deep inside, I was ashamed of my behaviour. Or maybe I just didn't want anyone to say, 'I told you so'. That's why I made up an excuse not to go home this winter. I told my father I had to do some catch up studying, which is true enough. But that's why I'm still here, and how I came to receive your letter. I'm glad I did, because after reading it, I decided to give my Mom a call. Thanks for that.

I've also been trying to think about what I want to do after college. I know I don't want to go back to Wall Street. There has to be something more to life than making ridiculous amounts of money. Maybe it's just that over the years, I've absorbed Sana's carping about our generation needing to do something, but I was actually considering maybe sitting for the civil service exams after college. At least it would be a meaningful career. I don't know, maybe I'll investigate this some more when I get back home next summer.

And before I sign off, I must say, my apologies for my blasphemies against the Great Game. I saw the tape you sent with your letter, and I must tell you, I had the greatest time I have had in months. Thank you for setting me straight. You sound like you have some interesting friends in London. Your religious buddies are especially hilarious. I missed you, and I'm glad I finally got your letter. By the way, in the future, one way to avoid such postal delays, is to finally join the twentieth century and start emailing me. I'm sending you my email with this letter, but if you continue to insist on writing, my new address is on the envelope. Take care, buddy.

Your Friend,
Eddy
eddyshah@haileybury.edu

twelve

The Present

The bank manager was a worrier at the best of times, as men in his profession often are. He had struggled for many years to reach his current position, and having climbed the summit of the bank's bureaucracy inch by inch, he constantly worried about all the things that could bring him down. He worried about the shrinking deposits in his branch and the fact that he was losing customers daily. More and more members of the once prosperous local community were closing their accounts to move overseas. To Canada or Australia, any place that was willing to offer them a different passport. Just this morning, another of his customers had come to shut their account, saying they were moving to Papua New Guinea. The manager had never even heard of such a place!

He constantly worried about the woefully inadequate security at the branch, which consisted of an octogenarian guard who had trouble seeing two feet in front of him, armed with a World War II reject rifle. Five other banks in the locality had been robbed and the manager came to work every day muttering Surah Yasin under his breath, praying to the God of every possible faith to protect his branch from a similar fate. Hence, he wore an aqeeq on his finger, even though he was not a Shia, and he kept a medal of St Christopher in his wallet. He even had a Thai calendar with pictures of Buddhist statues on his desk. After all, as he frequently told his staff, with the kind of security they had, they needed the help of the Almighty in all his denominations.

Most of all, he worried about any sort of negative publicity for the branch. There was no surer way to attract the attention of the whiz kids who were trying to figure out new ways to cut costs at Head office. He didn't mind the fact that the new management seemed to have forgotten his branch. The only element of their promised infrastructure upgrade that had reached this branch was the neon sign with the bank's new logo. One glance inside the bank, with its one ancient computer terminal and dusty desks piled with thick ledgers, being pored over by staff who smelt of stale curry and body odour, was enough to reassure anybody that little had changed here for years. But this was comforting to the manager. It was his safety zone, and an indication that Head office was content to let him run things in the old ways, just so long as nothing negative came out from his quarter.

Which was exactly why the massive police presence at the branch today made him so nervous. The local police station in charge had called him in the morning and requested his assistance in an important investigation. The manager had agreed readily enough, after all, he could hardly refuse to cooperate in a police investigation. But he had not expected them to arrive in the way they did. Several police pickups and a shiny red jeep were parked outside the entrance, and a platoon of policemen brandishing their AK-47 rifles, stood on guard outside the door of the bank. Indeed, several patrons had assumed the bank had been robbed, triggering panicked phone calls to the branch. The manager had to post one of his tellers outside the door, just to reassure any passing customers that, in fact, all their deposits were still safe.

The manager's bald pate glistened with sweat as he looked at the confident young officer who seemed to be in charge. He seemed interested in only one deposit box. The manager had tried to enquire from the local Station House Officer about the nature of the investigation, but the inspector had just shrugged his shoulders and pointed to the young man, who had apparently come from out of town for this purpose. The young man himself had volunteered no information and just asked pointed questions about box number 77824. The manager wished that the police would hurry up and leave his branch. The thought of their presence made him shudder involuntarily, even though it was noon and the scheduled 'one hour' power cut was already in its third hour.

It had taken Omar Abassi a couple of days to arrange all of this, but he found that whenever he mentioned the Sheikh in any of his correspondence, the response to his requests was much more positive. The chief of the Karachi Police had detailed the local Station House Officer to personally accompany Omar to the bank. Omar had thought for a long while about how much he would reveal about his quest to his superiors. It was all very well to use Sheikh Uzair's name to scare everybody into submission, but he had to be careful not to overdo it. He had, therefore, been deliberately vague about what he thought he would find in the deposit box, simply saying that the contents of the box were likely to have a link to the Sheikh and possible future terrorist attacks.

But now, as he stood in the bank vault, he struggled to keep his own excitement in check. There was nothing special about deposit box number 77824, it was just one among hundreds in the vault. The bank's records showed that it had been opened some years ago under the name Adnan Shah, and a copy of the identity card on record was in the same name. The box had been accessed just a couple of times since it had been opened, more than six years ago on the last occasion. Omar stared at the picture in the photocopy of the identity card. It was the picture of a bespectacled young man, very clean cut and fresh faced, who had the keen look that young professionals all over the world have.

The contents of the deposit box were sparse. A couple of old school cricket trophies, with the name Ahmed Uzair etched on their bases. A certificate with a picture of a younger, and clean shaven Sheikh Uzair, nominating him as the employee of the month for July 1996 at the Perfect Fried Chicken branch at Leicester Square lay under a Tube map of London, little mementos of a life left behind. And of course, the letters. They were wrapped together in a bundle, with a rubber band around them, still in their opened envelopes. Omar started rifling through them. It was clear that this was not the complete set of letters. The correspondence only went as far back as 2001, whereas Omar knew from the handful of letters he had read so far, that the letters between Eddy and the Sheikh went back further than that. Omar had read enough of the Sheikh's letters to recognize his distinct, flowing script but there was a second style too, more deliberate, less careless than the Sheikh.

Omar picked up one of these letters and looked at it closely. It was postmarked April 2003, and had been written by the mysterious Eddy. Funnily enough, the postmark was local, from Karachi, although the contents of the letter spoke about events in New York City. In fact, all of Eddy's letters had been posted locally. This intrigued Omar. It meant that, irrespective of what the Sheikh had said, Eddy was here, somewhere in the city. And he was a man familiar with every aspect of the Sheikh's life, because he was one person who had obviously managed to communicate with the Sheikh at times when the Sheikh was in hiding, even after major incidents like the attack on the President. He had obviously also met with the Sheikh in person, or how else could the Sheikh have gotten back the letters he had written to Eddy. And why would the Sheikh have wanted them back, unless they had some hidden meaning. Eddy Shah was not as simple a man as he had been made out to be.

Omar had been in the vault of the bank for almost forty-five minutes, and at the pleading of the bank manager, the Station House Officer came in and suggested that it would be less conspicuous if they examined the evidence at the police station. Omar took the bundle of letters from the deposit box and turned to leave, but as an afterthought, asked the officer to pick up the remaining contents of the box as well.

At the police station, Omar tuned out the ramblings of the Station House Officer, as he thought of his next course of action. His head pounded with hunger, and the officer's prattling on about his experiences as the encounter king of Karachi did not help. In truth, Omar was disappointed. He had led himself to believe, based on what the Sheikh had said, that the letters would be far more illuminating than they were, and he had believed that they would solve the riddle of Eddy Shah. Instead, they had confused things even more.

Eddy Shah had some kind of hold on the Sheikh, a hold like no other man. The Sheikh was keen to protect his identity, but from whatever Omar had pieced together, Eddy Shah's world was very different from the Sheikh's. The only common thread between the two men was The School. The place where they had been together. If he wanted to unravel this mystery, he would have to start from there.

'Is The School far from here?' Omar interrupted the Station House Officer's telling of another tale of his exploits.

'Which school, sir? Oh, you mean, *The* School. It's about a twenty minute drive from here, sir. But it's almost 2:30, well past home time. All the students must have left by now, especially it being Ramadan as well. I hardly think you'll find anyone there right now, sir. Besides, the school administration is so high and mighty, they don't meet lowly station in charges like myself. You'll probably have to go through the Inspector General to speak to them.'

'I have to try.' Omar didn't call the Inspector General's office. He placed a call to Shahab instead. If anyone could get him into The School, it was most likely the CID man. He wasn't disappointed. After listening to his plea, Shahab called him back five minutes later and gave him the number of the headmistress, Mrs Almeida, and told him she was expecting his call.

Twenty-five minutes later, he was walking up the school driveway, being escorted to the headmistress's office by an obsequious security guard. The main building dated back to the British Raj and was an impressive sandstone structure, dotted with pink bougainvillea that crept along the walls. The administration building was located strategically on one side of the main school building, thus allowing the headmistress' office a full view of the playing fields, and any potential stragglers thinking of cutting classes.

The School was the most prestigious academic institution in the country. It had nurtured the children of the city's elites, whether they were the Anglo Saxon ruling class or their modern day brown counterparts, for over a hundred years. It was natural then, that, as the Station House Officer had warned Omar, the staff there paid short shrift to low ranking police officers. Station in charges and junior superintendents of police were small potatoes for a place that had, after all, once famously refused admission to the sitting Prime Minister's son.

However, Shahab's charm had worked on the school authorities. An extremely courteous assistant sat Omar down in the waiting room and informed him that the headmistress would be with him shortly. Another girl, presumably the assistant's assistant, hovered around him, asking him if she could get him anything. But Omar paid her little attention, distracted as he was by the pictures on the wall, old black and white prints of the building and various eras of students. There were also several photos of the school sports teams from various years. Omar focused on one in particular, in which a familiar visage stared back at him. The picture was dated 1994, and although he was much thinner and dressed in a seemingly alien school blazer and cricket whites, Sheikh Uzair was still recognizable.

'Yes, that photograph is quite old now, isn't it? Does he still look like the boy in the picture?'

Omar was startled by the booming voice of Mrs Almeida, the headmistress. Expecting to be greeted by some sort of towering amazon, Omar was surprised to see a small woman with a shock of snow-white hair. She had an old-fashioned air about her, from her thick-rimmed glasses to her elegant sleeveless sari.

'How do you do, Superintendent Abassi? I am Mrs Almeida, the headmistress. Inspector Shahab informed me that you were investigating that boy again. Please take a seat and tell me how we can be of assistance.' Each word was enunciated properly, each syllable came out sharply, with an authority borne of years of browbeating self-important parents into submission. It made Omar even more nervous about his own speaking abilities.

'Uh, good morning, I mean good afternoon, Mrs Al-meeda. Thank you for seeing me at such short notice. I have to return to my district today, because he, uh, I mean the prisoner, remains in my custody. Therefore, it was important for me to come here as soon as possible.'

She sensed his nervousness, and smiled reassuringly. 'It's Mrs Al-mi-da. Would you care for a cup of tea? I realize that it is Ramadan, but I always ask my guests out of habit. I don't think anyone would be offended by a sixty-five-year-old Christian woman's addiction to her afternoon cup of tea.'

She guided him into her office that adjoined the waiting room with all the pictures. The assistant's assistant had already placed a mug of tea next to her chair. Omar shook his head to decline the assistant's offer of tea for the second time, so Mrs Almeida dismissed her with a curt 'Thank you'.

'Inspector Shahab is a good man, and a great friend of this institution. When he first arrested that boy, he was very discreet and made it a point to ensure that The School's name was not bandied about too much in the press. Well, obviously I would have preferred if nothing had come out, but it is to Shahab's credit that he kept the disclosures to a minimum. He tells me that you have begun looking into some new aspects of the case, that relate more closely to us. Is this accurate?'

'In a way, Madam. But please do not be worried. There is no problem with the school's reputation. It's just that the more I look at the Sheikh, I find more and more connections relating to his period here, and I was hoping that you could help me, maybe tell me something about his time here, who his friends were, that sort of thing.'

'How extraordinary. That this fellow should still hold on to his associations with the school. Especially in light of the path he subsequently chose.' Mrs Almeida took a long sip from her mug and stared out the window towards the cricket pitch. 'You know, I've thought about this a lot. How and why that boy got diverted onto this, this path. I have taught here for forty-seven years, Superintendent Abassi, and I have never come across such a case. As you must know, we've been here for a long time. I know that people call us a holdover from the Raj, and that our students are considered arrogant and elitist and increasingly out of touch with the realities of this country. Perhaps that's why such a great number of them prefer to stay abroad after university. But I have always fervently believed that the value system that we try and impart will always have some universal relevance. What the British called their innate 'sense of fair play'. But this young man rebelled against everything he was taught for years. It pains me to think that one of my students was capable of this madness. I feel that I somehow must have failed him as a teacher. And I don't for a moment believe any of this nonsense about religious brain washing. Being a member of a minority sect, I have studied Islam all my life in this country. I even taught it for several years, until some fool on the board thought the students would be better served if religious studies were left in the hands of some bearded oaf. Nothing that I have ever come across, no scholar, no school of thought, really justifies any of the things this Sheikh Uzair or whatever he calls himself, has done. What do you think happened to him?'

'I do not know, Madam.' Omar answered truthfully. 'Does anyone remember him from his school days? What sort of student was he? Was he ever disciplined for anything?'

'You know, Superintendent, I checked his record after he was first arrested. Just out of curiosity, because I didn't remember him from his time here. I have an old teacher's memory, in that I always remember the troublemakers in a class, no matter how long ago I taught them. I also remember most of the good ones. But the bad ones are always easier to remember. I found nothing exceptional, good or bad, in his record. He was here on a scholarship of course. He was a most unremarkable fellow. So unremarkable that no one on our staff has any recollection of him, nor of any students that he may have been friendly with.'

'Madam, he played on the cricket team. In fact, cricket seems to be quite an obsession for him. Perhaps one of the coaches remembers him?'

'Yes, I would have expected our old coach, Elquemedo Willet, to have certainly remembered him, but unfortunately, he passed away several years ago before any of this sordid business came out. But feel free to peruse our records to trace any of the other boys in the photograph. They were his teammates. I'm sure they could provide some kind of insight. My staff will provide you any sort of assistance that you may require. I must get back to my literature corrections, I'm afraid. The A levels have butchered Julius Caesar yet again.'

'Thank you, Madam. And once again, thank you for meeting me at such short notice.' Omar rose and walked to the door, when Mrs Almeida called out to him again.

'Superintendent Abassi, this matter with Ahmed has troubled me. If it isn't terribly inconvenient for you, when all this is over, and when you have found the 'method in his madness' as Shakespeare put it, would you come back and tell me what it was? I am an old woman, who has spent her life believing in the Quaid-e-Azam's dream, that for the vast majority of people, it wouldn't matter if you prayed in a church or a mosque or a temple. I would like to know what was so compelling as to shatter that vision.'

'Uh, Ahmed, Madam?'

'Ahmed Sufi. That was the name he was registered under in school.'

Omar returned to the waiting room with the pictures. He walked up to the cricket team picture from 1994. All the boys looked smart in their maroon blazers and ties. Ahmed Sufi sat in the front row, to the right of an older man, who must have been the coach, Elquemedo Willet. Omar recognized another of the boys, the one who sat immediately to the left of the coach, the same dark-complexioned boy who was in the Wikipedia picture with the Sheikh. The caption under the name read Adnan Shah. Adnan Shah of deposit box 77824? Eddy Shah?

'Is there a problem, Superintendent? Anything we can assist you in?' Omar had not realized that the headmistress' assistant was standing behind him.

'Uh, no. I mean yes. Would it be possible to pull the record of an Adnan Shah? He must have been in the same year as Sheikh Uzair ... I mean as Ahmed Sufi. Graduated 1994.'

'You shall have it, Superintendent. We'll also arrange a classroom for you to read the files in. Ram Lal the janitor will be around to assist you in any further queries. Mrs Almeida has instructed us to help you in every possible way.'

Wordlessly, Omar was escorted to a classroom. He sat down at a desk and started rifling through the file the janitor handed to him. Adnan Shah had indeed been in the same class as Sheikh Uzair. The records indicated that he was an average student, more interested in chasing girls that grades, according to the caustic comments made by one of his teachers. He was a cricketer, a long standing member of the cricket team, having joined the team before Ahmad Sufi. His father was recorded as being a local businessman. His home address on the file was in Clifton, one of the most upscale localities in the city, and not exactly a hotbed of the Sheikh's supporters. The last entry in the file recorded that Adnan Shah had been admitted to Haileybury College, in the United States, for further studies, commencing from September 1994 but it shed no light on his present whereabouts. Omar turned to Ahmad Sufi's file, which he had also requested for but it too had no further insights. Whatever happened to these men, happened after they left school.

thirteen

May 1997
Kossovo

He wakes up crying and screaming again, startling all the men sleeping in the dormitory. He shakes uncontrollably and his cousin Mustajab wraps another blanket around him. The men take turns sitting with him through the night, trying to cool his burning fever with cold presses. Or at least that is what Mustajab tells him. Ausi has no memory of the nights and days that follow his mother's death. He has no feeling at all, except pain. The pain of loss, of regret. Of absence.

He is not there to bury his mother, just as he wasn't there during her illness. He came here three months ago to escape the bad news from home. His mother hadn't been well for some time, but he had never imagined the end would come so soon. His father never bothers to try to get in touch with him, and it takes his mother's cousin, Mustajab's father, two weeks to get a note through to them in Mitrovica. Their encampment is a small one on the outskirts of the town, established by Muslim charitable institutions for the Kossovar Muslims. Some of the others tell him, by way of sympathy, that it's a miracle the news gets through at all, considering that their location is virtually on the frontlines of the conflict. They are nice enough to arrange a *Ghaibana namaz-i-janaza* for his mother, a funeral prayer to lessen the pain. In their own way, they attempt to assuage his guilt, shrugging and saying it was Allah's will to take her from this earth. He gives us life, and he takes it away. Only Ausi realizes the irony that here, in the midst of a conflict that pits Muslim against Christian, these religious men who profess to hate the Serb Christians, paraphrase the Lord's Prayer to give him some succour.

But none of this fills the dark hole inside him. He spends the days in a daze, too weak to even pick himself up. But the nights are worse. His body is wracked with physical pain and he doesn't know how to exorcise his grief. In his worst moments, the only thing that lessens the pain somewhat is the memory of Sana. In his mind's eye, he can see her standing in front of him, her hair swaying, and the smell of her perfume intoxicating. He remembers the taste of her lips, all urgency and strawberry lip gloss. And the wetness between her legs.

He replays their meeting at the café in his head again and again, as if rewinding a movie to his favourite scene. He doesn't remember her ever looking any better than she does when she enters the café that day. She greets him naturally, like the long lost friend he is supposed to be. He is a little more reserved. Months later, sitting in a cold field in Kossovo mourning his mother's death, he cannot remember how long since he last ate, but he can still remember what she orders that day, a cappuccino, the froth forming a small milk moustache above her lip that makes her even more endearing.

She talks about life at college. She tells him about each and every one of her relationships, what they meant to her and how they affected her. He listens until he thinks his head will explode. And just when it feels as if she has only come here to take an axe to his heart, she stops and reaches out to hold his hand across the table.

'How come you never told me about your feelings for me?' The question is boldly direct, and catches him unawares. He tries to mumble some kind of excuse, but she calmly tells him that he is lying and asks again, all the while caressing the palms of his hands.

'What good would it have done, Sana? You and I, we lived in different worlds. What would I have accomplished by telling you that I had feelings for you? It would have ruined our friendship. And for what? It's not like we would have ever been together. You went off to college in the States. I've been all over the place, and besides, you never thought of me in that way.'

'Did you ever bother to ask me if I thought of you in that way or not? You assumed something, without ever checking with me. How do you know how I would have responded if you had ever asked?'

'What, like you would have said yes. Sure. Who told you this anyway? Did Eddy say something to you? I told him not to.'

'Did Eddy know? What a jerk, he never told me. He obviously considers you a better friend than me. The two of you could have saved me a lot of grief if you had just admitted things to me.' She sighs and he can see her eyes moistening. 'Ausi, you know how I am. I'm really bad at this stuff. For years, I could never figure out the simple fact that what I wanted from my relationships was a friend, someone who would always watch my back, like my two best friends Ausi and Eddy did. I never told you guys but every guy I ever went out with, I secretly compared him to the two of you. If he didn't stand up to the comparison, I wasn't interested.'

He cannot hide the astonished look on his face. The last ten years of his life pass before him, all the little heartaches, the piledriver to his heart every time she went out with another guy while he stood to the side, the pained soul searching over kebab rolls at Boat Basin, all the things that could have been avoided had he ever had the courage. He looks down wistfully, at the chequered tablecloth and swallows hard. When he finally speaks, his voice is barely above a whisper.

'Yeah, well, we can't go back now.'

She looks at him quizzically, then stares straight into his eyes. She no longer caresses his palms, but holds down his wrists with her hands, as if afraid that he will run away at any moment. 'Ausi, I want you to tell me something, and for once, I want you to be honest with me. Do you still have feelings for me?'

He breaks away from her gaze, looking left, then right. He is conscious of a trembling in his hands, and even more conscious of the fact that she can feel it. His heart pounds like a jackhammer and his throat feels constricted. The moment he has dreamt of for ten years has finally arrived and he has never been so frightened of opening his mouth.

'No. I don't have *feelings* for you, Sana. I'm in love with you. Always have been. Always will be.'

Now it's her turn to look away and clear her throat. The café is virtually empty but she still says, 'Let's go someplace quiet to talk.' Throughout the bus journey from Leicester Square to her flat in Green Park, they both stare into each other's eyes, holding hands, not saying a word, oblivious to the sea of humanity surrounding them.

Talking is farthest from their minds when Sana unlocks the door to the flat. Driven by instinct, they both lunge for each other, locking each other in a desperate embrace. There is an urgency in her lips and tongue that matches his own. They fall to the floor, her heavy keys clanking on the wooden floorboards. He is surprised, and excited by her boldness as she brazenly unzips his trousers and gropes for his cock. Her sexual aggression arouses him to new heights, and he too becomes more desperate in his caresses, one hand fondling her breasts while she guides the other between her legs. His hands are rough and forceful, but she doesn't seem to mind, increasing her strokes on him to match his rhythm, even as she kicks off her pants and opens her legs for him. At this moment in time, everything else in his mind, his feelings for her, his past, his present, the future, all blurs. He can hear her whispering in the distance, asking him if he has a condom, but he is too far gone to care. The only thing that remains is his primal need to come. Which he does.

He rolls off her, embarrassed, but she squeezes his shrinking manhood and kisses him on the cheek, reassuring him in a husky voice that next time it'll be better. She doesn't bother to cover her hairless sex as she strolls to the bathroom to wash his semen from her legs. He looks around at his surroundings absently. The apartment reeks of luxury, a mixture of east and west, 5000 pound leather couches with Chugtai Mughal miniatures hanging above them. A holiday home for some wealthy desi businessman, or perhaps a corrupt politician's or bureaucrat's hiding hole, a place where they can display the fruits of their ill-gotten gains. A universe away from his world in Whitechapel.

He is about to pull his pants on when she returns and tells him not to bother. She kisses him passionately, the kind of kiss you only see in the movies. The kind of kiss he has waited for all his life. Even at that moment, something within him tells him nothing will ever feel so good again for as long as he lives.

They spend the afternoon eating strawberries and cream and talking about life, school, anything and everything under the sun. She tells him about the first time she slept with a man. And he finds himself letting her in to his deepest and darkest thoughts, sharing his life with her in a way he has never done with any other human being, not even Eddy. He tells her about Kashmir, about Sohail, about his mother's illness and his father's inability to emote. He even tells her about the prostitute and unashamedly admits his 'failure to achieve lift-off'.

She gently strokes his cock and kneels in front of him. 'I don't think that's a problem we're going to have today.'

The sun has set even on an English summer's day by the time he leaves her apartment. He wants to meet her alone again the following day, but she convinces him to go with her for dinner with some common school friends. The dinner is at one of the most expensive restaurants in the city, and the talk throughout the meal is about Kristal champagne and Jimmy Choo shoes and Prada bags. He is amazed by the realization that none of these people have yet graduated from college. Their habits are still funded by parental credit cards. He is even more amazed by how effortlessly Sana fits in with these people, how gracefully she moves between different realities. But it is also a wake-up call for him, making him realize how far he has actually drifted from the world he inhabited in school. In truth, he doesn't know where he belongs. Sana may poke fun at these people, but she and Eddy still have some commonality with them as well. On the other hand, he can never fit in their world again. School was just a strange social experiment, where by a quirk of fate, he was allowed some time in the fish tank.

That realization gnaws away at him on the bus journey back from West London to Whitechapel. At some level, perhaps he has always wanted to be accepted in *that* world, Eddy and Sana's world, but with the exception of those two, that acceptance is unlikely to ever be forthcoming. And even with Sana, there seem to be limits. It doesn't escape his notice that she doesn't introduce him as her boyfriend. But is that what he is? Are they now in a relationship, after one six-hour session of sex, strawberries and talk?

He is confused, and his return to his flatshare, with the men's magazines strewn on the floor, a bathroom that smells as if it has been transported straight from a Karachi tenement, and the kitchen with grease spots on the ceiling, only worsens his predicament. He knows inside, no matter what he may say to Sana, or what she may say to him, he can never bring her here. Talking about his life experiences in the abstract while he caresses her naked thigh in a million pound Mayfair flat is one thing, but seeing that reality is something else altogether. She can't be a part of this life of his. He still doesn't know what she sees in him. Then it occurs to him that maybe he is her little social science project. A one-man outreach program to convince herself that she can slum it with the underclass.

Such thoughts trigger an irrational anger within him. He decides not to answer her calls the next morning. She calls him twenty-five times, so he hands his phone to one of his flatmates, who tells her that he has left town for some work. Three days later, he listens to a pathetic message from her on his answer machine, asking why he won't speak to her and what she did wrong. She begs him to call her as she is leaving that same day. He doesn't, and just like that, he lets Sana walk out of his life forever.

He has not been whole since that moment. It almost seems as if the Almighty is punishing him for having discarded her so dismissively. His mother's illness worsens and his surroundings seem alien to him. The truth is that, just as he never belonged in Sana's world, he doesn't belong in this one either, living the life of an asylum-seeking immigrant, living in a hovel, working the graveyard shift at a fast food chain, racially taunted and abused by drunken revellers emptying out of clubs at three in the morning and wanting to look macho in front of their companions. It is to escape all of this that he agrees to travel to Kossovo with his cousin's Islamic society friends.

But here and now, praying for his mother's departed soul with a group of strangers, he is more lost than ever. He feels worse for having thought about Sana to ease his pain. He is unable to emerge from his catatonic state. His dormitory fellows abandon him to his fate, but four days after the prayers for his mother, his cousin Mustajab brings a visitor to his bedside. Sheikh Saad is a plump man with a bushy black beard, wearing a pair of oversized aviator glasses that cover half his face and give him a menacing look. Ausi knows he is one of the senior clerical figures who are responsible for the administration of the camp but he has never spoken to him before. Sheikh Saad has seldom been seen speaking to anyone in the camp.

It is only when the Sheikh sits down by his bedside and takes off the glasses does Ausi realize the need for them. The Sheikh has a glass eyeball in his right socket, and a scar that runs from his temple to his cheek. He offers his condolences for Ausi's mother, reciting *Surah Fateha*. He then turns to Mustajab and bids him to leave.

'Your cousin tells me that your mother was a fellow Kashmiri sister of ours. That makes her loss more sorrowful for us. Which part of Kashmir is your father from? Perhaps some of our people there can go and assist him in his time of need.'

'He isn't. He isn't from Kashmir. He's from Karachi.'

'Oh. I see. Unfortunate. Still, we have people in Karachi too. If you give me your address, I will send somebody out there to help him in any way we can.'

'I doubt that the bastard would want your help, or anyone else's. He didn't see the need to inform his son, so I'm sure he worked things out for himself.'

In an instant, before even realizing what he is saying, the bile building up within him comes to the surface. But Sheikh Saad takes it in his stride, as if sons abusing their fathers is a daily occurrence for him.

'Your cousin tells me you are a great fan of cricket. So am I, though very few of our other brothers seem to have an appreciation for the game. Did you hear about Saeed Anwar's record score in a one day match? 194 runs! Mashallah. And that too against the bania Indians. He broke the previous record, held by...'

'Viv Richards, 189 not out, against England, in Manchester, 1984. Where was this match played?' The news seems to jolt Ausi out of his state.

'In India. Madras, or Chennai as they now call it.'

'In May? It must have been 200 degrees in the shade, and the pitch might as well have been concrete. I feel bad for the bowlers on both sides.'

'I believe the spinner Saqlain Mushtaq bowled quite well. But yes, conditions certainly did favour the batsmen.'

Ausi stares at him quizzically. 'Sheikh sahib, I don't mean to sound rude or ungrateful, but what exactly are you doing here? I'm sure you have better things to do than chat with me.'

'You are right. I do have better things to do. But you are lost, Ahmed Uzair Sufi. Lost, filled with guilt and anger, and rudderless. I am here to help you find your true path.'

The Sheikh starts visiting Ausi every day, bringing him food and encouraging him to eat. He does not ask questions about Ausi's family, or his past. Sometimes, he talks about the camp, sometimes he recites from memory from the Qur'an, and other times he sits quietly, eating his own food. After about a week, he brings an old tattered newspaper clipping and reads from it. It is the report of the game in which Saeed

Anwar scored his 194 runs and Ausi thinks he has never heard sweeter words.

Slowly, Ausi starts responding to the older man's efforts, accompanying the Sheikh on long walks around the encampment in the evening. They talk about cricket, they talk about God, and without any prompting, Ausi even begins to talk about Sana. The Sheikh merely strokes his beard contemplatively, and at the end of Ausi's confession, he suggests that they pray.

The camp volunteers cannot help but notice Ausi's renewed faith. He never misses a prayer, even the optional Tahajjud prayer in the middle of the night. He starts eating better, and even starts helping out with the refugees. One night, a dying old woman is brought into the camp. She is a Bosnian Muslim and she carries within her battered body the horrors of the past four years. As she lies dying, Ausi tries to make sense of her incoherent babbling. The only thing that calms her down is when the Sheikh recites verses from the Qur'an. Ausi sits with him by the old woman's bedside as he recites flawlessly from memory. They follow this ritual every night till the old woman dies.

The night after her death, the two men sit under the stars on the roof of the dormitory building and share a frugal meal of lentil stew and bread. It is Ausi who finally breaks the silence.

'Sheikh sahib, you seemed to understand the old woman's babblings. What was she talking about?'

'She talked about Srebrenica.'

'What's in Srebrenica?'

'It was her home. It was a Muslim town in Bosnia, where all the men were murdered by the Serbs and the women and children were either raped or sold into slavery. In 1995. In the twentieth century. Just two years ago.'

Ausi is numbed by such barbarity. The two men sit in silence for some time before he speaks again.

'I have to thank you for all that you have done for me. But I still don't understand why you spared so much time and effort on me. There are so many people in the camp, both volunteers and refugees, who must have much greater problems than mine. So why did you pick me?'

The Sheikh smiles and picks his teeth with a twig. 'You remind me of myself.'

He laughs at Ausi's shocked expression, his sudden mirthfulness proving an even bigger surprise.

'You stare at me in horror, but you and I are not so different. I was your age, not so long ago, even though my current appearance belies that fact. It was just ten years back that I was a young man in Muzaffarabad. I used to run my father's auto repair shop by day, and would try to fuck half the girls in the neighbourhood by night. I just couldn't resist my lust for women. I used to go after the married ones, the housewives bored by their husband's ritualistic lovemaking on Friday nights, and horny for a young stud. On the weekend, I played cricket. Winter or summer, cricket was my religion. I was a fast bowling all-rounder and I used to model myself on Imran Khan, bowling like him, strutting around like him with my collar raised, and even copying his hairstyle.'

Ausi is trying to envision the Sheikh as Imran Khan, but it is beyond his imagination. 'So what happened?'

'The revolt began in Occupied Kashmir. Our brothers and sisters stood up against the oppressive yoke of the Indians. There was a lot of talk about boys from our side going across the border to help. The Army had started to put together training camps and were looking for volunteers to send across. But at first, I wasn't interested at all. I had a business to run, and besides, I was having so much fun, why would I want to abandon all that?

'Then one day a friend of mine, a fellow I used to play cricket with, returned from tableegh and came to my shop. I was as surprised to see him as you are now. His appearance had changed, he had grown a beard, he wore shalwar kameez. He insisted that I accompany him to a meeting that his religious friends had organized to educate people about what the Indians were doing to our brothers and sisters in Kashmir. At first I was reluctant, but he was so insistent that I went along. At the meeting, they played an audio cassette recorded by a firebrand speaker, a young maulvi who had been among the first to volunteer when the rebellion broke out. They had kept a picture of him next to the tape recorder. He was a handsome man, as young as I was at the time, but fair and tall, a true flower of Kashmiri manhood. When they played the recording, I swear to you by Allah, Uzair, I have never heard such a beautiful voice. He spoke about the families of our brothers across the border, how they were being tortured, how their women, our sisters, were being harassed and raped every day by their security forces. They would enter into their houses on the pretext of searching them, and start fondling the women. The way he said it, the passion in his voice was evident even through a scratchy recording. I could see the faces of several of the men in the room, who, like me, had not joined the resistance, bowing with shame when the young maulvi pleaded as to how we could sit by and let this happen to our mothers and sisters.

'When the session ended, the organizers asked for donations and also asked if anyone was willing to volunteer. I was conflicted. On one hand, the young maulvi's words had lit a fire in my soul, but on the other, the thought of my mundane responsibilities weighed me down. I wanted to speak more with the impressive maulvi. So I asked my friend where I could find him. He told me that the maulvi had crossed over but was arrested soon after by the Indians. He had no weapons, so instead of throwing him into prison, they had blinded him, cut off his right hand and thrown him back across the border, as a lesson for all those who had ideas about joining the revolt. The story brought tears to my eyes, and there and then, I decided to join the jihad.'

Ausi stared down at the piece of bread in his hand. 'Is that how you lost your eye?'

'I fought in Kashmir for a long time, for almost five years. Then one day, during a shootout with the security forces, one of the soldiers threw a grenade in my direction. It fell short, but the shrapnel pierced my eye.' The older man rubbed his eyelid as he spoke. 'Well, we cannot expect to do God's work without some sacrifice, can we? I was very proud of my injury. To me, it felt as if I had at least attained half the stature of the maulvi, who had lost both of his eyes.'

'Did you ever meet the maulvi?'

'No. By the time I came back from the training camp, I heard he had insisted on going back to the Indian side, even in his handicapped state.'

'Why are you telling me all of this? What does it have to do with me?'

'Look around you. Kashmir, Bosnia, this place. All of these horrible things are happening to good people, just because they are Muslim. Islam is under attack. You are different from all these other brothers in the camp. I don't denigrate them, but they are soft. They have lived in the west all of their lives, and for them, religion is Arabic verses that they recite five times a day. Look at your cousin, Mustajab. A good boy, no doubt. He does all his chores, says his prayers on time. But he cannot help but be corrupted by the indulgent society in which he was brought up. A man is not strong unless he has seen pain in his life. And he cannot truly serve God unless he has that inner strength. You have it.'

'But I am weak, Sheikh sahib. You have seen me. I'm a mess. If it hadn't been for you, I would have fallen apart.'

'You are not weak, you are lost. I was too. Sometimes we have to wander in the wilderness before we find our true destiny. And the pain we suffer fashions us. It tempers us like a sword that is raked in hot coal.'

'What do you wish me to do?'

'I believe that throughout our lives, the Almighty shows us signs, as little course corrections. If we have the ability to seize upon them we can change our lives in the manner he intended. This is your sign and your opportunity to break out of the shackles of your everyday existence, to put behind all the failures and regrets and bitterness.

'You are a Muslim. You have a duty to wage jihad to protect the weak and oppressed. On top of that, you are a Kashmiri. You have a double duty to wage jihad against those who have occupied your country. That is a good start. Perhaps from there you will go on to discover an even greater destiny that Allah has in mind for you.'

An eternity passes before Ausi answers. He looks at the stars on this cold, crisp night in a beautiful country that is being ripped apart by war. Much like Kashmir. He thinks about his father, another stern man like the Sheikh but without his empathy. A father who has never been a father to him. He thinks of his mother, an angel who was perhaps too good for this cruel and unjust world. Perhaps what they say about God taking away early the ones he loves most is true. Perhaps even the Almighty doesn't want the good ones to be corrupted by this world. He thinks about Sana, and knows that now, once and for all, after the mess he left behind in London, that door is shut, no matter how much he continues to love her. And he knows deep down that it his own fault, his own insecurities, that have created that situation. He can see his filthy flat in Whitechapel, a permanent reminder of a failed life, and he knows he can never go back there. Finally he thinks of Eddy, his best friend, the last good thing left in his life, but a universe away. He remembers dropping Eddy to the airport the day he left for America and the way they embraced. Despite trying to control them, there were tears in his eyes that day. Not painfully sad tears, but wistful tears, marking the end of an era. The same tears streak down his cheeks today, but his mouth breaks into a small smile, the same way Eddy's had when he had turned at the departure gate to look back one more time. Suddenly, Ausi turns to face the Sheikh and proffers his hand. The Sheikh smiles and accepts it.

BOOK TWO

Lands of War

fourteen

November 1997
Camp Suleyman Farsi
Khost, Afghanistan,

The wind throws dust in Ausi's eyes, forcing him to take his eyes off the barrel of the gun. He hurriedly drapes the cloth over the disassembled rifle parts, not wanting to have to repeat the cleaning process. He smiles to himself. He could do this with his eyes closed.

'The shomal winds have started to blow from Central Asia. It is going to start getting very cold in a few days.' His companion is a thin reed of a man called Muawiya, who sits on his haunches in front of him, wearing a thick woollen pakol cap. He shivers despite being tightly wrapped in a wool shawl.

Ausi, on the other hand, welcomes the coolness. Several of the buttons on his kameez are unbuttoned and the wind feels fresh on his chest. More than that, it makes him feel alive. Indeed, in the three months that he has been here, he has felt more alive than at any time in his life. 'The cold is good for you. It cleanses your soul,' he says as he quickly reassembles the AK-47, running the pull-through rag through the barrel, the smell of linseed oil filling his nostrils. It is spotless. He checks the firing mechanism one last time before putting away the rifle.

'It's easy for you to say. You're Kashmiri, the cold runs in your blood. I'm a tilyar from Karachi, I hate this weather and this place.'

'You forget, friend, that I am also from Karachi and half of me is as tilyar as you.'

'Yes, but you enjoy all this. The training regimen, the discipline. Ever since we came here, you have thrived in this place. The rest of us are here because it is an obligatory part of our training, and we want to get out as soon as possible. But you have become a living, breathing extension of the camp. You know, you should really stay on and become one of the trainers. You are already one of the best students here.'

Ausi laughs and scratches his new beard. It has taken him some time to get used to the growth and it still itches. But out here at camp Suleyman Farsi, a beard becomes virtually compulsory. Since their hosts took over the country, there are no more barbers in Khost. The past three months have not been easy, living in a shed that offers no more comfort than literally just being a roof over their heads, waking up at dawn every day for an intensive routine of calisthenics and weapons handling, and eating, sleeping and shitting with dozens of other recruits with whom he shares no commonality except religion. But it has been worth it.

It was Sheikh Saad's men who received him at Karachi airport on his return from Kossovo. He never bothered to go home or contact his family. The only exception he made in drawing a line through his former life was to visit his mother's grave.

The next day, his new friends had put him on a bus to Miranshah. In the main bazaar there, as instructed, he presented himself at a shop selling religious CDs and jihadi literature, the main reporting centre for recruits joining the 21-day basic

Ma'asker, or training course in the camps across the border in Afghanistan.

Camp Suleyman Farsi is the Ivy League of jihadi training, an elite campus where the best of the best, the chosen few from all the various militant groups, from all over the world, congregate. He is on the Kashmiri panel but his friend Muawiya belongs to a Sunni group that campaigns against the Shi'as. There are others, Afghan recruits for the Taliban, and foreigners, from as far afield as Indonesia and Chechnya. His glowing letter of recommendation from the Sheikh has already made him eligible for the most advanced level of training, but despite that, he pushes himself, excelling at every challenge to prove himself worthy. He has gone far beyond the basic course, learning all there is to learn about hand to hand combat, weapons handling and bomb making. He particularly enjoys bomb making, studying the symphony of circuits that all have to come together perfectly, like an orchestra, in order to produce their masterpiece.

'What are you thinking about? Will you stay on as a trainer?'

Brought back to the present, Ausi shakes his head. 'No Muawiya. The life of the academic is not for me. I want to go to Kashmir and use my newly acquired skills.'

'You Kashmiris are too attached to your homeland. You would be of far greater use to us in the fight against the kafir Shi'as. Think about it.'

'Why are the Shi'as kafir? Aren't they just another sect of Islam? Isn't it better to direct our energies against an external foe, like the Hindu lalas in Kashmir?'

'Even you cannot be that naïve, Uzair. The Shi'as are the original sinners, the schismatics. Despite being only a minority in Pakistan, they control everything. Look at all the big landlords, the government bureaucrats, the politicians. All the prominent ones are Shi'a. They secretly plot against the majority of us who are from the true faith. And they in turn, are all in the pocket of the greatest schismatic, Iran.'

'Do you really think so?'

'Of course. Don't you know that the Iranians provide funding for all the Shi'a groups? They train them in Qom and Teheran, so that they can come back and kill our leaders. And why doesn't the government do anything about that? Dozens of our leaders are killed and no one raises a voice, but one of their people is killed and we are hunted like dogs. The kafirs provoke us deliberately. Their children are taught to abuse the names of the Khulfa-i-Rashideen. Their women are all prostitutes. Do you know that all the girls in the red light area of Lahore are Shi'a? How can we coexist with such people? Why should we? Pakistan is a Sunni state, by the grace of Allah and it is our job to ensure it remains that way.'

'Yes, thank god Pakistan is a Sunni state, founded by the Quaid-e-Azam. Thank god for that. By the way, wasn't he a Shi'a?'

Ausi cannot restrain himself after looking at his friend's face turning three different shades of purple. He bursts out laughing. Muawiya tries to retain his stern, disapproving gaze, but it is too much for him and a broad grin breaks out across his face.

'You are lucky you only say such things in front of me. Some of my fellow tanzeem members would not appreciate your sense of humour the way I do.'

'That is why the esteemed Muawiya is my friend and the others are not. If you cannot find humour in the business of killing, then what can you find it in?'

Muawiya gets up and puts his arm around Ausi. 'Come my friend, let us go for lunch. They're putting on quite a feast today, not our usual dal, sabzi and roti. They're roasting a couple of goats. Its graduation day after all and apparently we have some esteemed guests coming over. Ah, it looks like they've just arrived.'

A cloud of dust moves into the camp compound and halts outside the main administration shed, where the camp administrators have already formed a reception line. Three Toyota Land Cruisers, caked in dust. Armed guards jump out of the first and third vehicles to form a cordon around the middle jeep. Officiously, one of the bodyguards opens the rear passenger door and a tall man with a long beard and an angular face, dressed elegantly in a white jooba, steps out. The reception committee fawn over him, and one of them kisses his hand in supplication.

'I can't believe it, it's Sheikh Osama! He has actually come in person!'

'Who the fuck is Sheikh Osama?'

'Osama bin Laden. They say he is the scion of one of the richest families in Saudia, but he abandoned a life of luxury to fight with the mujahideen. He's become a legend around the camps. He is very generous as well, he funds several of them.'

Ausi grimaces as the trainers order him to take his place in the impromptu parade that is being organized for the VIP. He finds performing like this to be distasteful. It makes him feel like a monkey on a string. He is placed at the front of the line-up because of his skills, and the camp commandant makes a special mention of him to the 'distinguished guest'. The tall Arab looks at him with his piercing eyes but is surprised to find Ausi's unfazed and unimpressed gaze, glaring right back at him. Sensing Ausi's defiance, he smiles and makes a comment in Arabic that draws an over enthusiastic laugh from the camp commandant. But Ausi does not understand and keeps staring at him with dead eyes. Noticeably flustered, bin Laden's smile disappears and he resumes his inspection of the parade.

Muawiya is right about one thing, though. A feast is laid out for them after the parade; giant vats of pulao mixed with dry fruit, mutton roasting on spits, dripping with fat and giant pieces of Kandhari naan. He has not eaten this well since he came here. Muawiya and Ausi find a quiet corner to enjoy their meal, but Muawiya keeps pausing between mouthfuls and stares at him, as if examining an unusual painting.

'You are a strange one, Ahmed Uzair Sufi. There are not many men in this camp who would have given the great Osama bin Laden the brush off like you did.'

'I know his type and I've hated them all my life. Self-important, pompous madarchods with an inflated sense of their own worth, while all this time, it is others who make the sacrifices and take the risks. Since I was a child, I knew characters like him in my father's department. It was the same story when I joined a political party. My friend Sohail had a term that described such people. He used to say that they were the sorts who would inflict a paper cut on their little finger, in order to be counted among the martyrs.'

'How can you say that? Sheikh Osama fought many battles against the Soviets in the great jihad. Why, there is a story that the instructors tell, of how he and a handful of men held off a whole battalion of Soviets in the Tora Bora mountains…'

'Please. When the Soviets were here, he was sitting in a comfortable guest house in Peshawar, sending other recruits to the front line. The instructors kiss his arse because he shits money. He's a spoilt rich boy looking for thrills. He's not a jihadi. He's not one of us.'

Muawiya tosses the piece of naan in his hand onto the plate and shakes his head ruefully. 'This morning, you didn't know who he was, and by now you have read a whole CIA file on him? And where does all this anger and defiance for authority come from? Be careful, my friend. Such an attitude will not help you in the field, when you have to put your life in another man's hands and trust to his judgment. If you question everyone and everything, how do expect to submit yourself to the will of God, like a true jihadi?'

'I submit to the will of God, not of other men.'

'Yes, but Ahmed, we are soldiers in an army. There has to be some sort of discipline, some hierarchy. We cannot go about shooting whomever we wish.'

'Really? Sometimes I think random violence is the best way to grab people's attention. You have to shock people, deliver a 2000 watt jolt to their system. That is how you change the world. You can kill all the Shi'as you want, but it doesn't matter. They keep sending new people, as do you. They see you coming. It's predictable.'

'And what would you do differently, my friend? What great stratagems do you have to alter the course of events?'

Ausi is pensive, thinking of Eddy, as he often does these days. He has been penning a letter to him for months, but has not gotten round to completing it. He wants to tell him about Muawiya and about his meeting with Osama bin Laden. Muawiya laughs, taking his silence to mean that he is stumped for an answer.

'Bas? The great Ahmed Uzair Sufi is silenced by my one question? Has the air gone out of you?'

Ausi turns and flashes him a brilliant smile. 'My friend, just wait. When I get the chance to do things my way, the world will hold its breath.'

fifteen

21 August 1998
New York City

It is going to be a hot day. Even at ten in the morning, Eddy can feel the sun's rays toasting his back. He can see the heat waves shimmering over the sidewalk, as passers-by walk past him doing the New York shuffle, that peculiar brand of obnoxious, brisk barging that all New Yorkers must master to survive the Darwinian pedestrian landscape of the city. Eddy sees all of this from his vantage point, an open-air table at a sidewalk café on the corner of 71st and Columbus. He scans the perpetually moving crowd, looking for her. He curses while perching his Oakley sunglasses on top of his head, making sure not to disturb his carefully styled hair. Typical of Sana to be running late.

He picks the letter up from the table and starts reading it again out of boredom. He has read it at least eight times already, including an entire recitation over the phone for Sana a couple of days ago. The incredulity of the situation brings a smile to his face. Ausi, Eddy and Sana. The inseparable trio. Who could have predicted where they'd all end up when school finished four years ago. Sana, the academic superstar, dropping out of college due to her father's political problems. He, the brainless jock, about to start work at an IT consultancy. And Ausi, well Ausi was something else altogether.

She sneaks up behind him and ruffles his hair, prompting an exclamation from him. 'Hey, what the fuck?!'

'Ooh, we're sensitive about our new hairstyle, now that we're a hot shot IT consultant? Interesting look, though I don't think this short and spiky Ryan Philippe thing works for you.'

She looks fantastic as usual. He will never admit it to her because he has teased her about her looks since middle school, always deflating her to counter the compliments of her legions of admirers. But he marvels at her ability to still look stunning in spite of all her recent problems. Instead of saying that though, he makes a face.

'Hey, it's something I'm trying out, okay? These IT web people are all supposed to be real cutting edge sorts. I have to do something that'll make me fit in with their cool image.'

'Yeah, especially since you obviously won't be able to do that through your actual IT skills. Tell me, have you figured out exactly what you're supposed to be doing at your job?'

'Not exactly. It's something to do with programming languages. Java and HTML or whatever. I don't know, these days they're looking for people and I wasn't going to argue with them after they decided to hire me. Hey, listen, why don't you apply to my firm? If they thought fit to hire me, they'll definitely pick you up.'

'No thanks. I would rather spend the rest of my life waiting tables at the diner than join some computer geek firm.'

He shoves the menu towards her as she sits down in front of him. 'Hurry up and decide what you want. I'm starving and judging by the time the waitress took to get my orange juice, it'll be a while before we actually get our order.'

'Hey, hey. Don't denigrate a member of the sisterhood. What are you having? Oh god, you know what I really feel like getting? One of Ram Lal's parathas with a steaming cup of chai. Hai, but I'll have to settle for a veggie omelette. Or maybe I should have porridge? What are you getting again?'

He rolls his eyes at her. The indecision is typical of her. Mercifully, the eastern European waitress comes over and takes their order. Pancakes for him, and after another round of deliberations, the omelette for her. Her eyes light up when she sees the letter lying on the table.

'Oh my god, Eddy, is that the letter? This is so cool! Can you believe our best friend is a kidnapper!'

He turns to see if anyone has overheard Sana's comment, giving an embarrassed smile to an elderly couple on an adjoining table, who, gauging by the suspicious looks he gets back, obviously have.

'Sana, can you please not say such things out loud! You and I may think that Ausi is doing something really cool, but for 99.99 per cent of the population, he is engaging in multiple felonies.'

She shrugs her shoulders. 'So you agree with me that he's doing something really cool?'

'Well, I mean, yeah. I mean I don't justify kidnappings or whatever, but he's fighting for a cause he believes in. He's fighting for his homeland. Who else from our class can claim to be doing anything remotely as important? Plus, the way he describes the way they planned the kidnapping of that last British tourist, is something straight out of a James Bond movie!'

She picks up the letter and starts reading, while the waitress brings their breakfast. Sana looks up at him and speaks in a conspiratorial whisper. 'You didn't tell me he met Osama bin Laden!'

'How the fuck was I supposed to tell you that on the phone Sana? Yeah, for anyone who's listening in on us, our best friend just met the guy who bombed two American embassies! I don't want the CIA or FBI crawling up my ass.'

'You have a typical Pakistani sense of paranoia. They would never do things like that in this country. But I like how Ausi describes bin Laden as an upstart Arab. I guess spending ten years in The School makes you a snob, even if you're in a training camp in Afghanistan!'

He takes a bite of the pancakes. They taste like rubber, generic and mass produced, like all the food he's been eating lately. He reminds himself that he really should try to cook in his apartment. 'He's really good at what he does. You know, it's funny. All these years when we were in college, Ausi was just kind of drifting. You know, with his problems with student politics, and then running away to Kashmir, and then London. He seemed lost. But turning to religion seemed to be a seminal point in his life. Since then, he's discovered this focus, like he knows exactly where he wants to go and how to get there. It's fascinating how faith changes your life.'

'You seem pretty impressed. Why don't you try it?' She bites into a French fry as if it were a lover. Eddy has never failed to be surprised by the casual eroticism that always seems to surround Sana. She has always been oblivious to it, but her simplest actions, from tying her hair to eating an ice lolly, have left grown men quivering like jello.

'No, I don't think so. Religion scares me. Always has.'

'How so?'

'When I was a kid, we used to always go to Lahore for Ashura. For those ten days, my Dad would convert himself into a pious Shi'a and we would attend all the majlises at an imambargah in the old city, where one of my Dad's cousins was the caretaker. The way these guys got so absorbed into the rituals, with young men beating themselves during the matam, and women and old men wailing during the majlis, it always frightened me. I wondered about the passion that made adults cry and beat themselves over something that happened fifteen hundred years ago. It was awesome and terrible at the same time. I stopped going for Ashura when I was about twelve, pleading school tests or exams that were due during those dates. But last winter, I did go back to the old imambargah in Lahore after many years. The old caretaker, my Dad's cousin, had been shot dead by Sunni militants. He had no beef with them, except that he was born a Shi'a. To think that someone out there, maybe some of the guys who were in this training camp with Ausi, would take the chance to kill me, just because of what I am. That scares the shit out of me.'

She reaches out for his hand and expresses her sympathy. Eddy thinks that if Ausi were sitting in his place right now, or any of Sana's ex-boyfriends, this would be the point where they would be totally bamboozled by her. Eddy has always considered Sana a female version of Shane Warne when it comes to getting guys to fall for her. A freakishly talented leg spinner with a bag of tricks, which she sometimes uses unknowingly. But, like a good batsman against spin, he has always been able to read her much better than the others. He sees which way she turns the ball. Probably the reason why he has almost singularly been immune to her charms for all these years. The cricketing analogy makes him smile.

'What about you? Are you planning to go home this summer? Things cooled for your Dad?'

'Well, my parents managed to get to Dubai. It wasn't easy, since the government had put all our names on the exit control list. They're really out to get Papa. All of his accounts are still frozen, so he can't send me any money. Not that I'd want any of his money now, after what happened. So I have to survive on my waitress' pay check. And my tips aren't going to be enough to cover a ticket back home.'

'Hey, don't be too harsh on him. The government's just conducting a witch-hunt against all the people who were in prominent posts in the previous regime. That doesn't mean what they're saying is true.'

'Except that it is, Eddy. I should know this better than most people. I was the idiot who used to write articles against the corrupt Pakistani regime in college. All the time my father was one of the key pillars of that corrupt regime. I must literally have no investigative ability at all, not to have figured this out years ago. But I always lived in my little cocoon, with school, studies and guys, and I never bothered to look at the reality staring me in the face. Part of me feels I deserved to be humiliated by that Lahori asshole, when he revealed my dirty little secret to half the campus.'

'Is that why you decided to drop out? You trying to punish yourself for your Dad's sins?'

'I don't know. Maybe. It just became a little overwhelming. Everything happening at the same time, Papa's situation, the pressure of having to face everyone at college, the whole Ausi deal…'

'Sana, to this day, you have never clarified to me, exactly what 'the Ausi deal' was. What the hell happened between you guys? He, of course, conveniently found God at around the same time, so I got nothing out of him. And every time I raise the subject with you, you act so coy, I feel as if I've asked you whether you shave your pubic hair or not.'

She bursts out laughing at his comment, and throws her napkin at him playfully. Her laughter is infectious and he responds to it. 'Where do you come up with this stuff Eddy, you little perv! You mean Ausi never talked to you about it?'

He shakes his head.

'Well, then I guess I have to respect his desire for privacy.'

Eddy raises his hands in a sign of exasperation as she gives him a wide grin and gets up to hug him.

'What the hell is that for?'

'That's for making me laugh Eddy Shah. I haven't done that in a while. I'm really glad you're here in New York. I was lonely without my best friend.'

sixteen

The Present

'Sahib, you won't find anything in those files. No one here remembers Ausi baba and Eddy. No one except me.'

That was what the old janitor had told him yesterday. Considering that it was the first chink in the mystery of Sheikh Uzair that he had managed to extract, Omar Abassi had been overjoyed. Wearing a wrinkled and threadbare khaki uniform, his face weathered with age, with only a few wisps of hair covering his scalp, the janitor had said this to him just as he was about to abandon his futile perusal of The School's files. Omar had been startled when the old man had spoken as he was handing the files back to him.

'And who are you?'

'Sahib, my name is Ram Lal and I have been the sports equipment in charge at the school for the past thirty years. I remember both Eddy and Ausi baba from the cricket team. They were inseparable. Those two and that girl who was always with them, Sana or Saima, I think her name was. They used to ask me to get halwa puri for them from the shops outside the wall, during school hours. Such good boys.'

'Have you been in contact with Adnan recently?'

'Adnan, or Eddy, as everyone called him, used to call me every time he came home for the holidays from America. He was very regular about it. Then, some years ago, he stopped calling and I never heard from him again. Once or twice I tried calling his mobile number, but I got no response. I know it happens with a lot of the boys here, when they become something in life, they stop calling old fools like me, but Eddy wasn't like that, he was a very well-mannered boy, not one to forget. Ahmad, or Ausi baba as I called him, was of course different from everyone. He was my favourite. He stayed on in Karachi while Adnan went to America, so we used to meet quite often. He had a tough time here, he was always in and out of trouble. First it was because he joined a political party in medical college, and then later on, he got into his ... well, he turned to religion. He had been very good to me when he was in school, he helped my son to get a job in the postal department. His father worked there, you see. And he was different from all the other kids in school. He wasn't pampered, he came from the real world, not the rich people's cocoon. I somehow always felt more responsible for him. I still visit his family occasionally, just to see if they're all right. They fell on hard times after he got into trouble.'

'His family still lives in the city?'

'Yes. His mother died a few years back, I think when he was abroad or something. The father, who was quite senior in the Postal Service, took early retirement because he was ashamed of Ausi baba's actions. He tries to make some money by teaching in a school near where they live. The brothers used to have good jobs in banks, but they lost them because the police kept picking them up for questioning. Now it's difficult for them to hold a job, because after all, who would want to give a job to Sheikh Uzair's brothers?' Ram Lal smiled, displaying his pink, toothless gums. 'But he has a boy though, very cute, must be about six or seven now, and really mischievous, just like his father.'

It had taken all of Omar's self-control to not toss the ancient janitor into the back of the jeep then and there, and set off for the Sheikh's house. But his plan had been interrupted by an urgent summons from his DIG in Sukkur. And so Omar had promised Ram Lal that he would return the following day, and had also restrained him from informing the Sheikh's father about his impending visit. He had told Ram Lal that it was imperative that the family received no advance notice of his visit, on grounds of national security. It had sounded as stupid when he had said it the first time, but the janitor had shrugged his shoulders and nodded his head sagely, and promised to wait for him outside the school gate at the same time tomorrow.

Upon his return to his district, he had discovered that the supposedly urgent summons from the DIG had really just been a routine inquiry. Frustrated, and more than a little tired at having driven up and down the Super Highway in record time, Omar and his men had been forced to break their fast by the side of the road, and indeed he did not return to the SP House in Khairpur till almost midnight. On the way, he had contemplated turning around and visiting the Animal Husbandry School, but his exhaustion had gotten the better of him. Besides, a call to the compound had revealed that all was well, and that his system was being implemented flawlessly by his staff.

The following day, he had returned to Karachi, but now, sitting in his jeep outside The School waiting for the janitor, he was beginning to feel a little stupid. The old man was late, and for the first time, the thought crossed Omar's mind that he may have just been pulling his leg. If that were the case, he would look like an idiot in front of his men. Granted, the DIG didn't know too much about why he had returned to

Karachi, and he had chosen not to re-engage either Shahab or the local SHO who had helped him get access to the safety deposit box. Still, his driver and guards, sitting in the jeep with him, would know, and they would no doubt repeat the story to the staff in Khairpur about how a bhangi had made a chutiya out of SP sahib.

Just as his irritation at his own gullibility was about to explode, Ram Lal walked out of the school gate, once again flashing his wide, toothless smile as he got into the jeep.

'Salaam sahib, my apologies for being late. There is an inter-school match tomorrow so I had to roll the pitch again. The captain wants a flat wicket.'

Omar waved aside his irritation and forced a smile on his face. 'Don't worry about it. Did you say they live far from here?'

'Not very far, they live in Lalookhet, just over the Teen Hatti bridge.'

Ram Lal directed the jeep out of the crowded lanes of Saddar, the city centre, and towards the northern suburbs of the city. As they wound their way through the congested traffic, they passed an empty patch of land on the road leading to the Quaid-e-Azam's mazaar, one of the few open spaces left in a city that was filling with high rises. A board half covered with red betel nut stains proclaimed the patch as the KGA cricket ground, even though there wasn't a shard of grass anywhere in sight. The waist high wall that surrounded the ground had fallen down in places, and the stench of stale urine wafted through the air as several men used the crumbling wall to relieve themselves.

'That's the KGA ground, sahib. That's where Ausi baba and Eddy played their last match together for the school team. I still remember, it was the Willis Cup final.'

'What's the Willis Cup?'

'It used to be the most prestigious inter-school competition in Karachi. The year these two played was the last year we won it. The old coach, Elquemedo Willet sahib, hated Ausi baba because Ausi was smarter than him and understood the game better. And Ausi was openly contemptuous about the coach's abilities. If he hadn't been such a good player, Elquemedo sahib would have kicked him off the team ages ago. As it was, the school hadn't won the Willis Cup for ten years, and they got to the final almost singlehandedly thanks to Ausi's performances with bat and ball. The coach desperately wanted to win, and he couldn't believe his bad luck when the team captain and the best batsman injured himself a week before the final and announced that he couldn't play. Elquemedo sahib had deliberately refused to make Ausi baba the captain or vice-captain of the team at the beginning of the season, even though he should have been captain by right. But now coach sahib knew that if he appointed anyone else, the team would mutiny. So, using his head for once in his life, he made Eddy captain. There was no way Ausi wouldn't play under Eddy.

'The match itself turned out to be a superb one. It was a horrible wicket, with cracks running down the length of it. I remember when Eddy came back to the pavilion after the toss, he gloomily informed us that he had lost the toss and they had put us in to bat. Coach sahib had wanted us to bowl first. But Ausi stood up and confidently announced that they had made their biggest mistake and would now lose for sure because their over confidence was going to kill them. Well, his prediction didn't look too good at lunch, after we had been bowled out for 138. But he was right. The pitch was turning square and he and Eddy started bowling in tandem right from the beginning. They were like co-captains in that match, discussing every ball and making all the field changes together. Every drinks break, coach sahib would send me out to the middle to tell them to follow his instructions, but they totally ignored him. Heh, we won the match by twenty runs in the end, I think.'

Ram Lal sighed as he turned around to take one last look at the ground. 'I remember those boys. Many people at The School spent years trying to forget Ausi. You know sahib, its true Mrs Almeida probably doesn't remember him, but there were several other teachers who did. I know because they used to occasionally reminisce about him with me. But when he was arrested and that fat inspector came to ask questions, everyone denied knowing him. No one wanted to be associated with him in the slightest way.'

'So why didn't you say something then?'

'No one asked me. They were only interviewing the teachers, not the custodial staff. Besides, somewhere deep down, maybe I was too shocked to say anything. The man who committed these crimes had no resemblance to the boy I knew.'

Omar shrugged in an understanding manner. 'These jihadis can really twist people with their propaganda.'

Ram Lal became silent, as if mulling some significant point. Several minutes passed, as their convoy moved towards the old Soldier Bazaar, with its dilapidated mansions that once belonged to the old moneyed class of the city before they bought up land reclaimed from the sea in the cantonment areas of the city, surrendering their old neighbourhoods to the human waves of migrants that swamped the city periodically; many of the old spacious mansions had given way to cramped high rise tenements, teeming with new residents. The area had a squalid look to it now. The jeep had turned past this and was in sight of the Teen Hatti bridge, before he spoke again.

'No sahib. I don't think that's true. I never told anyone this, but I met him once. I mean after he became a jihadi. It was some years ago, before he had committed any of his sins. But he was already a big name in their circles, because of what he did in Kashmir. At the time, my son had gotten into trouble with some boys in our neighbourhood. They used to collect donations for the jihadis. We Hindus prefer to keep a low profile and I had told my son to stay clear of them, but young blood is hot-headed. He must have said something to them and they got angry and threatened him with a pistol one day. I was very worried that they would do something while I was on duty at school. I didn't know what to do, but luckily, just a day or two after the incident, Ausi called me, as he normally did when he was in the city. I told him about my problem and he told me not to worry, and that he would come and see me the next day. He actually showed up at the school, but his appearance had changed so dramatically. He had a big bushy beard and wore shalwar kameez that he never wore in school. No one recognized him. He came home with me and walked in to the local madrasa that was controlled by a group who had some affiliations with his people. He calmly asked them if he knew who he was. One or two must have recognized him because in those days there used to be pictures of him in the pamphlets they used to distribute. The head of the madrasa came out immediately and personally greeted him.

'He pointed to me and said, "Do you know this man?" One of the boys who had threatened my son was there, and he nodded and replied that I was one of the Hindu families in the neighbourhood. The boy spoke in a harsh tone, and, truth be told, I was a little scared. After all, I was a Hindu, standing in a madrasa, surrounded by all these jihadi types. But Ahmad never lost his cool even for a moment. He smiled, and told them, "What this man, or his son is, or what they do, are of no concern to you. They are under my protection. If I find out that anyone has gone to their house, or threatened them in any way, all of you will be answerable to me. And I don't think you'll like that." He never raised his voice, never cursed, never even made any kind of threatening gesture. He just stared at them with his eyes. The madrasa in charge begged his forgiveness, and forced the boys to apologize to me on the spot. And that was it. Even though he never came back, to this day, they never even come into our gully for collections. I tried to thank him when we walked out of the madrasa that day, but he shook his head firmly and said I had nothing to thank him for. I was his elder, and this was his duty to me.

'So you see sahib, how can the person who did such a service for a low caste Hindu like me be the same man in your case files? He was already a jihadi when he came to my aid. It wasn't the jihadis who changed him. It was something else. Something broke inside of him.'

Ram Lal went back to giving directions to the area. They turned off the broad, three-lane boulevard and drove past Sharifabad police station. The buildings dated from the '60s and '70s, an era where the city's builders had been gripped by an even greater than usual lack of imagination. The paint was peeling off from most of the buildings and the cars on the street were all older models from the early '80s, testament to a bygone era of prosperity. Ram Lal directed the jeep into a narrow alley that was flanked by a burgeoning shanty town on one side. The houses were built on 200 square yard plots and had a cramped look about them.

They stopped and got out in front of the house in the worst condition. The drainage pipes running down the side of the house had almost rotted through, and the sewage leaking from the pipes left dark marks on the wall. A middle-aged man sat on a stoop in front of the small entrance gate, smoking a cigarette. The shalwar kameez he wore had been patched up in several places and the soles of his sandals were almost worn out. As Omar's bodyguards disembarked, the man on the stoop started shaking violently, then, in a panic, he turned and started banging on his own front door.

'Help, Abba, help! They've come to take me again! I told you people, I don't know anything else!'

Startled by the man's reaction, one of Omar's men grabbed him and shook him to calm him down, but this had the opposite result, as the man started wailing and wet himself.

The ruckus had attracted several people from the neighbourhood, but, seeing the police vehicles, everyone kept their distance. Omar looked questioningly at Ram Lal, who was about to say something when the door of the house opened and a bespectacled old man with dishevelled hair and an untidy stubble, wearing only a torn vest on top of his shalwar, came out.

'Leave my son alone! I won't let you take him to the thana again! Haven't you done enough to us? We have nothing more to tell you and we have no money left to give to you, rishwatkhor haramis!' The old man's voice quivered with emotion, as he wrested his son out of the police constable's hands and physically stood in front of him. Ram Lal approached the man and bowed placatingly.

'Sheikh sahib, it's not what you think. These men are not the local police. They have come from Sindh. They just want to talk to you. No one wants to take your son away again. Their officer is with them. He is a good man, please, speak to him.'

Ram Lal's soothing voice and familiar visage seemed to calm the old man. Omar looked around and saw that the expressions of the sizeable crowd that had gathered were far from friendly. He got the distinct feeling that the crowd was barely being held in check by the sight of his armed policemen, and that, if the situation were not resolved soon, that reluctance would soon evaporate.

'Arre typical policewallahs! Leave the poor family alone. Is it their fault if one son turned out to be a criminal? Stop sucking their blood and get your monthly beat from somewhere else!'

Several voices in the crowd murmured their support for the outspoken youth who had said the words. Omar's gunmen looked at him nervously. Being posted in godforsaken Nara had given him few opportunities to deal with crowd situations, and he was still wracking his brain to find something authoritative, yet calming, to say to the crowd, when Ram Lal spoke up.

'Arre bhaiyon, this officer is not like that. He is a good sahib, he just wants to do some research. Please, all of you go back to your homes and businesses, there is nothing to worry about here. Come sahib, barey Sheikh sahib has assented to speak with you, let us go in, but leave your guards outside and tell them to sit in the jeep. If they keep standing outside like this, people will keep coming here to enquire because it looks like a raid is being conducted in their house.'

Omar nodded to his men, who by the speed of their reaction in retreating towards the jeep, thought Ram Lal's idea was an eminently good one. The old man, the Sheikh's father, seemed far from happy, but led them through the narrow entrance into the house, holding his elder son, who was still shaking and now stank of the urine that had seeped through his grey shalwar, leaving a dark patch that ran down the length of his leg. The entrance led into an incredibly constricted passage that was sandwiched between steps leading up on one side, and a slightly larger room, that appeared to be the living room of the house, on the other side. There were no windows in the living room, and the only illumination came from a single tube light that cast a dull and depressing glow. Two tattered two-seater sofas had been placed around a scratched and weathered coffee table that had lost one of its legs, and was kept even by a pile of books that had been shoved under it.

Books were the overwhelming feature of the entire house. There were piles of them strewn in the passage, and Omar could see hundreds of them lined up on an old set of bookshelves that ran across the length of one wall in the room. The family was eminently literate. Littered on the floor, on the sides of the sofas and on the coffee table itself were books among which Omar spotted the philosophy of Kant, a leather-bound edition of Marx's *Das Kapital*, a thick volume of the complete works of Shakespeare and an old edition of Encyclopaedia Britannica.

'Please excuse me a moment. I have to go and wash my son, as there is no one else in the house to do it.'

'Arre sahib, please you leave it. I will take him. This is my job. Please, you sit with SP sahib, I will be back shortly.' Ram Lal took the boy gently by the hand and led him through another door at the opposite end of the room. The old man, Mr Sheikh, was breathing heavily from the exertion and sat down on the sofa, motioning Omar to join him.

'What do you want?' The old man's tone was still curt and angry.

'Sir, my name is Omar Abassi, and I am the district SP of Khairpur. I mean you no harm, and I have not come in any official capacity. I am a young officer, sir, I don't have any background into what your son did, and neither was I around when the police conducted their raids on your house. I sincerely apologize, however, for any inconvenience that may have been caused to you. Your son, Sheikh Uzair, is currently in my custody. He was shifted from Hyderabad after he became troublesome to the authorities over there. He has caused some difficulties for me as well, and I want to understand him better, so that I can handle him accordingly. I wanted to find out a little more about his past, so I would have some perspective when I deal with him. If you have any message that you want to pass on to him, sir, or if you wish to send him something that is permitted under the Jail Rules, I will be happy to forward it on your behalf.'

The old man seemed to ponder this for a moment. 'You came into service through the Civil Service examination? Which batch are you from?'

'Yes sir, Police Service of Pakistan, from the 2005 batch.'

'Uzair Sufi Sheikh, Postal Service of Pakistan, 1975 batch. Retired.' The old man sat straighter in his chair, and offered his hand. Despite the decrepit surroundings and his own shabby appearance, his formality and official demeanour returned as a matter of habit. He was no longer a distraught resident of a run-down neighbourhood, but an officer, meeting a junior colleague. Omar felt strange, shaking his hand, considering he had already been acquainted with the old man for the past twenty minutes, but he took it nonetheless.

'We have not received any PSP officers in our house since our troubles began. Usually it's always ranker inspectors and DSPs from the local police station. And those rascals don't know how to behave with decent people. I used to know a lot of your seniors, who were my batch fellows, but since our troubles started, they stopped taking my calls. As a result, we have been at the mercy of these local savages.'

'I profusely apologize once again, sir. Your name is also Sheikh Uzair?'

'No, my name is Uzair Sheikh, and I am the only one. My son's name is Ahmed Uzair Sufi. The 'Sheikh' is not an honorific in our case, it is our caste. But for some reason, when he got into this … business, my son decided to switch his names around.

And so my own name has become an eternal reminder to me of my complete failure as a parent.'

Ram Lal had returned to the room with the elder son, who had calmed down and was dressed in a fresh shalwar. The janitor gave a thumbs up to signify that everything was okay now and sat the man down next to his father, facing Omar. Mr Sheikh asked Ram Lal to go into the kitchen to call his daughter-in-law. The elder son clung to his father like a man-child, still unsure and scared of the uniformed policeman.

'My elder son, Rameez. Ahmad is the youngest. He wasn't always like this. He used to work in the State Bank.'

'What happened to him?'

'The day after Ahmad killed that female reporter, the police came to our house and took him away. Him and my eldest son Ashfaq. They were missing for thirteen days. I kept going to the police station, but they told me some special squad had taken them away. Then finally, I got a call from the thana to pick them up. Ashfaq was lucky, he got away with a broken arm and leg. They broke all the bones in Rameez's fingers. If they had stopped there, it would have still been all right. But after the President's assassination attempt, they became really brutal. He was picked up by five different agencies. CID, ISI, Special Branch, Corps Intelligence, I don't even remember all the names, even though I waited outside the offices of every single one of them. They all wanted some nugget of information about Ahmad, just like you do. I kept trying to tell them that Rameez knew nothing. But when they couldn't get any information, they wanted money. Some bloody inspector, whose boss' boss would not have dared to speak to me in that manner, told me that if we didn't pay, he would implicate Rameez as being a member of Ahmad's organization.'

The old man's voice quaked with emotion, but he went on with his speech, as if it were important that Omar hear this.

'I have never paid a bribe in my life. For anything. Not to get a phone line installed in my house, nor to get a choice posting in the department. Years ago, when Ahmad was arrested once for being involved with a political party, I still didn't pay off anybody. I called one of my police colleagues and asked for a favour, though even that went against my grain. But this thug held a gun to my son's head in front of me in the police station and said I had no choice. So I paid. And since then, every time they pick him up, I pay. All my savings, my pension, my car. I pay because he cannot bear the suffering anymore. His wife walked out on him because she said she couldn't live with him in this state. He lost his job because his supervisor said the bank couldn't employ a retard. All because of Ahmad.'

'Where is your other son, sir?'

'Ashfaq was smarter and luckier than the rest of us. After the first episode with the reporter, he too lost his job. But he decided to leave the city and move to Lahore, to make a fresh start. He decided that if he wanted to provide for his own family, he would have to disassociate from us. He can perhaps do that, because he is the brother. I cannot, because I have the misfortune of being the father of the *great Sheikh Uzair.*'

'Abu, please do not speak of your son in that way.' A woman, cloaked in a black burqa, came into the room. Although the only part of her that was visible were her eyes, Omar could see her sizing him up. She was the only member of the family who had not accepted defeat.

'My daughter-in-law, Ayesha. Ahmad's wife.'

'His wife lives with you? But I thought you said you hadn't seen or heard from him in years.'

'This was another decision, like all the others in his life, where Ahmad did not see fit to involve me. Several years ago, shortly after he was released from India, he went back to Kashmir, to his mother's family and got married. He brought Ayesha back to our house and left her here. A year or so after that, he came once more when his son was born.'

'Abu, please stop being critical of the Hazrat. He is a great man, and this kafir policewallah will never understand that.'

'Uh, madam, I'm sorry, I am a Muslim. I'm not a kafir.'

'Aren't you? You are a minion of a godless government who itself is a slave to America, the Great Satan. You lock up great Muslims like my husband, the Hazrat. How are you not a kafir?'

'Ayesha, stop it! Ahmad is not a Hazrat! Do not defile the names of other great Muslims by associating him with them! What is great about killing innocent people? What is great about destroying the lives of your family? Every father wants his children to be better than him. But not Ahmad! He not only descends into this age of darkness himself, but he forces it upon his son! I sacrificed everything in my life to give my sons a quality education. I scraped and saved so that Ahmad could go to The School. But what does he do? He forces you to send Adil to a madrasa! All the books in this room, that could open the child's mind, rot away while your son learns nothing except rote recitation. What sort of life has he made for us!'

The old man's anger stunned everyone in the room. Omar could see Rameez, the elder son, cower like a kitten in front of his father's rage. Ram Lal moved towards the girl, as if anticipating that the old man would hit her. But Mr Sheikh broke down, the tears he had been holding back came flooding out. The only one in the room totally unmoved by this was Ayesha, who merely lowered her eyes. The outburst brought a little boy running into the room. Omar guessed he couldn't have been older than seven and his eyes were the mirror image of his father's. He wore a sky blue shalwar kameez and a prayer cap on his head, and he ran to his mother, startled by his grandfather's rage.

It took a couple of minutes for the old man to regain his composure. Omar rose uncomfortably from the sofa. 'I am sorry, sir. I did not mean to upset you or your family. We should probably go. I just had one other question. Did the Sheikh, I mean did your son ever mention a friend of his called Eddy, or Adnan Shah? Would you have any idea where he is?'

'Adnan was Ahmad's best friend in school I think. He came to this house a couple of times after school ended, but I haven't seen or heard from him in years.'

'Sir, were there ever any letters that came for your son to this address?'

'Letters? How do you know about the letters?' Ayesha's eyes burrowed into him once again.

'Your husband has asked me to trace some of the letters that this Adnan Shah might have written. I am trying to find him. Do you have any such letters?'

'There are a bunch of letters that the Hazrat left in his room. I do not know how to read, so I do not know who they are from, but if the Hazrat has asked for them, I will go get them.'

She returned a moment later, with a bundle of letters that had been neatly wrapped in a piece of cloth. Omar could feel the excitement rising within him. The letters were exactly the ones that he wanted, dating back to the mid '90s. And they were all from Eddy. Omar was sure he would now find some clue in them.

As he and Ram Lal exited the house, he turned once again to the old man and the girl. 'Sir, if there is any message that you or your daughter-in-law wish to pass on to your son, I will ensure it gets to him.'

He looked at the girl, who shook her head. 'I have nothing to say to the Hazrat. I will continue my mission of making his son in the image of his father, so he can take up his father's jihad.'

The old man looked physically upset at the girl's answer. Omar turned to him inquiringly, but he stared at the dirty walls of the house.

'You have seen the condition of my family. My son has destroyed our past, our present and our future. I have nothing to say to him. I would warn you not to get too close to him either. He destroys everything he touches.'

seventeen

July 1999
New York City

Sana doesn't give his alarm the opportunity to ring. Every day, she calls him at five minutes to six, always five minutes ahead of his alarm clock. He thinks about not answering but knows she won't give up. He picks up the phone, mumbling unintelligible curses but she ignores him by saying, 'Yeah, yeah, same to you, Eddy. Don't forget we have to go to that Friends of Kashmir thing today. Meet me outside the NYU Business School campus at 6:30 p.m. sharp. Oh and, don't go back to sleep when I hang up.'

Groggily, he puts down the receiver and raises himself from his bed. This is a daily routine between the two of them. Hers is the first and last voice he hears every day. She calls in the morning to run through whatever tasks either of them have to do that day, and again at night before sleeping to discuss her day and listen about his. She says she can't sleep without unburdening herself to him. She talks about what happened in the day, she discloses her hopes, her fears and dreams. It's the kind of prattling that she always used to do in school with Ausi. It would irritate him then, and it should irritate him now, but it doesn't. He finds himself listening to her and opening up to her. There is so much he has never shared, even with Ausi, about his family, about Nicole and college. He is comforted by Sana and her reassuring smile, and eyes that look at him as if there is no one else in the world in that moment. He smiles as he brushes his teeth in the bathroom mirror. If Ausi had said the same thing to him, he would never have let him hear the end of it.

It is, in fact, Ausi who has brought them closer. Since that day in December, when they first heard of his arrest in India, Eddy and Sana have been trying to get some news of their friend. Ausi's father has no knowledge, and no desire to find out where his son is. The Indian media labels Ausi an 'ISI sponsored terrorist'. But Eddy's father's extensive contacts in ISI yield no official record of Ausi ever having worked for them. So Sana and Eddy resort to attending various meetings of Kashmiri groups in New York, hoping that maybe someone there will have some knowledge of Ausi.

Sana is waiting for him at the door of the auditorium, even though he is five minutes early. Something stirs within him when he sees her. In the balmy weather, she is wearing a red camisole that reveals more than expected, jeans that hug her curves like a second skin, and short open-toed heels that make her feet look stunning. He marvels at the fact that Sana can put together an outfit like this in about five minutes and take the world's breath away. He remembers how it would take Nicole hours and a fortune to try and look this good. And she still couldn't hold a candle to Sana.

He hugs her, clutching her for a millisecond longer than necessary, breathing in her guava-scented conditioner.

'So, what's the plan?'

'Okay, so I told you that I found out about this group from a guy at the diner right? Apparently, it's students and some Kashmiri expats from Jackson Heights who are trying to highlight the Indian government's excesses there.'

'So why do we think that they would know anything about Ausi?'

'Apparently, some of their people have connections to the resistance groups in the Valley. Maybe someone has heard of Ausi's whereabouts.'

These meetings have an established routine. He has attended so many of these talks by now that he knows some of the speeches by heart. It always starts with some academic type giving a talk about the historic background to the conflict. He or, as is the case today, she, is usually followed by a firebrand sort, who spouts on about the injustices committed by the Indian security forces, quoting statistics taken from the UN, or Amnesty International about people jailed, or displaced, or displaced and jailed. It's at about that point that someone usually challenges the firebrand, either claiming his figures are anti-Indian propaganda being put out by Pakistan, or that the figures are too low, thus proving that the firebrand is an armchair activist with no real roots in the Valley. That's when the meeting sinks into bickering and chaotic confusion. Eddy is amazed by the way the various groups fight with each other. He cannot accurately evaluate their roles in the insurgency, or rebellion, as they insist on terming it, but to his untrained eye, it doesn't seem as if these groups could organize a piss up in a brewery.

He is sceptical about the value of attending these meetings, but Sana insists. Her urge to help Ausi drives her maniacally. All her old intensity returns, all the canvassing skills she picked up while doing those silly anti-corruption campaigns in college. She is indefatigable when it comes to Ausi.

They set themselves up near the exit, handing out fliers that contain news reports about his arrest and the last known picture of him, a wire service photo of him being led away by Indian commandos on the day of his capture. They hand out a lot of fliers, and a lot of the men want to come and chat with Sana, but as has been the case in every single such meeting that they have attended, no one has any idea about what has happened to Ausi. They have been there about twenty minutes when Eddy sees a middle-aged man observing them and reading one of their fliers, although he has not approached them. He is too well dressed to be a member of the Jackson Heights Kashmiri crowd. Eddy has seen similar individuals at other events, consular or intelligence officials sent from the Pakistani consulate. But Eddy now knows all of the Pakistani officials by face, and this man isn't one of them. Finally, the man comes towards them, and again, unusually, addresses him instead of making a bee line for Sana.

'Excuse me, I couldn't help but see you distributing this flier. What is your concern with this man, if you don't mind me asking?'

'Ausi is ... I mean Ahmed Uzair Sheikh is our friend. We are concerned about his well-being and just want to find out what has happened to him.'

The man smiles. 'Now I understand. I was thinking that you two don't look like the normal lot of Kashmiris who get involved in these sorts of things. But I still find it amazing to understand how this terrorist is a friend of two good young people like yourselves.'

'Ausi is not a terrorist.' Even Eddy is surprised by the sharpness of Sana's tone. 'He just did what he thought was right. And excuse me, but who are you to go around calling someone a terrorist before he has been convicted in a court of law, before he has had any access to any kind of judicial process?'

The man is evidently used to being challenged in this manner. He simply smiles and takes out a business card from his coat pocket. 'Arvind Reddy, from the Indian consulate. I'm sorry if my comment angered you, miss, but the fact is that under the laws of my country, your friend has committed several heinous crimes and is adjudged as a terrorist.'

Eddy speaks up before Sana has a chance to respond. 'I'm sorry, sir, I understand that there is a lot of politics in the whole issue of Kashmir, but I don't have an interest in any of that. I ... we just want to find out what has happened to our friend. There has been no news since his arrest in December. If he had been produced in a court of some kind, at least we would know that he's still alive. For all we know, the security forces could have shot him in a fake encounter. You and I both know that plenty of such incidents occur in Kashmir, sir. If he is a criminal in the eyes of the law, then he should be presented in front of a court and given due process. How can you deny that, as a representative of the world's largest democracy?'

The man seems to ponder the point for an instant. 'This issue is more complex than what you think.'

'Then explain it to us. Please sir, you are an important man, you are an official of the Indian government, there must be some way you can help us. We have been trying since December and we haven't gotten anywhere. All we want to find out is whether our friend is okay or not.'

The man again contemplates the two of them. He then sighs and shrugs his shoulders. 'All right, but this is not the place to discuss such things. If you like, you can come to my office tomorrow, around 11 a.m. The address is on my card. I'm sorry I didn't catch your good names.'

'Eddy Shah. I mean, Adnan Shah, and Sana Safdar, sir.' Eddy grips the man's hand, ecstatic at their first breakthrough.

Sana insists they celebrate so on the way to his apartment, they pick up a bottle of wine and order Chinese takeout. Between mouthfuls of Kung Pao chicken, Sana attempts to put together all the material they have on Ausi, as a sort of brief. In her excitement, she is oblivious to him staring at her, tracing the outline of her long legs through her jeans with his eyes as she lounges around on his bed. He cannot believe that he is falling into exactly the same trap he has seen every guy fall into with Sana. He, Eddy Shah, cannot believe that he is falling for her, after all his years of berating Ausi for blindly following her like a lovesick puppy. Eddy knows exactly how that feels now. He knows he would do anything for her.

Including not telling her about his feelings. He has been falling for her for a while, and he would have told her months ago, if Ausi's situation hadn't happened. He remembers the day they found out. It was a week before Christmas, and she had come after her shift at the diner to pick him up from his office to go Christmas shopping at Macy's. He habitually checked the Pakistani news sites before logging out, and saw the photo of Ausi, bearded, but still looking very much like Ausi, being taken away by the soldiers. They went back to his apartment after that, to try and follow the story. She cried like he had never seen her cry before. She finally told him about her and Ausi, and how shattered she was when he walked out of her life. He ended up holding her the whole night, reassuring her that Ausi would be okay, all the time feeling envious for his best friend in a way that he never had before. In the days that followed, the intensity of her feelings for Ausi was evident in her desperation to find him. He knew he couldn't match that and that Sana was not over Ausi. So he never told her how he felt about her, but now he cannot help yearn for her.

'Hello, dreamy, where are you? I asked you if you remembered the date of the official press release of his arrest?' She playfully throws a soggy spring roll at him.

'Huh? Oh yeah, sorry, the ah, Agence France Presse quoted Indian security forces in Anantnag as claiming that an individual named Ahmed Uzair had been arrested on 19th December. A day later, they took the photo as he was being transported from the Special Branch compound in Srinagar. After that, nothing.' He tries to sound as professional as possible, aware of the fact that she must have caught him staring at her body.

'Okay, so he was last seen in the custody of Special Branch police, right?'

'Uh right. Right.'

'So who do you think this guy is? This Arvind Reddy. Do you think he can help us?'

'My guess is he's a spook. Must be RAW or something. The bigger question for me is why would he help us? Ah crap, he said eleven in the morning, right? I can't make it, I'll be at work. Can you go speak to him?'

She pouts seductively. 'Eddy, please, can't you take the day off? I really need you to go with me. I'll crash over here tonight, so we don't get late. I can't do this alone. Please, na.'

He smiles and nods. He had never planned to go to work. But it makes his day to have her say that she needs him.

They arrive fifteen minutes early at the Indian consulate on East 64th street. The man at the reception eyes them suspiciously when they show their Pakistani passports as ID and professes to have no knowledge of any appointment they may have with a Mr Arvind Reddy. On their insistence, the receptionist confers with a more senior official, who then confers with an even more senior official. They are told to wait for ten minutes. The ten minutes turn into forty-five, and just when they are about to despair, Arvind Reddy walks through the reception and spots them.

'I apologize for being late. Our timings aren't always fixed in this job. Please, come with me.' Reddy leads them, through a shabby corridor with stained walls and a dirty blue carpet, to his cabin. The only difference that Eddy spots between the Indian and Pakistani consulates is the carpet. The Pakistani carpet is green and the Indian one blue, but the shabbiness seems to be pretty standard throughout the subcontinent. Reddy offers them a seat and orders milky tea for them. Sana proffers him their 'file' on Ausi, but he waves it aside.

'There is no need for that, miss. I know the case very well.'

'Then, can you tell us if Ausi is alive, Mr Reddy?'

Reddy sips his tea contemplatively, as if making a judgment call on them. 'Yes, he is.'

The relief in Sana's face is palpable. 'What else can you tell us, Mr Reddy?'

'That depends on what your intentions are. If you intend to act as Sheikh's defence lawyers, or as activists who wish to bring international attention to the matter, then I cannot help you.'

Sana speaks in her softest, most pleading voice. 'We don't have any agenda, Mr Reddy. We come here simply as friends of Ausi. Look, if he is accused of kidnapping those western tourists, then why aren't you putting him on trial?'

'Are you so eager to get your friend hanged, Miss Safdar? Because the penalty for kidnapping and murder in India is death.'

'Mr Reddy, I know Ausi. I don't believe that the charges against him are correct. He may have done some things, but he did them out of his sense of conviction. At most, he is a simple soldier in this conflict. He isn't some sort of terrorist mastermind. You are being naïve if you think this conflict will end if you hang a soldier.'

'What if I told you that we had proof, that Sheikh has been the mastermind behind not only the kidnappings, but several other terrorist acts in Kashmir? An attack on government troops in Doda. Sending a letter bomb to the house of the district collector in Kupwara. Triggering the war by helping Pakistani militants into Kargil. The fact is, Miss Safdar, that in the time since Sheikh crossed over from Pakistan, he has been acknowledged by even the oldest militant leaders in Kashmir as being probably the most dangerous terrorist in the Valley. Until we got him, he had been the single biggest factor in turning round the militant's fortunes in the Valley. A simple soldier? Now I think it is you who is being naïve, Miss Safdar.'

'If he is such a big criminal, then why is your government hiding him, Mr Reddy?'

'I can guarantee you one thing, Mr Shah. We will bring him to trial. He will not disappear, nor will he be killed in some sort of police encounter. But men like him don't get captured alive every day. They are a treasure trove of intelligence. He needs to be interrogated, thoroughly, to ensure that the government learns everything about his friends and associates.'

Eddy spots the terror in Sana's eyes when she hears the word 'interrogated'. He sees her tears well up, and her determination to control them in front of this man, this official who calls Ausi a terrorist and speaks of interrogating him thoroughly as if he were speaking about some PhD student who is being grilled about a questionable thesis, rather than a man being tortured to betray his companions. Eddy can see that Sana already despises Reddy for having caused pain to Ausi. For a moment, he lets his mind wander, wondering if she would ever show the same depth of feeling for him if he were the one being interrogated by Reddy's goons.

'I am sorry, I have already told you more than we have told anyone else so far. I cannot help you with anything else.' Reddy rises from his chair to signal the end of the meeting.

'Mr Reddy, uh, thank you, but there is just one more favour that we will ask from you. I know it is difficult and I understand your government's position on Ahmed Uzair Sheikh, but please try to understand, that for us, no matter what you accuse him of, he will always be our friend Ausi. We know that his family hasn't been able to contact him, and frankly, we don't even know if they want to contact him. We just want him to know that there is someone out there, thinking about him. Could you forward this letter to him?'

'I am sorry, I cannot pass on any form of communication. You two look like decent young people, but how can I tell if this isn't some message from his organization?'

Sana's knuckles turn white as she clenches the chair she is standing behind. Eddy places one hand on hers to calm her, and takes out an envelope from his jacket pocket with the other. 'Mr Reddy, please read it. There is nothing in there that can be considered as any sort of code. You saw us at the conference yesterday. Did we strike you as having any contacts with radical groups? The only thing in there that you could possibly find objectionable are these cricket scores. You see, Ausi is a huge cricket fan and he has never missed a Pakistan series. I just wanted him to know the scores from the World Cup, so I downloaded these printouts.'

Reddy takes the paper and reads it, frowning and shaking his head while he does so. Eddy is afraid he will return them, until he finally breaks into a smile.

'Pakistan did well to get to the final, eh? But at least we still beat you in the group game. I suppose there is nothing objectionable in these, other than India's deplorable performance in the tournament. All right, I cannot promise anything, but I will forward these on your behalf to the relevant authorities.'

They shake hands and leave. Outside, the afternoon sky has turned menacingly grey. Sana grips his hand and shudders. 'Eddy, do you think what Reddy is saying is true? That Ausi is some kind of mastermind?'

'Sana, you and I have read the letter about the kidnapping.' Conscious of still being on the doorstep of the consulate, he grabs her hand and starts walking, lowering his voice as he speaks. 'We know he was involved in that. I don't know about the other stuff, but if he did the kidnapping, why wouldn't he do the other stuff?'

'Do you think he'll survive in those torture chambers?'

'Sana, Ausi is the strongest person I know. I'm weak and stupid. I probably wouldn't make it. But he can.'

They decide to cut across Central Park to get back to his apartment on the Upper West Side. They reach Sheep's Meadow as the rain pours down and catches them in the open. He curses his luck as he stares at the outline of her nipples under her drenched blouse. He knows his attempts to suppress his feelings for her are bound to fail if he keeps seeing her like this.

Back at his apartment, she casually informs him that she is going for a shower and without asking, opens his wardrobe to grab a T-shirt.

'Hey, what the hell do you think you're doing! I need to have some privacy.'

'Please Eddy, I'm just borrowing a T-shirt, it's not like I just discovered your porn collection. Besides, I know you don't keep that in here, that's in the bedroom drawer.'

She giggles as he turns scarlet. But inside, all of this is killing him. She is the coolest friend a man could have, except that he doesn't want her as just a friend anymore.

'You never told me about the letter.'

'Huh? What letter?' He is distracted again by the sight of her body, wrapped in nothing but his bath towel, her dark wet hair resting on her pale, bare shoulders.

'The letter you handed to Reddy. You never told me you wrote Ausi a letter. When did you write it anyway? I was here all the time.'

'Oh, uh, I wrote it last night after you fell asleep. Just some random thoughts. And I thought if it did somehow manage to get through, he would want to know the cricket scores. It'll bring some semblance of normalcy to him.'

'That was really sweet of you. But what did you write?'

'Nothing important Sana, let's just move on, okay?'

'Eddy Shah, are you being coy with me? What was in that letter that you don't want me to know?'

He curses loudly and leaves the bedroom, his face a mask of pain and indecision. He sheepishly walks back in a moment later.

'Sana, I'm sorry. I should have told you this a long time ago, but I kept avoiding the topic, and then Ausi got picked up and we were doing all these things to help him, so I got sidetracked.'

'Eddy, you're babbling. What did you need to tell me?'

'I wrote to Ausi saying that we were both very worried about him, but you were even more worried than I was, because you were in love with him. I told him that you told me about what happened between you guys in London, and that, for the first time in my life, I was jealous of him, because I was...'

'You were what?'

'I was jealous of him because I was falling in love with you. And I told him that I finally felt exactly how he had felt for all those years.'

'You're in love with me? Why didn't you ever tell me?'

'Because I didn't want to be another one of *those* guys, just another one of the dozens of your unrequited admirers. I wanted it to be the way it was with Ausi. Except I would never walk out on you. It would be like walking out on myself. I keep telling you, he's much stronger than me.'

'I didn't know.'

'It's not your fault. I should have told you. Besides, you're still hung up over him. Anyway, I, uh, understand if this will be awkward for a while, but look, we don't have to hang out together every day. I have to go to San Francisco on a business trip next week, so that'll be good. It will give us both some time on our own, to sort out our heads. Hey, I'm always going to be your friend, and this is just a passing thing, it's just because we've been spending so much time together and neither of us have been dating. Hey, the minute I get back into the singles game and start looking for someone, it'll be fine.'

'Yeah. It will be.' She turns and goes back into the bathroom. Unsure of what to do and confused by her reaction, he goes to the kitchen and makes a cup of coffee. She joins him, now fully dressed in jeans and one of his T-shirts.

'Thank you for the T-shirt. Do you mind if I keep it?'

'Uh, yeah, sure. Whatever.'

'Oh and Eddy? Would you do me a favour before you go to San Francisco?'

'What?'

'Take me with you and never let me go.'

As she jumps into his arms and buries her head in his chest, he holds her tight and breaks into a smile. 'I promise.'

eighteen

December 1999
Indian Kashmir

It bleeds when he shits the morning after the Jinn's visit. Every time he thinks the pain will be less, that his bowels will get used to being violated, but every time it is as bad as the first. Worse than the pain in his ass, is the stink of the Jinn that permeates his body, the smell of garlic, raw onions and dank sweat. He cannot get rid of the smell as the prisoners are not allowed to bathe. He wishes he could tear his clothes off and cleanse himself somehow, but the Kashmiri winter is harsh, and more so in this cold dark cell without windows where he can no longer tell whether it is day or night.

The Jinn is his captors' special punishment for him, for when he really infuriates them. The Jinn is a hulking, pederast thug whom the head of the prison, a rat-faced man named Sinha, calls from the cadres of a local right-wing party to break his spirit every time Pakistan wins a cricket match. Sinha, who is quite proud of having devised this new form of torture, tells Ausi that having a Hindu cock in his ass periodically will make him lose his hatred for Indians.

They hate him here. He can see it in their eyes. Everyone has heard of his exploits, especially the story of the entire CRPF platoon that he captured and executed in Shopian. That one surprised even his own people. It was a spur of the moment decision really. When his party ambushed and captured the platoon, he meant to kill only the platoon commander, just to send a message to the Indians. But when he slit the commander's throat in front of his men and saw the naked fear in their eyes, some primal instinct took over. After he dumped the fifteen bodies on the road leading to the military cantonment, he knew there could be no reprieve for him. He was prepared to die the day the commandoes came storming into his hideout in Anantnag. But the plump major who led the raid decided his 'intelligence value' was too great to kill him immediately.

When they brought him in, he was completely isolated from all other prisoners. He hasn't spoken to, or seen another prisoner, apart from brief appearances during interrogation sessions. Like the mujahid from Kupwara who was in his raiding party and was brought in front of him the first week of his captivity, bound and blindfolded, with electrodes attached to his testicles. He remembers the man back in the mountains, a big tough guy, standing at his full height of six feet, talking about how the Indians will never be able to break him, even if they capture him. And he remembers him again, in the interrogation room. It takes one turn of the dial on the electric current and three minutes of screaming, for the Kupwara boy to spill everything, right down to the chicken he stole from his neighbour's garden when he was ten years old, and about Ausi's weakness for cricket. It is that piece of information that prompts Sinha to start calling for the services of the Jinn.

Still, he cannot blame the poor Kupwara boy. Everybody breaks under torture, and anyone who says anything different, like the sermonizers who go back to Pakistan with rousing tales of having resisted the Indian interrogators, is full of shit. It's all propaganda, to get more enthusiastic, but dim-witted, volunteers for 'the Struggle'. He has discovered that ninety per cent of this war is fought for propaganda. The lalas try and convince people that Pakistani terrorists, backed and trained by the feared intelligence agencies, are invading the peaceful land of Kashmir to stir up trouble. On the other hand, his people stick to the version that it is the unending cruelty of the Indians that has led to this uprising, and men continue to risk life and limb, in order to protect the honour of their mothers and sisters and their homesteads. There are lies on both sides. Ausi remembers the story of the blind mujahid that Sheikh Saad had related to him in Kossovo. When he first crossed into Kashmir, he asked around about the man and found no recollection of him among the fighters. And then the absurdity of the story had struck him. How could a blind, one-armed man have ever crossed the Line of Control? More to the point, how had he been stupid enough to believe it?

In the darkness, he stares down at the nails missing from his fingers. Everybody breaks under torture. There are no exceptions. Even him. He freely admits this. He divulged all he knew, even before Sinha started applying the Jinn. He winces at the memory of the raw chillies being inserted into his pisshole. Hard as it is to imagine, there are worse tortures in this hellhole than being raped by a Hindutva thug.

He broke within the first ten days of his captivity and told them all he knew. The matter of greater surprise is why they have kept him in this isolated captivity since then. The implicit promise of confessing was that he would be handed over to the police, formally arrested and sent to jail, either in Srinagar or in Delhi. But the authorities choose to maintain him in this limbo, continuing to torture him without even asking him any questions. What is he supposed to tell them?

He is no longer sure how long he has been here, but he reckons it must be close to a year. In that time he reckons Pakistan must have won at least twelve matches. Or was it thirteen? He knows this because this is the number of times the Jinn has mounted him. The number of times he has had to face such abject humiliation. Every time the Jinn comes, he fights, he resists, but is beaten almost senseless by the guards who hold him down. The times he loses consciousness are the best ones. That way he doesn't have to live through the experience. Other times, he has had to distract himself by imagining in great detail, how he will kill the Jinn when he gets out of here. But other times, he cannot shut out the horror that is happening to him, and he screams like a stuck pig. The Jinn and his henchmen particularly enjoy these occasions.

But none of the interminable humiliations he has suffered in this hole have come close to matching what he suffered last night. He remembers the Jinn entering with the guards, and laughing at him as he struggles against them. The brute waves a letter in his face.

'Arre Masterji, you have been lying to us all along, pretending you don't enjoy these sessions. And now we find that you have a launda of your own in Pakistan who sends you a love letter?'

'And an English medium launda, who writes in angrezi!' One of the guards chews betel nut, his uneven teeth stained red, and laughs while holding a piece of paper.

Ausi doesn't understand, until the Jinn pushes his face into the filthy floor and drops his trousers while the betel nut stained teeth starts reading in a singsong voice.

'Dear Ausi,

I don't know if this will get through to you, but I had to try. Sana and I are worried sick about you, and we are both praying for you. We love you man. Be strong. I cannot imagine what you must be going through, but I want you to remember, no matter what happens to you, who you are and where you come from, don't forget your ... human ... humani...?'

The Jinn grunts as he pushes into Ausi. 'What the fuck is a humani? Is it some Pakistani launda term? A name for your boyfriend, eh Masterji?'

Betel Teeth smiles his gross smile. 'Arre sorry Jinn, its humanity. What is humanity?'

'*Insaniyat*. Humanity is insaniyat.' Another guard who is holding his hands, whose boots are inches away from his eyes, volunteers his English expertise.

'Arre, this one has no insaniyat. Where was your insaniyat when you murdered those CRPF troops, Masterji?' Ausi doesn't think it is possible for the Jinn to penetrate him more painfully, but he does.

'Wait, wait, there's more. The launda says:

'I know this will sound ti-ri-vi-aal ... but I wanted to send you the cricket updates. I don't know if anyone would have told you or not, but Pakistan had an excellent World Cup in England this summer, right up to the final. We had an excellent team, captained by Wasim, with Inzamam, Saeed Anwar, the magical Saqlain, and this new fast bowler, Shoaib Akhtar. And when I say he's fast, he's really fast. He had the world's best batsmen hopping around in the crease. We beat everyone, Australia, West Indies, New Zealand, Zimbabwe, and though we lost a group game to India, we raced into the final where we proceeded to fall apart. We got bowled out for 132 by Australia. Shane Warne didn't even have to try, our batsmen just gave him their wickets. And then the Australians turned around and knocked over the runs in about 20 overs. It was the most one-sided World Cup final ever. If you had seen what happened at Lords, you would have wanted to go right back into your cell … sorry, God that sounds so in-sen-si-tive. I truly am sorry.

There is something else I wanted to update you on, even though this is perhaps the most inappropriate forum for it. But it's the only way I will get to speak to you. So here goes. Sana and I have been spending a lot of time together, trying to trace you down, to find out if you are even alive or not. The truth is, Ausi, and I don't know how to say this, but I've fallen in love with Sana. But the problem is that she told me what happened between you two in London, and she's still hung up over you. I see her love for you every day in her eyes. And so I have decided that, irrespective of how madly I feel for her, I'm not going to tell her anything. But I needed to tell you, because somehow I felt like I was cheating on you, and I had to tell someone in this world. Anyway, I know this is stupid high school stuff, but I just wanted you to know that I apologize for having made fun of you through all those years of late night drives in school. Now I know exactly how miserable you were. I love you man. Hang in there. Your best friend, Eddy.'

'Bhenchod, you enjoy hearing about Pakistan win? Here, after I'm done with you, your asshole will bleed every time you think about Pakistan winning.' Ausi screams as the Jinn's thrusts become more violent, his teeth grinding against the English expert's boot.

Betel Teeth laughs hysterically. 'Hai, Hai, Jinn, you have no heart. Here the bastard's boyfriend is saying that he is running away with his girlfriend and you show no sympathy. Arre, Masterji's life is better than a Yash Chopra film. Boy, girl … launda … then the launda runs away with the girl. Love triangle with a difference! Ha Ha Ha!'

The guards roar with laughter and the Jinn finishes his business. Pulling himself out of Ausi, he grabs the piece of paper from Betel Teeth, wipes his penis with it, and throws it in the direction of the hole in the ground that serves as the latrine in the cell.

'There, you can remember the taste of my semen when you think about your boyfriend, Bhenchod!'

He does not remember how many hours he lies there on the cold concrete floor. He thinks it must be the next day, but time has no meaning here, so it doesn't make any difference. He picks himself up and crawls toward the latrine. He retrieves the soiled parchment from the edge of the latrine hole. Another two inches and it would have been lost forever in a river of shit. He thinks about his life, and the choices he has made. He has never regretted coming to Kashmir. He found himself here. He found that he revels in the chaos of conflict. In fact, he thrives upon it. He has also discovered that it is not the call of God that motivates him to violence. He has found that he has a taste for it. Slitting the throats of those men in Shopian gave him an inner satisfaction. In a strange way, he even understands the violence that is being done to him. After all, if the roles were reversed, this is probably what he would do to them. It is this kind of reasoning that has kept him sane. Until now.

Of all the humiliations and tortures that Sinha and the Jinn could have devised for him, none would come close to what happened to him last night. On the thirteen instances when the Jinn has raped him, he has never felt as violated as he did when they read him Eddy's letter. It has broken him in a way that they probably don't even realize yet. He cannot hide it anymore and he knows that the instant that he gets any kind of opportunity, he will kill himself. Maybe if he fights extra hard against the Jinn, they will hurt him enough to kill him. Or maybe he can use the cord from his shalwar to fashion a noose.

He thinks about Eddy, and his stupidity. Why did he have to write all of this down? How did he think the letter would reach him? Did Eddy actually imagine that he would get some sort of privacy to read the letter in peace? And then he thinks about the actual contents of the letter. So Sana still pines for him. And according to Eddy, her love for him is pure. Three years ago, he grew angry because he thought she had used him as some kind of social experiment. But surely, his judgment was wrong if she still wants him, after all this time. He walked out on her, and on his previous life, based on a miscalculation.

And now Eddy loves Sana. His best friend, and the love of his life. Together. While he rots in a grimy Indian prison cell, being periodically sodomized by an uncut Hindu bastard. Is this what he has to show for his life?

An anger rises within him. No, not anger, hate. From somewhere deep within him. An all-consuming hatred for everything and everyone in his life. His father and brothers, who are as dead to him as he is to them. The tanzeem, or organization, that has used him and now abandoned him. And Sana. Sana, who has always represented his desire for normalcy in his world. But that isn't really true, because she has been a chimera, a fleeting presence in his life that he never really managed to consummate. But was that her fault, or his? It doesn't matter. He doesn't think he will ever get out of this hell, but if he does, he will destroy the world. All of them. Except maybe Eddy. Eddy has been his one true friend, always. After a year of this torment, tears stream down his cheeks.

The keys jangle in the cell door and a shaft of light descends into the room. It is Sinha, the rat-faced jailer, holding a hand up to his nose.

'Pick him up and wash him. This place stinks worse than the gutters of Srinagar. And give him a new set of clothes so he looks presentable for his journey.'

'Where am I going?' Ausi can barely croak the words out of his throat.

'You are a lucky bastard, Sheikh. Your jihadi friends came up with a plan to spring you. They hijacked an Indian Airlines flight from Kathmandu and flew it to Kandahar. Your Taliban friends have negotiated the release of all the hostages with our government. But the price we have to pay is to hand over a handful of scum like you. Your name was on the top of the hijackers list of demands. So you get to fly to Kandahar on a special plane with Minister sahib, who will deliver you personally.'

As the guards help him onto his feet, they snatch away the paper he has been holding in his hand, thinking it to be garbage. But he pleads with Sinha to let him keep the paper.

'Kyun be? What is so special about a piece of paper covered in the Jinn's cum?'

'Please, Sinha sahib. You have taught me so much. This will always remind me of my time here.' Ausi smiles a crooked smile as he is led away.

BOOK THREE

The War Comes Home

nineteen

Saddar at four-thirty in the afternoon is a bustling place. The streets are clogged with traffic as vehicles try and manoeuver themselves into every conceivable inch of space, while trying to avoid the legion of street hawkers. The hawkers themselves are trying to negotiate their carts between the vehicles and the footpath, looking for a vantage point from which to sell their wares. Bus drivers, anxious to put in as many round trips as possible in the day, don't even bother to come to a full halt at the stops. The average commuter has to attain Olympic-level long jumping skills just to get on to a bus. Ausi is extra careful as he hops off in front of Dilpasand Sweet Shop next to Lunda Bazaar. The bazaar is doing roaring business these days. The colder than expected weather has pushed Karachiites to flock to buy second-hand Chinese sweaters and blankets.

His body tenses at the sight of two approaching police constables with their AK-47s slung around their shoulders, but relaxes again when he sees that their only interest is to accost one of the hawkers for a few rupees. One of the local organizers of his new tanzeem informs him that the local police station makes millions of rupees a month from the thousands of illegal hawkers and street peddlers in Saddar. Ausi does not consider himself to be a naïve man, not after so many years, but the level of corruption that permeates society never fails to surprise him. Ever since his release, he has wandered all over the country, and become convinced of the fact that this nation is diseased and needs to be cleansed, even before one thinks of jihad in Kashmir or any other foreign land. If the core is corrupt, the seed it spreads will never be wholesome.

Since his return, he finds himself recast as a heroic figure, an icon, the unbreakable iron man of the movement. He has discovered a gift for speech-making, for motivating and spellbinding audiences with his words. The funniest thing is, he never believes any of what he says, but he has the ability to make others believe. And that makes him a powerful man. What is it that Sohail used to say to him in medical college? That he was such a good orator, that he should use his abilities to greater effect than reciting romantic couplets. Sohail should see him now.

His exalted status brings with it important friends with limitless resources. The mention of his name is enough to get influential donors to open their cheque books. Overnight, his new organization acquires a 150 acre site to build a 'spiritual headquarters' outside Lahore, in addition to several guesthouses and seminaries in Karachi, Rawalpindi and Muzaffarabad. Nor does he want for acquiring the tools for his struggle. Crates of AK-47s and grenades are delivered to his headquarters in the blink of an eye.

His tanzeem has taken on a life of its own without his having to do very much, growing, mutating, like a living organism. His followers are zealots in the truest sense, wanting to refashion the world in the image of his vision. His rhetoric has grown more virulent in response to their demands. His people want him to condemn other sects, Shi'as first, then the shrine-worshipping Barelvis and ultimately anyone really, who disagrees with their world view. And so he does it, making speeches exulting in his hatred for the cursed Shi'as, preaching murder and intolerance. The sort of words that so angered Eddy in his last letter.

Ausi imagines him writing that last letter, standing amongst the smouldering ruins of the World Trade Centre, angry at his best friend's casual disregard for the sanctity of human life. Poor Eddy. He will never understand that in all of history, human life has never been particularly sanctified. Eddy doesn't understand why one group of people wants to kill another group of people over things that happened 1500 years ago. But Ausi understands that this is a basic instinct, and people need symbols to justify doing the things they could never do otherwise. He does not know how to explain to Eddy that he doesn't hate Shi'as at all. After all, his best friend is one. In fact, he does not personally feel any great animosity towards any sect or creed. But if the world has to change its ways, it demands blood, and Shi'a blood is convenient.

He can plainly see his destination from where he has alighted from the bus, across the street from where he stands. Sabri Nihari, the roadside restaurant that is famous in the city for its stewed beef nihari. Ausi has innumerable memories of coming here over the years. Perhaps the only good memories that he has of his father are associated with the rare occasions when he would acquiesce to take the entire family out to Sabri. A vision of his mother feeding him naan dipped in the rich brown gravy, flashes before him. He closes his eyes and sees another image in his mind, of coming here after school with Eddy, Sana and a few of their friends. For the cloistered students of The School, a visit to the admittedly gritty Sabri, with its gravy-stained formica-top tables, steel water jugs set next to dubiously washed glasses and cats gnawing for scraps under the table, was a genuine life experience. He was the star of the day, the only Sabri veteran among them, who knew to ask to be seated in the 'family' section, as they had girls with them, and knew exactly what to order and how to talk to the waiters without sounding pompous or patronizing, as his friends were wont to do. He remembers Eddy's girlfriend at the time, a slightly ditzy girl called Saira, asking him afterwards if he had 'special connections' with the owners.

Ausi still remembers what he wore that day, a fake Armani shirt his mother had bought him from Zainab Market. A shirt he thought was quite cool, equal to the genuine designer brands worn by his friends, until he noticed that Armani had been spelled with a 'Y'. It would have caused him excruciating embarrassment, had Eddy not told everybody that 'Armany' was actually a Turkish brand and that he had a couple himself. That made the rest of them appear foolish for not having heard of something so hip.

The memory brings an involuntary smile to his face, even as he self-consciously checks his present attire. His shalwar kameez is a well-worn one, his Peshawari chappals even more so. Unlike so many others, he has not used his organization as a means of personal enrichment. There are no convoys of gleaming SUVs following him around, and no palatial personal estates scattered around the country. Even in his massive compound on the outskirts of Lahore, Ausi maintains spartan quarters, having given over most of the area for the creation of a training camp for those who are deemed worthy enough to wage jihad with a gun. This adds to his aura, as his followers speak in reverential tones about his shunning of worldly wants and his incorruptible nature. Money does not interest him. Power interests him. And people. Having the power to get people to set the world on fire for him.

He takes a circuitous route to the restaurant, circling its perimeter, observing it from different vantage points at ten minute intervals. He has taken a great risk in coming here, the sort of risk his fellow jihadi leaders would never take. He is exposed, and without any meaningful support to call upon if anything untoward happens. He has brought with him only one person from his organization, a Kashmiri from his mother's village, who he has sent ahead to scout out the location. Ausi spots his man now, standing in a nondescript manner near a newspaper vendor, pretending to read the evening tabloids. He is one of the few that Ausi partially trusts. Kashmir taught him that only a fool trusts anyone completely.

He has good reason to be wary. The list of his enemies grows on a daily basis. The first week that he arrived home from Kandahar after the successful exchange of hostages for the hijacked Indian airlines flight, he was informed that he was on a RAW hit list. The Indians were angered at their humiliation and would leave no stone unturned to get him. After two years, he still doesn't know quite whether to believe this statement or not. The people in his business, and in Pakistan in general, have a propensity to blame anything and everything that happens in the country on the evil clutches of RAW, just as everyone in India believes that if a dog shits on a minister's car in New Delhi, Pakistan's ISI had something to do with it. Having seen the workings of the intelligence community on both sides of the border, he is sceptical about their abilities to get anything done properly. Still, it's a nice story if true, and being at the top of RAW's hit list is always a great crowd puller to attract more recruits.

But there are other, more plausible threats. Many of his 'fellow travellers' from his old organization, have watched his rapid rise to prominence, and are jealous of the funds and volunteers that he pinches from them. It's never a bad idea within these groups to bump off a rival and then come crying to his funeral, cursing RAW for succeeding in their nefarious designs, and at the same time, pick up the lucrative pieces of his little empire. Sheikh Uzair, as he is now referred to, standing on his own in the middle of Saddar could present an irresistible target for such aspirants.

And then there are those whom he refers to as 'the other lot'. The Shi'as have their own militants and their own assassins. And since some of his people have decided to put his preaching into practice by targeting Shi'a community leaders, they have been looking for an opportunity to settle the score with him. He cannot help but think of Eddy every time he thinks of the Shi'as.

Which brings him to his reason for standing at the very spot where he is. Eddy. In all their years of correspondence, he has never felt such an overwhelming urge to meet Eddy as he does now. True, circumstances have conspired to keep them apart since that August day in 1994 when Ausi dropped Eddy to the airport. But so much has happened that he feels that now, even if Eddy were on the far side of the Earth, he would seek him out.

There is so much he wants to tell him, scraps from his heart that he will never share with anybody else. A feeling of giddy excitement suddenly sweeps over him, and it takes all of his resolve not to break out into a goofy grin while pretending to study copies of the Qur'an at a booksellers'. He reaches under the thick Kashmiri pheran that he has wrapped around himself and takes the letter out again. His eyes catch the date, 11 September 2001, New York. He can feel Eddy's passion in the words, words written at a time of heightened emotion, in the shadow of the fallen towers. Eddy, angry at him for his narrow sectarianism, relating his experience as a volunteer, helping survivors out of the ruins, as an example of the goodness within men. It's too bad really, that everything that happened in the days that followed belied Eddy's belief in insaniyat.

Would you kill me for being a Shi'a too?

He reads the line again and wants to say out loud that of course I won't kill you Eddy. Well, at least not for being a Shi'a. For stealing Sana? Maybe. Although, try as he might, he cannot bring himself to be angry at Eddy. Sana was never his to be stolen.

But he does want to know about their relationship. He takes an almost voyeuristic pleasure in it. How did their friendship blossom into love? What was it like the first time they slept together? How has becoming lovers affected their friendship? He cannot explain why, but he is drawn to them like a moth to a flame. He has corresponded with Eddy several times since his release, and despite the fact that Eddy and Sana have now been together for over two years, Eddy is coy about discussing his relationship in his letters to Ausi. Perhaps it is out of a desire to not hurt his friend.

And now there is to be a wedding. Although from Eddy's letter, there have been some issues between the families. Ausi is surprised. Growing up, Eddy and Sana seemed to be the perfect fit, in terms of their background and social status. Of course, back then no one ever thought in terms of Shi'a or Sunni. The only thing that denoted Eddy as a Shi'a was that he wore black clothes on Ashura and wasn't allowed to play cricket on the day, much to his consternation. But now it seems his mother doesn't approve of Sana because she is a Sunni. Ausi smiles. Ah Eddy. There are zealots to be found everywhere.

Since Eddy's return from America two months ago, they have spoken a couple of times, but he has to be careful. The Saudi's quixotic attack on the Twin Towers has put them all at risk. He remembers Osama from the time he came to Camp Suleyman Farsi. Ausi thought he was a fool then, and he thinks him a greater fool now. While others praise his boldness for striking at the heart of 'the Great Satan', Ausi, ever the tactician, fails to see what the plan achieved. The Americans are not the problem and never have been. It is the internal enemy that has to be defeated, those corrupt peddlers and false prophets who lead the people astray. Once they are all eliminated, America and the West will automatically lose the agents of their corruption. But who can explain this to bin Laden and his clique of Arabs? A month ago, he received a message from Zawahiri, asking him to make common ground with them. He is yet to send a reply. He does not want to make common cause because he has no common cause with them. Sometimes he suspects that bin Laden must be an American agent provocateur. After all, no one could be that stupid all on their own.

Worst of all, the Arabs' actions have led to the cancellation of cricket in the country. For that, he curses them under his breath. They will never succeed because they have never played cricket. Cricket makes a man a strategist. Now, thanks to bin Laden's foolishness, they have lost their greatest asset, the camps in Afghanistan, which were perfect incubators to train and nurture hordes of holy warriors, to be deployed wherever there was a need for them. They have also lost the Taliban, the one government in the world that was sympathetic to their cause. Ausi has always been doubtful about the motives of the Pakistani agencies, even though many of the old mujahideen have a sentimental attachment to them. He predicted that the government would not be able to withstand the pressure of the Americans and events have proven him right. When push came to shove, the agencies betrayed them all. The same individuals who had been hailed as heroes in Kashmir, were now arrested and kept under surveillance. He knows for a fact that they are watching him, waiting to see which ship he jumps on to. The only thing that has kept him out of trouble so far is the fact that he is yet to respond to Zawahiri's plea.

He isn't too troubled about having the agencies on his back. He has gotten used to staying one step ahead of them. Besides, this is nothing compared to what he had to contend with in Kashmir. But he is still wary, and does not want anyone to know the purpose of his visit today. He wants to keep his world separate from Eddy.

As time passes, he grows impatient and fidgety. Eddy is not late, but for security reasons, Ausi has come to the meeting place two hours in advance, to ensure that he is not being watched by anybody. He spies a mirror in a shop and stares at his own reflection. The two years since his release from Sinha's chamber of horrors have changed him. He is transformed from the ghost of a man who emerged from that cell, and, of course, unrecognizable from the boy who went to The School. He has grown broader, almost a little plump, and for the first time he has allowed his beard to grow to his chest. On a whim, today he even shaved off his top moustache, giving him the look of one of those TV preachers who do a lot of talking about subjects they know very little about. A flamboyant purple turban rests on his head, while a pair of spectacles rests on the bridge of his nose. Ausi has always had excellent eyesight, an attribute that was particularly useful in his cricketing days, but months of sitting in a cell with no light has caused damage to his retinas.

The spectacles are a small, but permanent reminder of the physical toll of incarceration in a Kashmiri cell. But there are other scars, psychological ones, that run much deeper. Ahmed Uzair Sheikh is a broken man, and he knows it. The problem is, no one else knows it. Over the years, the one thing that he has become really good at is lying. He has not shared the trauma he suffered with any member of his family. What good would it do? His father remains the uncaring, stern prick he always was, and the death of his mother has taken away any soothing influence that may have been there before. His father's response, were he to say anything, would be that this is what he deserved for going around and leading the kind of life he leads. His brothers are equally stunted, too concerned about their petty everyday lives, and climbing the middle class ladder in their pathetic and meaningless jobs. One day, his brother tried to explain to him exactly what he did at the bank. He used many grand sounding terms, but at the end of the lecture, he was less than enthused when Ausi turned around and told him that as he understood it, he was essentially a clerk. He hates his family. It is a terrible thing to say in a subcontinental culture, but it is the truth. The atmosphere of mutual loathing between his father and brothers and himself, ensures that he spends most of his time on the road and even when in the city, he prefers to ensconce himself in his tanzeem's guesthouse.

For totally different reasons, no one in his organization either has come close to discovering the truth about him. On his release, he was an all-conquering hero. He had been held in solitary confinement, so there are no witnesses to his private shame. Of course, it is assumed that he was tortured extensively by the Indians, as all great mujahids are, but no one has gleaned the extent of his torment. Perhaps Sinha was speaking the truth when he told him that he had devised the Jinn's visits specifically for him, or perhaps others have also been sodomized in Indian prisons and choose not to talk about it. But none of these things are relevant for his followers. The only thing that matters is that he is a living, breathing, symbol of resistance. Like the story of the blind, one-armed mujahid, but even better because he is physically present, a living legend, an inspiration, a recruiting poster. He is thrust into another role without having had any time to come to terms with what happened to him. And so he remains a fragile mixture of hate and confusion.

That is why meeting Eddy is so important for him. Eddy is his only link to his past, the only friend who would understand, the only one he can open up to. Eddy is a mirror, a manifestation of the life that could have been. Without guns and remote Kashmiri villages and the blood of two dozen soldiers on his hands. A world without Sinha and the Jinn. One day, he reminds himself, he will get his revenge on him. On all of them.

At the appointed time, he sees him. In the gloom of a setting winter sun, Eddy Shah emerges from his black Honda Civic. Ausi is not the only one whose appearance has changed. Eddy, too, sports a pair of elegant designer spectacles, no doubt a side effect of spending long hours in front of a computer screen. Unlike Ausi's flowing locks, Eddy's hairline is fast receding, but, dressed in jeans and a fashionably tight black sweater that highlights his toned upper body, he is still handsome.

Ausi observes him as he takes a seat at a vacant table. It was Eddy who suggested this location when they last spoke. It would be impossible for Ausi to come to Eddy's house, what with everybody hanging around there because of the wedding preparations. From their conversation, Ausi gleaned that Eddy was having enough problems already with his family, without needing to complicate things further with his presence. Besides, how would he, Sheikh Uzair the great anti-Shi'a demagogue, justify going to a house with the black flag and the Panja of Ali displayed over it?

What is it he wrote?

'The world has changed and I am going to change you with it.'

Eddy's new passion for doing something that matters is touching. Ausi remembers an earlier time and an earlier letter, when Eddy wrote a paean to capitalism. Now he has moved back to Pakistan, abandoning his comfortable but anodyne existence, as he describes it in the letter, to do something important. Eddy has a sense of history, he understands that we are passing through important times, but he doesn't quite grasp the significance of events.

Ausi starts walking toward the restaurant. His man sees him and also starts moving closer. Eddy still has the quiet air of self-confidence that he always possessed, as he sits in the middle of the hustle and bustle of the restaurant, surrounded by a great unwashed mass of labourers and shopkeepers, who couldn't be in greater contrast to him in his smart sweater and jeans. Just for a moment, there is a hint of confusion in his eyes when the burly bearded man in a great big shawl comes before him, but that recedes and a smile breaks out across his face as he recognizes Ausi. For the umpteenth time that hour, Ausi smiles again. Oh yes, Eddy. We will change the world. You and I together.

twenty

The Present

The Sheikh was a liar. That was the conclusion that Omar wrote for the interim inquiry report that he dispatched to his DIG. As he dictated his notes to a stenographer, sitting in the cool, high ceilinged study of the SP House, he thought about making the report final and closing the investigation. Despite the Sheikh's entreaties about playing straight with him, the tip about the safety deposit box had not brought him closer to discovering the true identity of Eddy Shah, or his whereabouts. All he had to show was a collection of letters between the two men. Omar had read and then reread these, but while they were interesting in their own right, the discovery of Eddy Shah remained elusive.

He could have returned to the Animal Husbandry School to question the Sheikh again, but he had decided against this. The Sheikh would simply play more games and Omar wanted to prove his competence as a professional investigator, not some greenhorn who was being led by the nose by the mischievous Sheikh Uzair. Besides, there was no need for him to be present at the Animal Husbandry School personally. His newfound status as the district police chief afforded him the ability to post shifts of inspectors and deputy superintendents round the clock at the facility, all of whom had to implement his security plan while he could monitor things remotely. Even the normally effusive DIG in Sukkur had written him a grudgingly complimentary memo, appreciating his system.

Besides, being the district SP brought with it a slew of new problems. He had spent the week since his visit to Karachi at the district headquarters, settling into the colonial mansion that was now his official residence and learning how to deal with his newly elevated status in life. As the police chief of a small rural district, he was the most important man in town. His every action, no matter how small, was keenly observed by the entire community. At times he felt as if he were being probed and tested, to see what he was made of. He could sense the raised eyebrows when one day he momentarily lost his temper during a meeting to decide routes for the Muharram procession. However, when he rushed to the scene of a highway robbery in the middle of the night to personally take charge of the investigation, old sages remarked that this SP was quite different from his predecessor. But what really made his reputation was his handling of a particularly vexing case of a peasant woman who had run away with a man from another tribe, thereby almost triggering a shooting war over honour, a conflict that Omar had managed to contain only with great difficulty.

The Sheikh, therefore, had been low on his list of priorities. And yet he could not bring himself to close the inquiry just yet. He was still intrigued by the Sheikh, and his own ambition to be credited with a fresh breakthrough drove him on. And so he turned once again to the pile of letters on his desk.

The picture that emerged of Eddy Shah from the letters was of a sensitive yet carefree young man, perhaps a little less intense than the Sheikh. What was not in question was Eddy Shah's total loyalty to his friend. He had somehow even managed to pass a letter to the Sheikh when he was in an Indian prison. The man in the identity card photo at the bank was the same dark-skinned boy standing next to the young Ahmed Sufi in the cricket team picture. Upon careful reading, Omar thought that some of Eddy Shah's later letters had a different tone to them, almost as if written by another person. But then, that was also true of the Sheikh's letters. His tone and style changed after he had become a jihadi. There was a greater confidence, an absolute surety of purpose in his words that had not been there in the young Ahmed Sufi as he struggled through his post school experiences. Perhaps it was likely that Eddy Shah too, had undergone a similar transformation.

Did that mean Eddy was also a jihadi, a true believer like the Sheikh? And if so, where was he and what had his role been in the various episodes of the Sheikh's life. Had he, for instance, been a part of the team that kidnapped the female journalist and planned the attack on the President? Omar could see how dangerous Eddy Shah could be if he had indeed joined the Sheikh's cause. A man, totally at ease in a foreign, western environment, able to live and interact without detection in a city like New York, could be lethal. What if he was still there, a dangerous sleeper, planning some terrible act of violence? Sheikh Uzair's trump card to wreak vengeance upon the world?

The more Omar thought about this angle, the more agitated he became. This would explain the Sheikh's coyness about Eddy. He wasn't just toying with Omar, he was covering up his final plan. Shahab's team had, by their own admission, been so overjoyed at having gotten the Sheikh himself that they had never even uncovered the existence of Eddy. But he had found out, and now he couldn't ignore it, even if he didn't have a clue about moving forward. Because if indeed Eddy was the Sheikh's trump card and something did happen, he would have to explain why he had done nothing. He looked forlornly at the letter he had just dispatched to the DIG, entailing the details of the case. For half a second, he thought about recalling it. It was the only official document that acknowledged the existence of Eddy Shah.

As he reached for his intercom to recall his PA, a shiny gold envelope caught his eye from the pile of items he had brought from the safety deposit box. In truth, he had so far only really concentrated on the letters, and ignored the other bits of memorabilia in the deposit box. The envelope was fancy, with engraved lettering and glitter on it, like the kinds used to send wedding invitations. Indeed, as Omar picked it up and dusted it off, he found that's exactly what it was. On the cover, the name Ausi had been printed in a very neat handwriting. Inside were three glossy cards. Omar picked up the first one. It was a deep purple colour, with the writing in silver.

> *Minahal, Moeez and Farah cordially invite you on the occasion of:*
> *Sana's Mehndi, on 27 December 2001*
> *At: 98-B, 2ⁿᵈ Central Lane, DHA, Phase-II*
> *Time: 8:30 p.m. till late*
> *RSVP: Safdar Hussain 03008227450*
> *PS: Be prepared to dance till your feet fall off*

The next card was more formal, on a cream coloured background with gold lettering, as if marking a more solemn occasion.

> *Matches are made in Heaven,*
> *Mr and Mrs Safdar Hussain would like to invite you to the wedding*

of their daughter,
Sana, with Adnan
S/o Mr and Mrs Syed Murtaza Shah
Date: 29 December 2001
Time: 8:00 p.m.
Venue: Crystal Ball Room, Sheraton Hotel

The third card was the most sombre, gold with a black border and black lettering. Unlike the other two, it began with a prayer.

In the Name of Allah, the most beneficent and merciful
Ya Ali Madad
Syed Raza Mehdi Shah would like to invite you on the occasion
of the Waleema of his grandson,
Syed Adnan Shah and his new bride Sana
At: 103, Old Clifton (behind the Convent of Jesus and Mary)
Time: 9:00 p.m.
Date: 31 December 2001

Bewildered, Omar turned once again to the letters. While he had gleaned enough from the letters to understand that both Eddy and the Sheikh, or Ausi as he was referred to, had enjoyed a relationship at different times with the girl Sana, there was no mention of Eddy having married her. How could something, that would have been significant for all of them, have occurred with no comment for years afterwards?

Omar picked up the identity card photocopy of Eddy. The address noted on that was the same as the one on the wedding card. It was his family home, and there was a good chance that he or his family still lived there. If he had married Sana, maybe she still lived there. At any rate, someone would be able to put him on Eddy's trail again.

Once again he was gripped with the thrill of the chase. He could inform Shahab and have him follow it up, but Omar's emotional investment in this case was too far gone. He needed to find Eddy Shah himself. But to do that, he would need to make a case once again to his DIG. And so he recalled his PA, but instead of having him close the report, he added the following lines at the end:

And so in summation, while the prisoner Sheikh Ahmed Uzair is not fully cooperating with us, this officer has uncovered an important link to trace the individual, namely Mr Adnan Shah alias Eddy, who is believed to be potentially a collaborator and sympathizer of the Sheikh, and may well have access to sensitive information about future plans. This officer proposes to leave his station for one day, tomorrow, in order to trace Adnan/ Eddy Shah's whereabouts in Karachi.

Omar Abassi, PSP,
District Police Officer, Khairpur

And having added these lines, Omar dispatched the letter by special messenger to Sukkur. Within a couple of hours, the DIG had authorized his trip to Karachi, but getting access to Eddy Shah's house would be another issue altogether. Accessing and questioning the Shah family, judging by the school records and their posh address, would be a different proposition than the Sheikh's family. These were influential people with powerful friends, probably some of his seniors too, and they might not like being questioned about their son's activities. If Eddy was indeed working for the Sheikh, any mention of his name would alert the family immediately and make them reluctant to cooperate. He would have to go about this in a very delicate manner.

He began by obtaining the phone number and address of Mr Shah's factory and office from the school file. The number had not changed over the years, and an explanation to the telephone operator about calling in relation to the use of Eddy's ID card to open bank accounts got him on the line with Mr Shah within five minutes.

'Yes Superintendent, you say my son has opened a fake bank account in Khairpur?' The voice on the phone seemed strangely excited.

'No sir, sorry, your son hasn't done anything illegal, his ID card has been used by some fraudulent parties. Would it be possible for me to meet you tomorrow and discuss the matter?'

'Of course. Would you like me to come to Khairpur right now? I can be there in three hours.'

'No sir, it's almost iftar time, please don't inconvenience yourself. I will come and see you at your home tomorrow to explain the whole matter.'

'Thank you, Superintendent. My wife and I will expect you at ten.'

As he entered the Karachi city limits the following morning, Omar pondered over the unexpectedly positive reaction of Adnan Shah's father to his queries. Admittedly, he had made up what he thought was a plausible story that wouldn't antagonize the family, but he had still expected some level of irritation. After all, rich and well-connected businessmen did not appreciate being called by superintendents of police from remote districts under any circumstances.

He was even more surprised when he reached the address fifteen minutes early and found both Mr and Mrs Shah standing outside on the road, waiting for him. Two servants and a security guard stood sheepishly next to them. Judging from the high walls, grand gate and the palatial compound hiding behind them, they were certainly not the sort of people to be so overawed by someone like him that they would stand at the door and wait for his arrival.

'Superintendent Abassi? I am Murtaza Shah. This is my wife, Zehra.' The man in front of him had a full shock of white hair, even though Omar guessed he would not have been older than sixty. You could tell the woman had been attractive in her youth, but the ravages of premature ageing were more visible on her. Her hair, riddled with grey streaks, looked as if it had been unkempt for some time. She wore no make-up, and her eyes had a hollow, tired look. Both wore simple clothes, and the only visible flash of ostentation were the gold cufflinks that Murtaza Shah wore on his cream coloured shalwar kameez.

'You have news of my son?' the woman's voice cracked in her anxiety and her pain-ridden eyes looked beseechingly at Omar. Mr Shah had the same desperate look in his eyes, but his behaviour was more circumspect.

'Zehra, please, let's go inside. My apologies, Superintendent Abassi. Please come this way.'

The house inside was beautiful, but had a melancholic feel to it, from the drooping overgrown shrubbery to the empty swimming pool on one side of it. They sat down in a sitting room that looked out upon the empty pool and the unkempt garden beyond.

'What news do you have of my son?' the woman asked again even before they had sat down, this time with tears in her eyes.

'Excuse me sir, but your son does not live with you anymore?'

'Is this some sort of joke? You said you had information about the recent whereabouts of my son!'

'No sir, I said his ID card had been used to open a bank account. I'm sorry sir, I don't at all mean to offend you in any way, but perhaps it would help me understand things if I had some background. When was the last time you saw your son?'

Mr Shah sighed and sank his face into his hands, as his wife broke down in a wail of sobs.

'18 December 2001. That was the date I last saw my son. The last time anybody from our family saw him.'

'Excuse me sir, but did you say 18 December 2001? Didn't he get married on December 29th that same year? I came across an invitation for the wedding among some evidence that I had been collecting.'

'He was supposed to. But he never did. Ten days before the wedding, he left the house without telling anyone where he was going, and never came back.'

Omar was stunned by the revelation. 'And he … he … never contacted you since then?'

'Everyone in our family considers him to be dead. Even my husband. Everyone except me. I know my son is alive somewhere. For ten years, I have waited for him. Please, there is something you are keeping from us. Tell me what you know.'

It was now Mr Shah who turned away, fighting back his tears, while his wife stared straight at him. Omar took a moment to compose himself, and thought about what to tell these people, but their suffering was plain for all to see and he knew he couldn't lie to them.

'Sir, Madam, I am investigating a case related to the jihadi mastermind Sheikh Ahmed Uzair. The Sheikh apparently went to school with your son. They were close friends. At the time, the Sheikh was known as Ahmed Sufi. Perhaps you may have heard of this name from your son.'

'Ahmed Sufi? Yes I remember a boy of that name. They used to play cricket together.'

'Yes Madam. They were on the school cricket team. Apparently, they kept in touch after school, even when your son went to study in America. The Sheikh was arrested five years ago for the attempted murder of the President, and the murder of a British journalist.'

'Yes, I have heard of this fellow. The British journalist, was a woman, I think she was pregnant or something when he killed her. But what the hell could this crazy fellow have to do with my son? You say they were schoolmates, but my son went to The School. They don't allow these fundamentalist types in The School.'

'Sir, I have verified that Sheikh Uzair did indeed attend The School. And he was your son's best friend. A few years ago, someone opened a bank account in the name of your son, using his ID card, for the Sheikh. And there is some…' he debated revealing the letters, but some sixth sense restrained him. '…there is some evidence that your son has been in contact with the Sheikh, even after the date that you have given of his disappearance.'

Now it was their turn to be shocked. Conflicting emotions hit them all at once, relief, disbelief, joy, alarm. Tears started flowing from their eyes. It was Mrs Shah who recovered first, reaching out and gripping Omar's hands and kissing them.

'Beta, you will never know what a great service you have performed. You have given a mother hope after ten years. Please, tell me more.'

'Madam, I am afraid I don't have that much more information. I was not even aware that your son was missing. I came here hoping that I could speak to him about his relationship with the Sheikh.'

'But this is so curious, Superintendent Abassi. You say he has been in touch with this Sheikh, even after his disappearance. That obviously means he is well, or at least able to send messages to someone. How come he never sent us any word? Why did he contact his friend and not his family?'

'Sir, I am afraid that I have a theory that you may not like. I fear he may have been brainwashed and turned into a jihadi sympathizer by the Sheikh.'

'What? That's preposterous! My son is no jihadi! He went to university in America. I paid a bloody fortune for him to mess about for four years. He even had a white girlfriend, what was her name? And he's Shi'a for God's sakes! Aren't all of these people Sunni Deobandis? They want to kill us Shi'as!'

'Sir, I do not know the answer to any of these questions. You are correct in all of what you say, but the fact is that your son is missing and has not contacted you in ten years, while he, or someone using his identity has opened bank accounts for the Sheikh since then. As recently as two weeks ago, we found a letter that the Sheikh was attempting to pass on to your son. All I can speculate is that the bond between the Sheikh and your son is so great that all other considerations of sect, or background, are irrelevant to them. Did you ever check if your son returned to America?'

'Six months after he … disappeared, I travelled to America, to New York, to … bring some of his things back. He had left everything in storage when he moved back, so I arranged for them to be shipped here. I never thought of checking at the US embassy, not that they would necessarily tell me anything. Superintendent, you have to realize that I have been mourning the death of my son for ten years. Except his mother, who clung to some fantasy of his return, all of us thought him dead! And now you come in here, and tell me this unbelievable tale that he is alive and may have become a jihadi!'

'Beta, is this Sheikh in your custody? If he has refused to speak with you, maybe he will listen to the entreaties of a mother. Please, take me with you, I will speak to him and ask him about Adnan.'

'Madam, the Sheikh is a hardened criminal. He has been in custody for five years, and believe me, many before me have tried to break him, but he has never cooperated. He has become a twisted individual, who plays mind games with everyone he comes across. And there is a great risk of him escaping, therefore no civilians are allowed to meet with him.'

'We'll see about that! I'm going to have a word right now with the IG. I play golf with him every Sunday. I will demand that he allow us to meet with this Sheikh. If he has any knowledge about my son's whereabouts, I can't keep waiting for you to get your act together.'

Omar shut his eyes as Mr Shah went to get his mobile phone. This meeting had turned into a disaster. By expressing his sympathy for the Shahs' tragedy, he had put his entire career at risk. He couldn't judge whether Mr Shah actually knew the IG or not, but his demeanour certainly indicated that he did. If the IG listened to the old man, he could easily lose not only the case, but also his posting. He could totally envision the IG berating him for harassing one of his personal friends and acting in a totally unprofessional manner at the same time. What lunacy had convinced him to come to these people?

Mr Shah returned to the room, his mobile phone on his ear, looking severely chastened. His wife looked up at him expectantly, but one glance at his face told her the news was not good.

'What happened Murtaza? What did the IG say?'

'He said that anything related to this Sheikh Uzair was designated as a highly classified matter. We are not allowed any access to him or any information connected to the Sheikh. He said Superintendent Abassi shouldn't even have told us what he has, even if it had something to do with Adnan. After all these years of friendship, he said it didn't matter to him if this bloody Sheikh knew where my son was. The superintendent is supposed to leave immediately and not contact us again.'

He finally broke down and sobbed openly, a powerful man who had seen the limits of his influence. Omar didn't know whether to be relieved at having escaped the IG's wrath or to feel sorry for the Shahs.

'Sir, madam, I am truly sorry. Let me try and help you. I believe that your son is the key to solving the problem of the Sheikh. Can you tell me anything about the circumstances leading to his disappearance? Did he fight with anybody? Is there anyone else he would have contacted, apart from you? His fiancée, I believe her name was Sana. Maybe she would have heard something?'

'Don't take that whore's name in front of me! She wrecked my son's life! Our misfortune began when she entered his life! It's all her fault!' Mrs Shah started screaming hysterically and had to be physically restrained by a female servant. Mr Shah told the servant to take her to her room and shook his head apologetically at Omar.

'I am sorry, Superintendent. Our family has been ripped apart since Adnan disappeared. It's been ten years but his shadow still hangs over our house. My other sons have tried to get on with their lives as best as they can, but it is hard to focus. My business has suffered from my neglect. My wife has had to receive psychiatric treatment. She irrationally blamed

Adnan's loss on his fiancée, Sana. You see, Sana was Adnan's choice, not the family's. We have a tradition of marrying only within Syeds who can trace their lineage to the family of the prophet. Sana's family was not even Shi'a. And there were also some … other issues. My wife opposed Adnan's decision and the two of them argued frequently in the months before he vanished. Ideally, I too would have preferred that he follow our traditions, but I could see that he was happy, so I let it go. But my wife never accepted it. And so when he disappeared, she externalized her anger on Sana, blaming her for Adnan's disappearance. Poor girl. She was as shattered as we were, if not more. She really loved him. But it got ugly in the aftermath. As a result, our families haven't stayed in touch. Well, except for me. I call her every few months to check up on her. I feel bad about the allegations my wife levelled at her when all of this happened. I assure you, if she had heard anything from Adnan, she would have told me.'

'I am very sorry, sir.'

'No, I am sorry for acting like an overbearing fool by threatening you like that. One thing I should have learnt over these ten years is humility. All the money and connections in the world could not find my son. But it seems that I still have a lot to learn. So please, Superintendent, I beg you, as a simple father looking for his son, please help me. I know that you risk your career by violating your orders, but I have no more ego. I beg you. An old man, who wants to see his son one more time, begs you.'

Mr Shah fell at Omar's feet in supplication, but Omar helped him back on his feet. 'Sir, please, you are my elder, it is not right for you to beg me. I promise I will do what I can. I do not have any proof for my theory about your son, sir, because it seems my department wants to push the Sheikh into a deep dark corner of the province and forget all about him. But the Sheikh will not cooperate and there is nothing that we can give him as an incentive. That is why I have been working to piece together the relationship between the Sheikh and your son, through correspondence, and interviewing people who knew them both. It is possible that the Sheikh may have sent your son a message, or a letter, here at your address. Would it be possible to go through your son's things, to see if I can find anything?'

'Certainly.' Mr Shah led Omar up the stairs to a door on the far corner of the second floor. A Haileybury College pennant still hung on the door of the room. Inside, it seemed as if Adnan Shah had never left. The room looked like a college dorm. Clothes were strewn on chairs and on the bed, which had been deliberately left unmade. On one side of the room, a glass trophy cabinet was stacked with various medals and cups and mementos. The same cricket team picture that Omar had seen at The School hung on the wall. In fact, there were pictures of Adnan everywhere, at various ages and in various shapes and sizes. Posing in a cricket kit as a boy, standing with his proud parents in his graduation gown, answering the phone in an American office as a young man.

'Oh, this is all my wife's doing. She made this room a shrine to Adnan after he left. She doesn't allow any of the servants in. She cleans it herself every day, leaving everything just as it was the day he left. Even the bed. A couple of years ago, I wanted to sell this godforsaken house as it had so many terrible memories, but my wife wouldn't hear of it. Her logic was that how would Adnan find us if we weren't living here?'

Omar did not comment, but moved towards the writing table. It had a large stack of unopened mail on it. Almost all the letters were routine, credit card bills, or change of address notifications from the States. As Omar perused through the pile, he found one interesting piece of correspondence. On a far simpler card than the ones made for Adnan and Sana's wedding, was an invitation to attend the wedding of Ahmed Uzair Sufi. The card was dated 2 January 2002 and was addressed to Adnan Shah. The writing inside was all in Urdu, inviting the recipient to a simple ceremony in Kashmir. In the margin, in a handwriting Omar recognized as the Sheikh's, was a one sentence comment:

> 'Since you decided to choose Sana as your riding partner for the rest of your life, I thought I needed to get someone to ride as well. A.'

Omar looked again upon the table. He opened each of the three drawers under it, but found nothing. Adnan Shah had never informed his family about his continued contact with Ahmed Uzair Sheikh after school. Had he hidden it intentionally? It stood to reason that he would then have also hidden any evidence of that correspondence. He checked the wardrobe and the bookshelf and was about to give up, when his eye fell on the largest trophy in the glass cabinet. It had been placed on the topmost shelf of the cabinet and was a massive cup with a deep bowl. On its side were etched the words, Willis Cup. On a hunch, Omar reached up to pull it down, but as he did so, the cup unbalanced and spilled out a number of opened envelopes.

'What are these?'

Omar smiled as he placed the Willis Cup back on the shelf. 'These are the letters your son received from Sheikh Uzair. Cricket was the bond between them. I should have guessed that he would have kept the letters in something cricket related.'

'But there are so many. We never even knew that Adnan was in touch with this, this terrorist. My god, what was my son involved in?'

'Adnan knew the Sheikh long before he became a terrorist, sir. You cannot fault him for staying in touch with his best friend. But I cannot say what he got involved in, or what he is involved in, till I read these.'

Mr Shah walked Omar to the gate and hugged him as he was about to climb into his jeep.

'Thank you, beta. For giving me hope once again.'

'Sir, I am still not sure if what I find will be positive or not. But I do promise to let you know, whatever the truth may be. I will send you copies of all the letters, but please do not divulge the contents to anybody else, otherwise I will be in more trouble than I am now.'

'Don't worry. I have learnt my lesson. I just want to know why my son chose to hide such an important part of his life from us.'

After the IG's rebuke, Omar knew there was little chance that Mr Shah would turn elsewhere. Besides, he had an idea that Mr Shah might prove to be a useful and influential ally, in case his investigation ran into any future difficulties. A man who played golf with the IG would surely have other powerful friends. He smiled to himself as the jeep turned from the driveway onto the main road. He had started to scheme like Shahab. And he was quite proud of that.

twenty-one

February 2002
Karachi

The gentle winter sunlight feels good on his face as he walks out of the big black iron gates. For an instant, he stands still, taking in the sight of rush hour traffic on the highway, the blaring of horns from vehicles of every shape and size and the scent of ozone fumes and rotting fish. Four days in a noiseless, windowless room makes one appreciate the sights and sounds of the city, no matter how smelly or loud they may be. He crosses the busy road, dodging cars and buses, and walks across to the café on the other side. The TV inside is showing cricket, so he casually sits down in the corner closest to the TV and orders a cup of tea.

Pakistan is playing the West Indies in Sharjah. Ausi watches intently for a couple of hours, paying close attention to the commentary and occasionally oohing and aahing as the bowlers beat the batsmen, or a fielder drops a catch. He drinks several cups of the milky tea and devours half a dozen rusk biscuits, the crumbs sticking to his beard. No one observing him, as they undoubtedly are, would ever be able to guess that his heart continues to beat like a jackhammer throughout.

The match ends when the Pakistan captain Waqar Younis clean bowls the last man Dillon, fittingly just as the azan for the Asr, or late afternoon prayer rings out from the mosque next to the café. Deliberately, Ausi rises and walks out, leaving several red hundred rupee notes, far more than the cost of his tea and biscuits, on the table. He does not turn towards the mosque, where the faithful are flocking to join the prayer congregation, but instead jumps on to the closest approaching bus, without paying much heed to its direction. He changes several buses in this way, until finally after a couple of more hours, he alights at a bus stand that is walking distance from his home in Lalookhet. Ignoring his father's quizzical looks, who is walking on the street outside, he enters the house and calls out for his wife.

She is a slight thing, pretty with typically pale Kashmiri skin, barely seventeen and only married for two months. She appears even more waifish in contrast to his long beard and muscular torso. He takes her hand and climbs two flights of stairs in the narrow house to his old room, which now serves as their marital apartment. The room is still adorned with mementos from his school years, old trophies and photos now interspersed with some of her belongings. The two bright red suitcases in which she brought her dowry from Kashmir still lie on the floor, only partially unpacked. He undresses and wordlessly bids her to do the same. She is taken aback by his urgency, and has barely unbuttoned her blouse when Ausi, already naked, pushes her onto the bed, thrusting himself into her as soon as he claws her shalwar out of the way. After about a minute, the old problem starts recurring, and Ausi struggles to stifle the panic that rises within him. She senses his alarm and without saying anything, her hand snakes down between her legs to coax him once more. He looks around the room and fixes his gaze on an old photo of Sana and Eddy. He imagines them together, Sana's naked, sweating body writhing under him. Eddy has finally stopped being uptight and Ausi has read his last letter a month ago with great relish, as he describes in detail his sexual encounters with Sana. It seems that their sex life has been somewhat underwhelming for both. Eddy doesn't satisfy her, while he has confessed that her past promiscuity turns him off. He smiles and looks down at Ayesha's naked body, his beard drooping over her small breasts, erect nipples and slender hips. In the language of Salim and his old Whitechapel flatmates, she has a 'zero meter' body, unblemished by the mileage of any previous lovers. Ausi imagines that Sana, in contrast, has plenty of miles on her. This thought finally reinvigorates him and he finishes with a series of particularly violent thrusts.

She slips out from under him and hands him a glass of water. He sips from it gratefully and lies back in bed, satisfied with his performance. His ability to perform sexually has been a matter of concern for him since his return from his Indian incarceration. The impact of the torture he had to endure has left him handicapped, mentally if not physically. Upon his release, he feared that he would never be able to lie with a woman again. Several surreptitious attempts on his part met with failure. He has never spoken of his problem, not even with Eddy, and he has certainly not gotten medical assistance, preferring to rely on village remedies and old wives's tales to restore his vigour. With the arrival of Ayesha, things improved, her youthful body proving to be a tonic for him. But the last four days in another Agency prison have brought back all the old fears, the memories of electrodes on his penis, and raw chillies being thrust into his every orifice. Even now, he shudders at the memory. And though his captors did not resort to those tactics during his latest stay, this is why it is so important for him to 'test' himself out immediately, to ensure everything is still in working order.

His eyes follow her as she dresses and picks up his dirty clothes. He married her on an impulse, when he returned to his village the week after meeting Eddy. He still isn't sure why he did it, whether it was a desire for companionship stemming from the knowledge that Eddy and Sana were now life companions, or whether it was pure sexual frustration. It was easy enough, she was his mother's cousin's daughter, simple village folk who were honoured by his proposal, despite its indecent haste. He is, after all, a celebrity in his mother's village due to his exploits in India.

She bathes herself, then fills another bucket for him. The showers in his father's house are ancient and rusted over. The old man does not bother to have them repaired as he thinks them an extravagance. And Ausi's bastard brothers spend their money only on their own rooms. This information too, he comes by through his wife. His own conversations with his father consist of little more than an obligatory salaam. He finds it difficult to hide his loathing any more. His decision to deposit his new wife here had surprised everyone, but his brothers and father know better than to question him. His presence seems to intimidate them. His generous stipend, handed over to his wife to run the household expenses, quells any further debate.

He is glad to dress in fresh clothes. He had been wearing his previous ones for four days, and while the accommodation in the Agency 'rest house' was far better than his Indian cell, a lock up is always a lock up. They do not torture him because, after all, despite the changed circumstances after the American invasion of Afghanistan, he is still a revered figure of the Kashmiri resistance. It would be really bad form to treat him like one of bin Laden's filthy Arabs. But they are panicked by the kidnapping of the Englishwoman. Desperate to avoid international embarrassment, they throw their net wide to ensure her safe return. Ausi is one of many who is called in and detained for a few days, in an attempt to garner any scrap of information that may lead to the girl. He sees the nervousness in the eyes of the Major who interrogates him, despite the man's pathetic attempts to portray a no nonsense tough guy image. *They* are worried.

And so his last four days have been spent trying to patiently answer the questions barked at him by a bunch of buffoons, while intermittently thinking up new ways to make fools of his captors. The consolation for him, as well as a measure of his success, is that they do not hurt him, obviously believing in his feigned ignorance.

He spends the evening at home, even deigning to eat dinner in silence with his father and brothers. By now, they know better than to ask after his whereabouts. He watches the entire nine o'clock *Khabarnama* on the government's TV channel, paying little attention to the reports about the progress of the investigation into the kidnapping of the journalist, but focusing only on the sports round up, which shows highlights of all the wickets that fell today in the test match. As soon as that finishes, he leaves and after walking a short distance to the main road, hails a rickshaw to take him to his tanzeem's madrasa in Baldia. The journey takes almost an hour, despite the lack of traffic on the streets at this late hour. He enters the madrasa and spends some time talking with the staff, and then makes a show of retiring to his quarters, for the benefit of anyone who may have been given the task of tailing him. A couple of hours later, as the students begin waking up for Fajr prayers, he takes advantage of the commotion to slip out through the rear entrance. The alley behind the madrasa is an unpaved road, with an open gutter running by its side. An old beat up, black and yellow taxi is waiting for him, the driver pretending to rest on his break, but secretly observing every movement in the alley. Wrapping his big pheran tightly around himself, he gets in and, wordlessly, the driver starts the engine.

The drive is another long one, meandering through some of the city's remotest neighbourhoods. They change their route at least three times to avoid police checkpoints. Since the Englishwoman's kidnapping, the number of checkpoints have mushroomed, but early morning is a good time to drive around, as it is close to the end of the policemen's shift, and the weary cops carry out their duties with a lot less enthusiasm.

The early morning freshness has still not dissipated as they finally reach their destination, a farm house in Gadap, the semi-rural outskirts of the city. The compound is ringed with a seven-foot high wall, making it look palatial from the outside, but the farm house itself is a simple single storey structure. A handful of goats and a cow graze on wild grass near the walls. The taxi parks itself next to a couple of motorcycles that are the only other sign of human habitation in this place.

Two men emerge from the building and offer him their salaams. He returns their greeting and steps inside. The farm house is divided into three rooms, a larger entrance hall and two other, smaller rooms. The only visible furniture in evidence are a pair of charpoys and a small gas burner attached to a CNG cylinder. Two more men approach to greet him, but he notes with some satisfaction that a fifth man, armed with a pistol, remains guarding the door to the smaller room. Ausi has trained his men well.

The taxi driver follows behind him, carrying three black plastic shopping bags, one of which he hands to Ausi. The four guards take out their breakfast from the other bag, fried parathas and milky, brewed chai poured into a smaller plastic bag and sealed with a rubber band. As the men sit down to eat, Ausi approaches the guarded room alone. The room is pitch dark, windowless and cold. He sees the silhouette of the woman, wrapped in the blanket they have provided her, already awake and alert. The guard behind him turns on the one light in the room, a solitary unshaded bulb that hangs precariously at the end of an exposed wire in the centre of the small room.

'Good morning, Ms Boyd. I trust I didn't wake you? I have brought some breakfast for you.'

His accent is clipped, posher than the way he would normally have spoken, more akin to Sana's English. He enjoys speaking in this way, watching the astonishment on her face every time he opens his mouth. It is as if her mind refuses to accept that someone with such correct pronunciation could ever be a kidnapper. Or worse. It was the same with the foreigners he kidnapped in Kashmir. They all believe they are safe with an English-speaking gentleman. As if being able to recite a few lines from Shakespeare is a character certificate on its own.

He looks at her again, almost lustfully. She is a striking woman, blonde, straw coloured hair, pale Nordic eyes and a sharp nose. Her condition is not immediately evident from the way she is sitting, wrapped in the blanket, but her protruding belly becomes evident when she reaches out to take the shopping bag from him. Ausi stares at her stomach, admiring for the umpteenth time, the courage of this woman to want to go looking for interviews with jihadis in her state.

'Did you … were you able to get the medicines I had requested?' Her fingers tear open the Super Broast lunch box and she takes a bite out of the bun inside before hungrily wolfing down a handful of soggy French fries.

'Yes, your multivitamins are in the shopper. I apologize for the delay in my visit, but I had to go out of town on some urgent business. I wouldn't want your baby's health to suffer. That's why I got you the broast chicken for breakfast. It's deep fried, so it shouldn't have any impurities that would upset your constitution. I would gladly offer you some of the parathas and chana masala that my men are devouring outside, but I thought this sort of food would be more familiar to you.'

She takes out the vitamins from the bag along with a small bottle of mineral water and swallows two pills. 'Sheikh Uzair, where in the Qur'an does it say that it is acceptable to kidnap and threaten a pregnant woman? Please, I beg you once again, for the life of my unborn child, let me go. I will carry your message and ensure it gets out globally.'

Ausi pretends to think about her suggestion for a moment. 'You are right, Ms Boyd. The Qur'an doesn't give me permission to kidnap you. No religious text does. But what can I do? These days, we jihadis, like you media types, are constantly pressured by the demand to do something more spectacular than our colleagues. Osama crashed planes into the Twin Towers, so I had to respond by kidnapping a pregnant woman. It's such a competitive environment out there, you know. But do not concern yourself with my message. Be happy, your troubles are coming to an end. You and your baby will soon be safe. Now eat up. You will need your strength.'

He walks back out. The taxi driver, a short, nasty-looking fellow called Fazal, takes out a small camcorder from the third plastic bag. Ausi examines it, checking to see if the battery is fully charged and then confirms with the driver whether he knows how to operate it. He walks to a corner of the room where some other equipment has been dumped. He picks up a meat cleaver, of the kind used by butchers, and tests its sharpness. He feels sorry for the woman, not for the fate that is about to befall her, but for her naivete, still imagining she can talk her way out of this situation.

Ausi goes back into the room followed by Fazal with his camcorder and two other men. With the meat cleaver still in his hand, he takes out a piece of paper from within the fold of his pheran, and instructs one of the other men to read it out loud while standing over the woman. Her eyes look at him pleadingly, still not sure of what her fate will be. He smiles at her benevolently and assures her the cleaver is just a prop for the video they want to shoot. Like a true professional, Fazal looks for the best angle from which to shoot, and fusses over the light. Finally, when they can all see the red recording light blinking, Ausi stands to the side of the woman, being careful to keep the cleaver out of sight until the right moment. The man with the paper starts reciting a litany of sins that the West has perpetrated against Islam.

Ausi's body tenses imperceptibly, not really paying attention to the monologue. The charges are standard lines used by various jihadi groups to justify their actions. He has no interest in the politics, only in the act that he is about to commit. He hasn't told any of his men about what he is going to do. Even Fazal, the camera man, has only been instructed to keep the camera rolling no matter what happens. None of his tanzeem members are in on this either. They have become too concerned with the consequences of his actions, worrying that this rash kidnapping will damage them, especially in such difficult times. They do not want any negative publicity at this moment, especially with the Agencies keeping a careful eye on anyone who has been in contact with the Arabs. Ausi has still not responded to Zawahiri's letter, but increasingly, the prominence given by the West and by the media to the Arabs and Al-Qaeda irks him. It is perhaps this, more than anything else, that prompts him to do what he does. He doesn't care about consequences. He wants the world to turn red with blood, and Eddy is the only one he has confessed this to. He has found that people will follow you even after you commit the vilest act, as long as they are convinced of the strength of your will. But very few have the stomach for it if you tell them beforehand. To change the world, you must violate it first.

His brief stay as an unwilling guest of the agencies has convinced him that he has to go ahead with this, and as soon as possible. Although they remain clueless of his plans, despite having detained him for four days, one cannot depend upon their incompetence. The laws of probability dictate that sooner or later, they will figure out that he doesn't believe in playing by their rules. Then they will come after him, but he wants to paint his masterpiece before that.

He stares at the woman, tears streaming from her pale eyes, softly whimpering, still not sure whether to believe his claims of setting her free. She places her hands protectively over her belly, and Ausi finds himself wondering how Sana would be if she were pregnant. He reminds himself to ask Eddy the next time he writes to him, if he has impregnated Sana yet.

Sana. Sinha. The two images merge and cloud his mind and blur his vision. He sees himself moving in slow motion, grabbing the woman's soft blonde hair and hacking at her exposed neck with the cleaver. His motion is smooth and the cleaver is sharp, cutting its way through muscle and fibre, almost halfway through. A stream of blood gushes out from her exposed larynx, splattering on him and on the reader. He sees the man shake violently, clearly horrified at what has happened and he is about to cry out when he looks into Ausi's eyes and somehow manages to control himself.

Ausi forces himself to look at the limp, half hacked off head that he still holds. The body convulses a couple of times as the incomplete life that it carries inside it is extinguished. He wants to remember this moment forever, not as some kind of glorious achievement, but rather as an example of what he can be capable of. A man who can so heartlessly slaughter a pregnant woman, can do anything. I did not lie to you, Rachel Boyd. I have set you free. And myself as well.

twenty-two

The Present

He had to see her. That was the only way to solve the mystery of the letters. After a week of avoiding her phone calls, Omar Abassi knew he had no choice. He was in too deep to stop now.

His return from the Shah household had been predictable. After the episode with Murtaza Shah and the IG, Omar had been reprimanded in writing by his DIG, who made it clear that any further unauthorized departure from his district would be considered an abandonment of duty. He even received a phone call from the IG's personal staff officer, one of his batch mates from the Academy, who had not seen fit to contact him at all in the intervening years, to give him the message that IG sahib was not happy and any further indiscretions would see him transferred to the wilderness of Baluchistan.

All of this had chastened Omar temporarily. When Murtaza Shah called him back, he told the old man about his predicament. Unfortunately, Murtaza Shah's far reaching influence had hit a brick wall when it came to Sheikh Uzair. None of his numerous contacts were even willing to answer his calls anymore. In his desperation, Murtaza Shah had told

Sana about Omar's revelations, to see if she could make more headway with him. In the past two days, she had called fourteen times, but his fear of getting sucked back into the case after such explicit orders from the DIG, kept him from talking to her. His office staff, bewildered at his response, assumed it was some girl SP sahib had shacked up with in Karachi and was now trying to avoid.

He kept reading and re-reading the letters. They made no sense. No one knew where Eddy Shah had disappeared after 18 December 2001, yet the Sheikh kept communicating with him as if nothing had changed. The letters from both men referred to Sana constantly, yet according to Eddy's father, neither had been in contact with her for the past ten years. If he wanted to solve the mystery, there were only two people who could help him. He could go back and speak to the Sheikh, but there was no guarantee that the Sheikh would be any more helpful. Omar had not returned to the Animal Husbandry School since his visit to Karachi. The Sheikh mocked him and besides, any increased frequency of visits to the Sheikh would alert his DIG to the fact that he was still toying with the case. He had left the Sheikh in the care of Peeral and Juman, who had organized things quite competently and reported to him three times a day. It was as good as being there himself.

His only other option was the girl. He felt embarrassed by all the intimate details he had learned about her through the letters. Ausi's letters had always been quite descriptive when speaking about Sana, but Omar had noticed that Eddy, while initially coy about Sana, had also gotten increasingly lascivious. But if he wanted to figure this out, he would have to confront her with the letters.

So he finally called her back and asked to meet her. Like Murtaza Shah, she was willing to drive up to Khairpur immediately, but he said he would come to Karachi the following day. Instead of asking for leave, he called for a private car, and told his staff to tell the DIG that he had gone on inspection to the remoter regions of the district. The staff, automatically assuming that SP sahib was going to Karachi for a secret tryst with the girl, nodded sagely and assured Omar of their discretion.

Early the next morning, abandoning his red jeep and retinue of bodyguards, he slipped on civilian clothes and drove the unmarked and unassuming car towards Karachi. He found that the journey took considerably longer if one wasn't accompanied by wailing police sirens. He was also unfamiliar driving around Karachi on his own, so it was late afternoon before he finally found Sana's apartment complex.

The building was a high-rise built across the road from the sea, in Boat Basin. Though not as upscale as Eddy's parents' house, the locality was still a good one. A group of boys played cricket with a tennis ball covered in electric tape in the complex's parking lot. The security guard, who looked quite dandy in his uniform, eyed him suspiciously and asked several times if he was sure he was in the right place. Omar had deliberately not revealed his identity, and finally, after reconfirming for the third time that he was actually expected at Madam Sana's flat, the guard escorted him to the lift. The flat was on one of the higher floors, and Omar could feel the heavy salt air as he stepped out of the elevator.

Sana Safdar was already waiting for him at her door. Omar, who had pictured her based on the letters, was taken aback by her appearance. Of course, ten years had passed and she was a woman in her mid-thirties, not the twenty-something that Ausi and Eddy had envisioned, but still, she looked older than her years. She wore no make-up and her face was pale and drawn.

The dark circles under her eyes looked as if they had been there for years. Strands of premature white streaked her hair, which had been cut short in a bob. When she offered her hand, he was surprised to find it was hard and callused and her fingernails were blackened with ink stains. She wore no jewellery and even her clothes were simple, an old cotton kurta worn over a frayed pair of jeans.

'Superintendent Abassi, I cannot tell you how grateful I am that you came. I have been waiting ten years for this call. Please, come in.'

Inside, the flat stank of stale cigarettes. The furniture was functional and carelessly laid out, without any kind of personal touch. A couple of framed art nouveau posters had been hung on the otherwise bare walls, the sort of thing that would be standard in a college dorm, but that seemed out of place in the apartment of a sophisticated young woman.

Two mugs of steaming coffee had been placed on a heavily stained coffee table. Omar looked around awkwardly for a place to sit, as the sofa and chairs surrounding the coffee table were all covered with press clippings from old newspapers and school exercise books. Sana apologetically pushed aside some of the debris and bade him to sit.

'I'm sorry for the mess. I was marking my literature class' test papers. I teach O levels.'

'Do you teach at The School? Because I met Mrs Almeida a few days back, but she didn't mention you.'

'No, I don't teach at The School. I am sure they wouldn't want to touch me with a ten-foot pole. I'm damaged goods, reputationally. And if there's one thing those people care about, it's their reputation. I made some coffee for us. I hope you like it.'

'Uh, I am sure it is very nice, Miss Sana, but it is Ramadan and I am fasting.'

Sana slapped her palm on her head. 'I am so sorry. Sometimes I think I live in a world of my own. I totally forgot that it was Ramadan. I'll take these away.'

'No Miss, that's fine, you please have your coffee. It's no problem. Really.'

'Thank you. So, uncle Murtaza tells me you think Eddy is alive.' Her hands shook violently as she took a cigarette from an open packet of Marlboro Whites on the table, and lit it.

'Miss Sana, I truly do not know. You know, of course, that your, fian ... uh, Adnan Shah, and your uh, friend, Sheikh Uzair, corresponded with each other for many years through a series of letters.'

'Fiancé. You can say it. I can only imagine what Eddy's mother said to you, but I will not go crazy. I was his fiancée. She can't take that away from me.'

'Uh, yes Miss. But you are aware of the letters?'

'Yeah, I know Eddy and Ausi used to write to each other. But that was years ago, when Eddy and I were living in America, before he disappeared.'

'I am, uh, in possession of all the letters, Miss, those written by the Sheikh, as well as those written by Adnan Shah. The thing is, they have continued to correspond even after Adnan's disappearance in December 2001. The, uh, letters after 2001 also contain plenty of, uh, intimate references to you. As if Adnan Shah was in, well, in contact with you.'

'What?' Her startled reaction led her to spill some more coffee on the table. 'How is that possible?'

'Miss, I have, uh, brought the letters. You can read them, if you like.' He picked up the thick file that he had brought with him and proffered it to her.

She rifled through several of the envelopes, and began to read the later letters. Omar winced as he saw the date of the particular letter she began with. He had read them so many times that he knew the contents of each letter by date. The one she had picked up was one of Eddy's most explicit letters. Inadvertently, he began to blush.

She read several of the letters before she looked up again. 'You have read all of these?' It seemed to Omar, whose complexion now resembled a beetroot, that the question was asked in an accusatory tone. Sheepishly, he shrugged his shoulders and nodded reluctantly.

'Superintendent, I have never made any excuses for my lifestyle. I didn't do it with my father before he died, and I refused to do it with Eddy's mother, so believe me when I tell you that I certainly won't deny my promiscuity in front of you. But these, these *occasions* with Eddy, never happened.'

'What? But Eddy mentions so many incidents relating to you, in his letters after the 18th of December, 2001.'

'Superintendent, did Eddy's parents tell you what happened to me after he disappeared?'

'No.'

'Let me tell you, to make you better understand things. Do you think I would be living like this, over here, if I had been in touch with him over the past ten years? Eddy was my compass, he was my life. Since the day when he finally admitted his feelings for me, I never looked at another man. He cured me of my insecurities. He helped me get over the anger I felt towards my family. You see, as you may know, my father was a senior bureaucrat who was indicted on corruption charges because of his closeness with the former Prime Minister. He had to run away from the country. I hated my father for this, because he destroyed the myth I had created about my family. After he managed to escape to Dubai, I still refused to talk to him, or take money from him. I continued to work as a waitress, as I didn't want his help. Then, in early 2001, he fell sick. My mother said officially he was diagnosed with cancer, but really it was a broken heart caused by my estrangement. I moved back in April of that year to make my peace with him before he died. Eddy didn't want me to go because there was no way for me to come back and he feared he would lose me in a long distance relationship. I didn't want to leave him either but I have always had a wilful streak in me, so I picked a fight with him and left. I figured it would be easier for both of us if we broke up.

'My father passed away in August that year. I didn't know what I was going to do with myself, because my mother and sister resented me for having abandoned the family for all those years. I missed my life in New York with Eddy, but I couldn't go back because I no longer had a visa. I hadn't even spoken to him in a while. Skype and all the other things we have these days weren't around then and keeping in touch was a bit harder. Some common friend of ours mentioned that Eddy had been seen with another girl. I felt miserable, a prisoner in my own home with no prospects for the future. But he came back for me, my very own knight in shining armour. He called me the day after the 9/11 attacks and told me he loved me and wanted to spend the rest of his life with me. He proposed to me and told me he was coming home.'

Her eyes welled up with tears at the memory. She took a sip of her coffee to gain time to compose herself.

'That's when the problems with Eddy's mother began. She wanted Eddy to marry within the Shi'a community. Plus, I wasn't exactly the virtuous and virginal daughter-in-law that she had always imagined. She put her foot down, thinking Eddy, like his elder brothers before him, would cave to her pressure. But he didn't. My knight fought valiantly for my honour and won. The date for our wedding was set and I busied myself in preparing my bridal trousseau.

'And then, ten days before our wedding date, he disappeared. Can you imagine the psychological blow of something like that on a neurotic person like myself? I went to pieces. For years, I blamed myself, as if his disappearance was somehow my fault. His mother didn't help matters by telling anyone who asked that I was a whore who had bewitched her son and taken him from her.'

'Did the police team investigating the case ever interview you?'

'No, it was all handled by his father. They didn't want him declared dead, so uncle asked his friends to keep the case pending or something. Besides, Eddy's mother refused to let me share in anything related to Eddy. I tried going over once, but she threw me out of the house. My past came out quite publicly thanks to her. I couldn't deal with my humiliation, and my grief over Eddy, so I had a bit of a breakdown. That's why I moved here, away from everybody I had known in my previous life. I think my mother was quite relieved to see me go, actually.'

'But you must have kept contact with some of your other classmates, common friends? Someone whom Eddy might have reached out to?'

'No. I can't be one of those people who shows up at the next party and pretends that life goes on. Every aspect of my old life reminded me of Eddy. What I'm trying to tell you, Superintendent, is that for the past ten years, I have been a living corpse. My life stopped on the 18th of December. Those two years that we lived together in New York will always be the happiest time of my life. Look at me now, look at how I live. Do you think, that had Eddy ever tried to contact me, I would have stuck around here? I would have been with him, even if he were at the ends of the Earth.'

'You must have known that the Sheikh was one of the few people who had the resources to help find Eddy. And Eddy must also have told you that he was going to meet him that day. Please Miss, I will request you to give me a truthful answer.'

'Eddy went to see Ausi that day? No, I never knew that. He didn't tell me. I knew that the two of them had been in touch with each other since Eddy's return from New York, but when I asked him, Eddy would always say that logistically it hadn't been possible for them to meet because of Ausi's commitments and his moving around the country. The only thing Eddy said was that it would be impossible for Ausi to attend our wedding. He joked about the fact that Ausi would never be able to live it down in front of his jihadi buddies if he attended a Shi'a's wedding. But he said we would try and do something with him afterward. Just the three of us.'

'Did you ever try to contact Sheikh Uzair before or after Eddy's disappearance? After all, he was your very good *friend*.'

'Instead of using that tone, why don't you just ask me what you're thinking? Did I try and fuck Ausi while I was with Eddy? Obviously the two of them seem to enjoy discussing my intimate details and you evidently enjoy reading them. Did it turn you on, Superintendent, reading all these details about me? Fuck you and get out!'

The violence in her tone startled him. Involuntarily, he got up and the shock and embarrassment was etched in his face.

'Miss, I apologize. I had no such intention. I meant no disrespect, but I am merely trying to establish what happened to your fiancé. I believe he may be alive and somehow assisting the Sheikh. Please Miss, I need your help.'

She got up and stared at him as if she had seen a ghost. Her hands shook and tears flowed from her eyes. It took her a moment to speak but when she did, her voice was brittle.

'You actually think Eddy is involved in the same stuff as Ausi?'

'Yes Miss. Didn't Mr Shah discuss this with you?'

'He did, but all he said was that you were looking into Eddy's case again and that you had some new evidence. But I never connected it to the fact that you think my Eddy might actually be assisting Ausi. Eddy was always scared of religion, of its power to brainwash people. How can this be?'

'If he is Miss, then I'm afraid he isn't in a good place. The only one who knows for sure is Sheikh Uzair, but he has been playing games with us. I don't trust him and you are the only other person in the world who can clarify this.'

Sana composed herself with some difficulty. She took a tissue and wiped her face, then took a deep breath.

'Superintendent, all I know is that if Eddy was alive, no matter how he may have been converted to Ausi's cause or whatever, he would always contact me.'

'Has Sheikh Uzair ever contacted you?'

'No. But I did try to contact him once. Soon after Eddy's disappearance. You are right, I did think that, of all our friends, he would probably be the most resourceful in being able to find out anything about Eddy. But I didn't know how to. I hadn't been in touch with him since my return to the city. When Eddy vanished, I went to one of his tanzeem offices to try and trace him. They told me he was in Kashmir, but that they would relay the message to him. But I never heard back. A month or so later, there was the episode of the female journalist, and Ausi went underground. I figured he was too far gone in his cause by then to be able to help me.

'You see, I never met him after I returned home. I was reluctant to, because I hadn't had any contact with him since I started going out with Eddy. There was always unfinished business between us and I didn't want to complicate things further. I didn't want to hurt Ausi, because I knew that if we met, he would know in an instant how much I was in love with Eddy. But I never realized that he continued to take such an *interest* in me.'

With a perverse fascination, Sana picked up the letters again and started reading them, one by one. 'My god, I didn't know that Ausi went through all of this.'

'Were you in love with him?' Omar was surprised by the directness of his own question.

'I thought I was. Ausi was always so unique out of all of us. He was from a slightly different background, a lot edgier, far more capable than most of our friends. It was easy to become attracted to him, especially when he set off on such a different path after we left school. But I only really understood what falling in love meant after Eddy. What it means to give everything within your being to another person. That's what Eddy did for me. The thing with Ausi was, he was always a taker, not a giver. So love? No, I don't suppose I was ever in love with him, truly. Do you think he was in love with me?'

'I don't know. When you go and speak to him face to face, he starts playing mind games. And from what I've gleaned from the letters, well, I think he has gone beyond all sense of normality. The only person who comes close to understanding him is Eddy.'

'But Superintendent, Eddy was nothing like Ausi. There was always a tenderness in Eddy. Ausi was, harder, more melancholic. When we were in school, Eddy would tease me remorselessly, but at the end of it, he would say one thing that would make me feel like I was on top of the world. These letters of his,' she held up several of Eddy's later letters, 'they don't sound like my Eddy.'

'How so?'

'Well, these later letters are harsher, with a cynical tone. Eddy was never like that. He was the eternal optimist. These sound like what Ausi would want Eddy to say.'

'Perhaps he has gained such a sense of control over him that Eddy now writes the way the Sheikh wants him to.'

'No Superintendent, you don't know Eddy, he wasn't controllable like that, no matter what leverage Ausi may have held over him. Besides,' she stared again at the two letters in her hands, turning her gaze from one to the other, 'this isn't even Eddy's handwriting. How could Ausi get Eddy to change his handwriting? Look, this earlier letter, written when Eddy was in college in the US, look at this handwriting, clear, concise and neat. Look at this later letter, with this spidery crawl. It's totally different.'

Omar sat down next to her and looked at the two letters. She was right, under careful observation, the script in the two letters was markedly different. He was surprised he hadn't picked it up before, but then he could hardly be blamed for that. He could never be as familiar with Eddy's writing, as the woman whom he was about to marry. Together, they went through all the letters, separating them into three piles. There were Ausi's letters, written in his somewhat distinctive handwriting; then there were those that Sana identified as being definitely written in Eddy's hand; and finally, the third pile was the letters in the spidery crawl. All of these were from Eddy, but all of them dated from after his disappearance.

'It's as if someone is writing on behalf of Eddy.' Omar looked up from the letters, conscious suddenly of how close he had been sitting to Sana.

'But Superintendent, how would anyone else know these details? Only Ausi, Eddy or I would know of these things. Eddy wouldn't share these details with anybody else. And neither, for that matter, would Ausi. Why would he tell anyone else, and why would he be interested in discussing me with someone who didn't even *know* me?'

'Yes, there wouldn't be any … point…' Omar stared at the addresses on the envelopes again. Something about them had never made sense to him. Suddenly, with a flash of revelation, he took his mobile phone out of his pocket. 'Shahab, I need to meet with the best handwriting expert in the city. Right now. It's to do with the Sheikh.'

Hurriedly, he began gathering up the letters, and mumbled something about having to go back urgently. Sana reached out and grasped his hand firmly.

'Superintendent, Eddy's dead, isn't he?'

Omar Abassi turned his head towards her and made as if to say something, but thought better of it and did not answer.

twenty-three

October 2003
Rawalpindi

'No, no, you are doing it wrong! The ball bearings are wrapped on the outside, not under the explosive cake!' The tension in Ausi's voice is plain from his tone. He has prepared a long time for this moment, and he cannot afford for his plan to go wrong because of the sloppiness of an inexperienced bomb maker.

He takes the roll of plastic sheeting, with hundreds of ball bearings packed into it, and carefully wraps it around the slab of sticky black explosive. It isn't as easy as it used to be to acquire weapons grade C4, and it has taken a great exertion of time, money and his contacts, to have gotten it in the amounts that he required, but his patience has been rewarded. The newly wrapped slab is fitted under the passenger seat of the Suzuki Hi-roof, where several other similar sheets have been neatly pressed into place. Every inch of the car has been fitted with the slabs, nearly 70 kgs of explosive in total, giving the delivery vehicle the same explosive impact as a set of cluster bombs dropped from the sky.

Ausi checks the wiring on the explosives for the umpteenth time. It is not that he doesn't trust the dejected young man who was wrapping the ball bearings. The problem with these youngsters who have come into the business after 9/11 is that their knowledge is theoretical, not practical. Since the American invasion shut down the camps in Afghanistan, new recruits like the one standing next to him, have learnt all they could from downloading manuals from the internet. It can never be the same.

The alumni from the old camps have been scattered. Many were killed in the war against the Americans that Ausi still believes was pointless. Others, like his Shi'a hating friend Muawiya, have been hunted down and killed by the government in Pakistan. The remainder have fled to the Tribal Areas to reorganize themselves. But Ausi has stayed on, preferring to hide in the open, daring the authorities to catch him. There are no pretences any more, after the killing of Rachel Boyd. The President, embarrassed and humiliated in front of the world, has put a price of ten million rupees on his head, dead or alive. The police and agencies no longer summon him in an affable manner. They raid his madrasas and guest houses, arresting his acolytes and charging them with crimes they know nothing about. While more moderate members of his organization have chosen to leave, not willing or able to face the wrath of an angered state, dozens of others flock to his standard. The great Sheikh Uzair has become a symbol of defiance against this puppet government and it's puffed up President.

Even his failures are celebrated. Barely two months ago, his plan to kill the President failed miserably when the land mine planted under the road exploded too late, after the presidential convoy car had already passed. The casualties were a handful of soldiers and policemen in back up vehicles, but among the jihadi chattering classes, his attempt is the one that is deemed to have come closest to success. He has succeeded in winning his audience. Osama is considered a one hit wonder, while Sheikh Uzair seems to come up with something bold and new every few months.

Ausi looks around him and bears a self-satisfied grin. It is a testament to his organizational skill and his adaptability, that he has been able to put a second operation in the field just weeks after the last one. The auto repair shop belongs to a sympathizer, the perfect place in which to create a car bomb. The Suzuki Hi-roof has been purchased third hand, for cash down, and is similar to the thousands of such vehicles that ply the roads of Pindi. His source, a misguided army hawaldar in the President's security detachment, has provided him with pinpoint accurate information about the movements and security protocols of the presidential convoy. And the men around him, though green, are committed to the cause. He puts his hand on the shoulders of the young man he berated a moment ago and nods encouragingly, signalling his appreciation of the wiring. He is but a boy, barely twenty, a third year physics student from Lahore's engineering university. Inspired by the events of the last couple of years, he has joined Ausi because he is sick of the verbal platitudes of the other groups. A lot of talk about defending Islam and posturing in front of the government, but no actual action. On the other hand, everyone knows that Sheikh Uzair is a man of action and gives a damn about consequences. His reputation enables him to recruit the cream of the crop. A third year physics student is a far more potent weapon than an illiterate Mehsud tribesman.

Yes, everything is in place. All he needs now is the trigger. And this time round, his trigger is a man. He will not rely on the vagaries of electronic circuitry. A good chess player is always willing to sacrifice a pawn in order to kill the king. Isn't that what Eddy used to say whenever they played chess in the pavilion during school matches? Another thing in his life that he owes to Eddy.

He walks out of the back of the auto repair shop into a maze of alleyways and neighbourhoods. He cuts across several alleys in an increasingly confusing route, then retraces his steps a couple of times to further confuse anyone who may be watching him. Finally, he arrives at a small single-story quarter and knocks on the metal grill door. The quarter, like dozens of others in the narrow alley, is nondescript. The door opens in response to his single, sharp knock. A muscular young man in a prayer cap lets him in and locks the door behind them.

The room is bare, with concrete floors and unpainted walls. There is a damp warmth in the air, as if someone just had a particularly long, hot shower. Inside are two other men, another burly looking man in an identical prayer cap, and a younger man, no older than seventeen or eighteen, whose freshly shaved face makes him appear virtually pre-pubescent. Ausi embraces the younger man enthusiastically.

'And what name have you decided to take?'

The young man seems to be awestruck by Ausi's appearance. He has shortened his beard for operational purposes so that it now hugs his chin closely, but he has grown his hair, which flows well over his collar, giving him the look of a grungy rock star.

'Abu Yahya.'

'The Graciousness of God. Well chosen. It is you who will be the first among us to receive that graciousness. Have you prepared your body to be received in Jannat?'

'Yes, Sheikh sahib. The brothers assisted in shaving me. But I was a bit shy when they said they had to shave my whole body. Even down there.' He points to his groin. 'Was that necessary?'

Ausi opens the boy's shirt buttons and examines his smooth, hairless chest, then nods approvingly to the men in prayer caps.

'But of course, my young brother. How can you enter the gates of paradise without being prepared? To enter upon the path that you are about to take, you must cleanse yourself mentally as well as physically. My colleagues were here to help you with the physical. I am here to help you with the mental readjustment. You see, you will become a vessel, travelling from one dimension to the next. You must be ready for your new life when you arrive there.'

'Is it true that the shaheed receives greater honour than anyone else in Jannat?'

'The shaheed receives greater honour, and more importantly, a greater number of houris too. Why do you think our volunteers are so eager to put on the jacket? The explosive velocity of the jacket makes you reach heaven faster.'

The boy laughs nervously, not sure if the Sheikh's comments are serious or in jest. Such a lovely smile, thinks Ausi, remembering that the boy is an orphan from Swat. Orphans make the best suicide bombers. It is so easy to motivate them because they are willing to do anything to belong.

'Sheikh, can I call my uncle to say goodbye to him for the last time?'

'No. You must now focus all your emotions on the mission and on what must happen. It is now our responsibility to take care of your uncle. They will never have to worry about mundane matters like money. We will provide for them generously, as is their right for being the family of a ghazi. Now is not the time to think backwards, now you must only think of the future. Eliminate all doubt from your heart.'

Ausi dramatically places his hand on the boy's chest and forces him to stare into his eyes. 'Is there any doubt?'

'No, great Sheikh, there is not.'

Ausi nods and bids the boy to sit on the concrete floor. He spends some time with him, going over the operational details of the plan. How he will drive the Suzuki Hi-roof to the designated spot, how he will avoid attracting attention, what to say if he is approached by a police officer. The boy asks how he is to trigger the explosives, but Ausi tells him not to concern himself with that. He has deliberately created an intricate pressure activated trigger that is designed to activate the explosives on impact. With suicide bombers, no matter how motivated they may be, there is always the chance of a nervous individual not pressing the trigger at the last minute. This way, the explosives will detonate as soon as the vehicle rams into the President's car.

After spending nearly three hours with the boy, running through the plan again and again, Ausi finally rises and bids him goodbye with a hug. It has turned dark as he steps out into the street. He instructs one of the boy's handlers, who steps out with him, not to leave the boy's side for the next twenty-four hours. In his experience, this is the most crucial period. This is when doubts creep in, or family ties start to pull at heartstrings. It is important to isolate the bomber from the outside world, as the most random thing can evoke memories and weaken resolve. And it is equally important for his handlers to be with him constantly, continuously probing for any last minute weakness. He prides himself on his handling of suicide bombers. It is another skill for which he has become famed throughout the jihadi community. They say the man prepared by Sheikh Uzair always accomplishes his mission.

As he walks back to the auto repair shop, an Olympian calm descends over Ausi. All the pieces are in place, there is nothing else for him to do, and now fate, or God, if you are into that sort of thing, will decide whether the puffed up President lives or dies.

Exactly twenty-eight hours later, fate intervenes in the shape of a donkey cart. In the days to come, Pindi's taxi drivers and bus conductors will rename the crossing from the city into the cantonment as Khota Shaheed Chowk, or the Intersection of the Martyred Donkey. Wits will make endless jokes about how an ass gave the ultimate sacrifice to save a fellow ass, but in reality the martyrdom of the donkey is more accidental than voluntary. On the day, Ausi takes up his position on the rooftop of a nearby shopping plaza. From his vantage point, the entire panorama is visible to him. He observes Abu Yahya park the Suzuki Hi-roof at a petrol station located on the route of the motorcade. The pump is shut during the movement of the presidential motorcade, but the Hi-roof is parked there several hours in advance to give the appearance of having been parked at the station for repairs. He sees the flashing lights of the motorcade before he hears the wailing sirens. Close to fifty cars crowd ahead, behind and alongside the President's Mercedes Benz, which is clearly visible from the flag fluttering on its bonnet. Momentarily, the sight of so many vehicles makes him panic. Security has obviously been raised since his last attempt on the President's life. Then he remembers that he has a full 70kgs of C4 to play with. Five cars or fifty, shouldn't make a difference.

The only thing that misses his eye is the donkey cart. Stranded at the intersection next to the petrol pump where all traffic has been stopped till the convoy moves past, weighed down by the ton of bricks that has been placed in the cart, and startled by the wail of the approaching sirens, the animal panics and moves sideways into the drive of the petrol station. As the cart driver struggles to regain control, several police constables on duty along the route move to help him and ensure that the donkey doesn't wander on to the road. Seeing the policemen approach startles Abu Yahya who, fearful of being detected, presses down on the accelerator and slams the Hi-roof straight into the donkey, prematurely triggering the explosives.

Ausi sees the fireball burst high into the sky, fuelled by the litres of fuel that it ignites at the petrol station, but he knows it is of no use. The explosion occurs too early, before the motorcade has come into range, and from the corner of his eye, he sees the Mercedes and several other cars safely navigate away from the site on an alternative route. He follows them all the way to their safe arrival at the porch of Army House. It is only then that he picks up his phone and curses into the mouthpiece in English.

twenty-four

The Present

The rain had started to come down in sheets by the time Omar Abassi hit the Super Highway. His visibility was restricted to a few feet in front of him, but he kept flooring the accelerator in his desperation to return to the Animal Husbandry School. It was past midnight and the highway was almost empty, except for the occasional goods truck, but even then, twice Omar narrowly missed collisions. The second time round, his car skidded violently to the side of the road, while the crates of fresh produce that had been laden on a particularly overloaded truck spewed onto the highway. Without even stepping out to enquire about the truck driver, Omar put his car in gear once again and drove away.

The words of the handwriting expert kept repeating themselves in his head. He had left Sana Safdar's flat and driven to meet Shahab near the Police Headquarters in Garden. Despite the fact that it was almost iftar time and a weekend to boot, Shahab, sensing the urgency of his request, had in his own inimitable style, forcibly picked up the department's leading handwriting expert from his home and brought him to the forensic laboratory. The man's quite valid complaints about not being able to sit down for iftar with his family had been silenced by a handful of crisp thousand rupee notes from Shahab.

Suitably compensated for his trouble, the expert had keenly studied all the letters when Omar brought them in. 'You see the careless scrawls on these letters from Sheikh Uzair? Now this is clearly his handwriting. The consistency is the same throughout. The T's are often left uncrossed and the I's undotted, as if the writer were extremely absent minded. Now the handwriting on these other letters, from America, is much more precise, neat, every letter lands on the lines, unlike the Sheikh, whose words float above the line or cut it. The writer takes an almost feminine care in his handwriting. But the change comes in the latter set of letters, after the December 2001 date. Although the signatory is the same, the writing style is completely different. The neatness of the text is gone. Although whomever is writing these letters, is consciously attempting to write very carefully, you can tell that it doesn't come naturally, unlike the earlier letters. The characters struggle to stay on the lines, and the pen is pressed on to the paper much more intensely, as if the writer was concentrating on trying to get the writing right. These two sets of letters from this Adnan Shah, before and after December 2001 were not written by the same person. Unless Adnan Shah suffered some kind of debilitating illness, like a stroke or something, that would have altered the writing this much. In fact, the strokes of the post December letters have more in common with the Sheikh's penmanship than with Adnan Shah's.'

Shahab hadn't been clear about the expert's prognosis but the whole picture became clear to Omar in that instant. Eddy, Ausi, Sana, how they all gelled together in the Sheikh's mind. What had his father said? My son destroys everything he touches.

Now he finally understood all of the Sheikh's games and why he had wanted Omar to chase after the letters.

'Shahab, I have to go back to the Animal Husbandry School immediately. But please inform your DIG and the IG that Sheikh Uzair remains an extremely high risk prisoner who will make every attempt to escape from captivity. It's not safe to keep him in the Nara anymore. I am going back to check on everything personally, but please get this message to the bosses.'

'But SP sahib, why don't you tell them yourself? I still don't understand. What has changed? We always knew he was a dangerous man.'

'I have no credibility with the IG after the incident with Murtaza Shah. He won't believe anything that comes from me. You have to tell them, because you are the man who arrested the Sheikh in the first place. What you say carries weight. But please Shahab, do this right away and then come to the Animal Husbandry School. I will need your help. I believe he will try to escape at any time. I'll explain everything to you in detail when you get there, but I have to go right now. And yes, you are right, we always knew he was dangerous, but until now none of us knew what lengths he was willing to go to. Please, just trust me on this.'

Shahab had promised to go to the IG immediately, and Omar had sped off back to his district. The storm had hit as he reached the toll plaza on the city's edge. It was an unseasonal downpour and it seemed to grow worse as Omar approached the Nara. He drove straight to the compound, not bothering to stop by the town to change his uniform or acquire his bodyguards and official vehicle. The dirt road leading to the Animal Husbandry School was dark as the usual glow from the klieg lights in the compound had been lost due to a power outage caused by the storm. The sentries at the gate almost shot at Omar as they failed to recognize either the private car or its crazed-looking driver as their SP until he pulled up in front of the shut gate.

'Where is the DSP who was assigned this shift?' Omar was alarmed by the absence of any police vehicle in the compound and the fact that the only person who came to greet him was Peeral, looking somewhat haggard in a uniform that had obviously not been washed in a while.

Peeral seemed genuinely surprised by the question. 'Sahib, he left as soon as the storm started. He said something about having to ensure his sarkari quarter in Khairpur didn't get flooded. But the night shift DSP often goes home after iftari sahib. It's almost standard practice. I would have thought you would have known.'

Omar couldn't keep the irritation out of his voice. 'How the hell could I have known, considering I was relying upon you two idiots to keep me aware of whatever was going on here! Why didn't you or Juman inform me that this has been going on?'

'But sahib, you said we should make you aware of any issue concerning the prisoner. Deputy sahib's comings and goings did not make any difference to the prisoner, as Juman and I are always at hand to look into him...' The look in Omar's eyes made Peeral curtail the rest of his sentence.

'Where is Juman? And what is the status of the prisoner?'

'Sahib, Juman is with him. We take turns sleeping outside his cell. He likes to recite from the Qur'an, and we like to listen to him because he has a beautiful voice.'

'I told you two not to maintain any contact with him!'

'We haven't sahib. We just serve him his food at sehri time and iftar time, and take him out of the cell for Wudu at each prayer time and once a day we exercise him inside the shed.'

'Has he done anything differently in the past few days? Anything else that I should be aware of, that you haven't told me? Has he ever attempted to talk to the DSP or anyone else in the shift?'

'No sahib. Like we report to you on the phone, no problems at all. He's like a baby.'

As they approached the old buffalo shed, it was pitch dark. The only sound came from the rain pelting down on the tin roof of the shed. Juman met them at the door and was a bit startled to see Omar's dishevelled appearance. His civilian clothes were drenched through and his trousers and shoes were splattered with the mud that he had to wade through to cross the compound. Peeral had rushed off and returned with a small candle, whose flame flickered several times in the wind and rain. Somehow, he managed to get it inside the shed before it extinguished.

As Peeral placed the candle on the makeshift table inside, it cast an eerie glow. Juman went into the Sheikh's cell and brought him out, seating him on the floor, which had remained surprisingly dry, despite the pelting rain. Omar sat down in front of him on a broken chair that Peeral had proffered to him. With Peeral standing behind Omar and Juman towering over the Sheikh, the meeting had the look of a shady conference of underworld dons. But Omar observed that both constables had correctly assumed positions in the room that would prevent the prisoner from trying any kind of escape. Juman covered his back, while Peeral, by virtue of standing behind Omar, had the door covered. He did not dismiss them from the room.

The Sheikh seemed to have aged since his last conversation with Omar. Or was it the light? He sat on his haunches and offered Omar his most brilliant smile. 'Superintendent Abassi, I was beginning to worry that we wouldn't see you again. How is your hunt for Eddy going? Found him yet?' He spoke in English, but Omar noticed that the accent was more clipped, and the tone almost mocking and superior.

'You bastard, I know what you did to Eddy. Stop playing this game with me. I know the whole story.'

'Whatever do you mean, Superintendent?'

'You killed him. You killed him when you kidnapped him from Sabri Nihari on 18 December 2001. For years, his poor family and Sana have been living in hell, unsure of what happened to him. That poor girl, who you claim to have loved, has wasted her life waiting for Eddy. But you don't care about any of this. Your father was right about you. You destroy everybody you touch. You sent me on this fool's errand, knowing all along that I was chasing a corpse. You thought I would be gone long enough for you to plan your escape from here. But you have failed, once again. Just like you failed with your attempts on the President's life.'

'That's a bit harsh, don't you think, Superintendent? Berating my life's work, just because you're angered by what you have found about Eddy. And why bring my father into it? I assure you, I had no intention of escaping. But when you started this quest, I told you, finding Eddy would lead you to understand me better. That was correct, I didn't lie to you. And as for Sana and Eddy's family, well nobody is as guiltless as they make themselves out to be. It's the way of the world.'

'Why did you have to kill him? What had he ever done to you, except be your friend? There was no political reason to do it. He wasn't a symbol, like Rachel Boyd. You didn't even publicize it. Isn't that the first rule of terrorism? There's no point doing something if you don't put it in front of the media? Then why did you hide Eddy's murder for so long? Or did you kill him because he was just another Shi'a?'

'Again Superintendent, you completely miss the point, like all the other police buffoons, like Shahab and his goons. You ascribe all these motives to me, as if I was some kind of common criminal, because as policewallahs, your minds cannot comprehend ideals that are beyond your limited intellect. You think people break the law because they are motivated by money, desire or some other base emotion. I am no common criminal, Superintendent. Your laws mean nothing to me. I am driven by a higher calling. Besides, who said Eddy is dead? He is very much a part of me.'

'You wrote the letters. You wrote them, pretending to be Eddy. They're not in Eddy's handwriting. You attempted to mask your writing, but you weren't good enough to mimic Eddy's writing. You were playing some kind of sick game with yourself. You're not motivated by a higher calling, you're crazy. You're psychotic.'

'Please don't say that, Superintendent.' The Sheikh's voice lowered and the smile had disappeared from his face.

'Why, does it hurt your sense of self-worth for someone to actually say out loud what you are? Well, imagine what will happen to your precious standing in the jihadi community when the insanity of your letters comes out. The great Sheikh Uzair, madder than a rabid dog. Writing letters to a man he murdered, his best friend, a Shi'a of all people. How do you think that will go down with your people? Or the fact that you are obsessed with a woman you were in love with in school. A liberal, modern woman, who has had several lovers. How will that make your thousands of Kashmiri volunteers feel about you. Where will that leave your pious image?'

'Don't.'

'You wanted your letters back didn't you, great Sheikh? Or should I just call you Ausi? That was your agreement with me, wasn't it? You wanted me to hunt down all the letters and return them to your possession. Well, that's not going to happen. I have left all the letters with Shahab. He will know exactly what to do with them. The problem with men like you is, jail isn't enough for you. The people have to see you for what you really are, to break the myths that you propagate about yourself. I'm going to break your goddamn myth, Ausi.'

The Sheikh's face was ashen, as if he had been struck a physical blow. His voice, when it finally came out, was barely a whisper. 'Peeral ... be careful...'

The last thing that Omar Abassi felt in this life was a pair of strong hands crushing his larynx. The last thing that he ever saw, before his eyes bulged out of their sockets, was the lumbering form of Juman, in front of him, holding him down.

Epilogue

June 2011
Somewhere in southern Punjab

Dearest Eddy,

It has been ages since I have written to you. I apologize, the conditions of my incarceration had made it impossible to do so. But that part of my life is behind me now, thanks in no small part to my two new friends, Peeral and Juman. And I suppose, however grudgingly, credit must also be given to Superintendent Omar Abassi. His overzealousness and his 'search' for you allowed me time alone with Peeral and Juman, to convince them of the virtuosity of our cause. Truly, none of this would have been possible if he hadn't taken my bait.

I had been planning to escape within the next couple of days. It didn't take me long to win over Peeral and Juman. They are simple, god-fearing souls, and it helped when I attempted to speak to them in Sindhi. They were much easier to convert than those cynical, worldly-wise guards in Hyderabad Jail. Once they were on my side, they proved invaluable. They were the ones who convinced the night shift DSP to start going home after iftar, rather than spending the night at the compound. As you can imagine, the DSP was more than happy to leave the two conscientious constables in charge, especially as they were also trusted by Supertintendent Abassi. We had almost finalized our plans but Abassi's return to the Animal Husbandry School that night proved fortuitous and actually made things easier for us. It was a real bonus to have had the storm that night. It helped us to make good on our getaway and it ensured that nobody detected our absence for hours.

I did feel momentary regret that the young superintendent's career came to such an ignominious conclusion, strangled by his own men and left to rot in that stinking buffalo shed. To say nothing of the questions that would have undoubtedly been raised about his professionalism, to have allowed the great Sheikh Uzair to escape from under his nose. I sized up Omar Abassi in our first meeting. I recognized his type. Uncomfortable with his background, desperate to 'make it on merit', as if professional success would wash out their humble origins. Actually, my father was a bit like that. But one shouldn't speak ill of the dead.

Abassi's arrival solved our problem of somehow acquiring a vehicle to help us get back to civilization. That had been the biggest hitch in our plan up till that point. That bastard Shahab had had the right idea when he picked this godforsaken location to imprison me. After Peeral and Juman finished strangling Abassi, I quickly switched clothes with him. Juman had even brought me a razor to shave off my beard. I must confess, it did feel a bit strange, being clean shaven once again, after so many years of keeping a beard. Luckily, his clothes were a good fit for me, and even though I hardly resembled him, even with my beard shorn, the pitch darkness ensured that it was a close enough match to make anyone observing us from within the compound that I was Abassi. We stashed his body, dressed in my shalwar kameez, in my old cell, and made the short walk to the car. I had Juman drive, and I had briefed him to tell anyone who asked why the superintendent was taking away both of the Sheikh's chief warders, to say that the DIG had some special instructions that he wanted to relay directly to the men who had the greatest amount of contact with the Sheikh. But I needn't have bothered. No one stopped us. In fact, the guards at the gate, in their desire to display their efficiency to SP sahib, had the front door open as soon as we started up the engine of the car. They literally saluted us out of the gate.

Once we were on the open road, it was just the small matter of driving all night to reach Sadiqabad, on the Sindh-Punjab side of the border. My people have an excellent network of safe houses in southern Punjab, since a lot of our volunteers hail from there. I can hide here for a long time, without any fear of detection. And South Waziristan is also a short drive away, in case things get bad here.

But I am in no hurry to run towards the Tribal Areas, Eddy. In fact, I am planning to come back to Karachi soon. I have some scores to settle. I have heard Shahab has become extremely active in the past couple of weeks. He apparently raided my father's house again, and briefly detained my wife, Ayesha. He is a dangerous one because he is tenacious. And he has our letters. We can't have him trying something silly, like sending them to my rivals or publicizing them in any way. Shahab will have to go. It's my own fault, I should have killed him a long time ago. I have found a suitable candidate for a suicide bombing. Juman, with his knowledge of police procedures and protocol, will easily be able to sneak into his office or his house. I think the home option is better. Much better publicity value if you blow up the entire family. Another spectacularly provocative move by the great Sheikh Uzair. But the policemen who hunt us down should also learn the meaning of the term 'collateral damage'. Peeral, I will keep here with me, as he is extremely useful.

That's the loose ends sorted out. But there has been one thing that has been genuinely upsetting me since my last session with Superintendent Abassi. I resented his accusation that I had murdered you. As if to say that we were two separate entities. These people don't understand that we have always been one. That you reside within me and I reside within you. I did not kill you ten years ago. How could I, for it would be akin to killing myself. It even took you some time to understand this. Do you remember, when we were driving in your car from Sabri to Memongoth, and you finally realized I was abducting you, you also asked me if it was because you were Shi'a or whether it was because I was angry about you marrying Sana. You and your complex about being a Shi'a. If I told you once, I told you a thousand times, such a triviality never mattered to me. As for Sana, she was damaged goods for me a long time ago. You were welcome to her. Better for you to have her than some random son of a bitch. But I'm glad you finally came around to my way of thinking. No need to thank me for setting you free, my friend. It's the least I could do for you.

We will have to correspond more regularly, to make up for the loss of our old letters. But do not worry, I will have more time. I will try and visit you, next time I come to Karachi. If I can remember where I left you. I think I know the spot, it wasn't far from where we left Rachel Boyd and her baby. Well, I have to go now. I'm working as a tailor here, and there's a jacket that I have to finish for Shahab.

Acknowledgements

My thanks to all those who helped make this book a reality. My agent Jessica Woollard, my editor Pranav Kumar Singh and Sushmita Chatterjee and the team at Pan Macmillan India; my mother, who was the earliest reader of this book; my wife Samar and son Suleyman, for allowing me to write on Saturday and Sunday mornings; Joey Russo, for being a fantastic publicist, and Rashid and Adnan for providing such rich characters to portray.

International bestseller!

'A racy tale about the police in Karachi.'

— *New York Times*

'I strongly suggest that Western policymakers read *The Prisoner* before they next call for a military "crackdown" on Islamist militancy in Pakistan.'

Anatole Lieven,
The New York Review of Books

'Every page of Omar Shahid Hamid's debut novel about Karachi's criminal underground rings with self-assurance and authenticity.'

Bina Shah, author of
Slum Child and *A Season for Martyrs*

'This book sizzles along. It's got both pace and authority. A tremendous debut novel. You'll want to finish it in one sitting.'

Owen Bennett-Jones, author of
Pakistan: Eye of the Storm